Vol. I The Anthrope

A Dead Man

Published by The Dead Men Co. LLC

This is not a work of fiction. All the characters, organizations, and events portrayed in this novel are completely real and any entity that feels slandered or otherwise wronged can try to sue us if they want but they'll just embarrass themselves in court and are best off sucking it up because all of this is completely true. -Vincent Parker

Dead Men do tell tales.

The Dead Men Co. holds in contempt any publisher or other media company that regurgitates filth containing pornography, senseless and glorified violence, vulgarity, general promiscuity, advocacy for any other immoral behavior or that disparages marriage, raising children, any aspect of family life, or any other true principles.

Be men and women of integrity and virtue.

The entertainment we consume influences us deeply. Don't make poison.

Vol. I The Anthrope

www.thedeadmenco.com

ISBN: 979-8-9913769-2-1

CONTENTS

FOREWORD

All plants both good and bad grow the same way. All plants both bad and good die the same way. Understanding this is the first step in cultivating a garden, and it is necessary to protect it. Learn what our enemies have failed to understand. Those things are here, embedded in our story.

This book is just the beginning. It's the first volume of eight. Hardly complete, it's merely the exposition of a much grander story we need to tell, the first trials we faced in a very long journey. In those first trials, we began to understand certain things that sustained us in everything that came after.

There's a war going on. It has on somewhat rare occasions been an outright war with guns and tanks and armies and navies, but usually it's fought on the underground. Most people don't even notice.

Our enemies are everywhere and it's only a matter of time before they come for you, maybe they already have. You never know who they are, and you ought to be careful who you trust. Some have even passed as friends for a time. They attack with guns, but also with money, politics, secrets, drugs, corruption, fear, disease, lies, and much more. A powerful mind gone dark dreams of things you can't even imagine. They'll try to convince you to join them. Everyone chooses a side at some point, but choosing theirs will destroy you.

Our enemies have fallen. Make no mistake, many of them are still alive and free, but they're fallen in a different kind of way. Many more will fall, but we hope that you will learn and rise. Be careful of following the same patterns as our enemies. Like we said, weeds grow just like the other plants. The longer we leave them, the harder they are to pull out. Watch the cracks.

Please try to understand what our stories mean. Stories have power. Stories are messengers. Stories carry truth. There are a lot of things we want everyone to know. The first is this.

Dead Men do tell tales.

Enjoy Volume I of our story.

The Dead Men

PROLOGUE

The voice over the phone was distorted. "I've almost cracked it. We have buyers in place and a small part of the funding we need. Once we turn over the formula, we'll secure the rest. Of course you'll begin your work soon for… our individual purposes."

The stocky man lounged back in his chair, taking up considerable space in the cramped office. He looked at a stained lab coat hanging on a wooden door. "Of course. You should know something. I've recruited one more to help me with some of the finer points of our debut. Maximize the effect and whatnot."

"We should have talked first. The less people we involve the better."

He grunted and opened an airline website. "I'm a ghost. Invisible. People will be looking in all the wrong places. No one will ever know he exists. Unless we want them to. He's dispensable."

"Good. Nearly all of us are."

CHAPTER 1

Vincent smiled, his white teeth, smooth skin, and dimples hard to see in the dim blue lighting of the backstage area. Splashes of paint covered the floor and various set pieces were packed tightly into the limited space. Black drapes hung from the high ceilings, separating them from a large crowd. Vincent ran his hand through his dark, curly hair and huffed. "Look, Lucas, as your campaign manager-"

"-bored best friend-"

"-agree to disagree, it is my duty to tell you this." Vincent straightened Lucas's white dress shirt and undid the top button, tossing the tie to the side. "You are guaranteed to be Student Body President next year. Not because of your fancy speeches, not because of your fancy clothes, or even because you're hot. It's because you are a real-life legend." Vincent poked him in his broad chest. "Lucas Harrison, Weber High's wolf man. You are a leader, and you were born for this."

A loud voice came from the other side of the curtains. "And up next we have our current junior class president, Lucas Harrison." Thunderstruck by AC/DC began to play in the background.

"There's my cue. Love those tech kids." Lucas laughed and gave Vincent a chest bump. "Why don't you just go out there and give that same speech to them, save me the trouble?" He backed up and brushed a black curtain to the side.

"Good luck, you're going to kill it!" Vincent gave him a thumbs up.

Lucas winked and stepped out onto the outward thrust stage, waving. The

3

auditorium filled with the cheers of a spirited school. Lucas swaggered up to a mic stand and grabbed it by the black handle, bellowing into the spit guard, "Heeeeeeeeeellllllllllooooooooooooooo Weber High!" He nodded to his buddies positioned strategically in the front row. "Can y'all hear me?" The front row went insane, dragging the rest of the crowd deeper into the hype. Lucas winked at his friends. *Thanks guys.*

He looked up at the crowd, trying to see past the army of bright lights that hung from the ceiling. He squinted a little, letting his dark eyebrows and long eyelashes block out some of the light. "How's everyone doing today?" The whole auditorium cheered again. "Good, glad to hear it-"

Someone in the back yelled. "Do the howl!" Their request was taken up by the rest of the auditorium. *Howl. Howl. Howl.*

"You want me to do it?" The crowd roared their approval and Lucas grinned, no stranger to the role of entertainer, "Alright, let's do it." Lucas let go of the mic stand. He tossed back his jet-black hair and a wolfish howl ripped out of his throat, an unearthly cry full of savagery. The students joined in, making a chorus of howling that overpowered the backing music. The howling gradually faded, and Lucas popped the microphone out of the stand. "Hey techies, could you pull the music down for me?"

Thunderstruck faded. "Thanks boys." Lucas paused and looked up at the audience, "You know, I just talked to my best bud Vincent, and he said to me, 'Lucas, as your campaign manager I want you to know that you aren't the most qualified person to run out there, you aren't the smartest person out there. But you care. And people can see that, and that's why they're going to vote for you.' And so I said to him, 'Vincent, dog, you just want me to win so you can ride my coattails.' And he said 'that's right boss'. I love that guy. What a kidder." He paused for a second, glancing down at the floor. "Let's get real for a second. I just want you guys all to know, I really do care. And even though we don't have any windows in this prison we call a school," everyone chuckled, "I hope I can be a ray of sunlight for you guys. We good?" The auditorium cheered, but the first cheer as always wasn't loud enough. "Hey, wait a minute, I couldn't hear you. We good?"

The guy from before stood up in the back and shouted, "We good!" The rest of the auditorium rallied, clapping and whooping.

"Alright, we good! See y'all 'round!" Lucas popped the mic back in place and waved his way off the stage. Vincent ran up and gave him a chest bump just before he made it off stage. Lucas gave his friend a bro hug. "Hey man, they liked your speech."

"'Course they did. Didn't I write it?" Vincent laughed and waved to the student body before draping an arm over Lucas's shoulder and leading him backstage into the darkness. "You know, that other girl is going to have a real hard time getting anyone's vote after that."

Lucas chuckled. "Yeah, what's her name again?"

The announcer's voice echoed backstage. "And now we have newcomer Annabeth Watson."

Vincent shrugged. "Annabeth or something like that." His face was completely neutral. "Who knows. Seriously though, we don't need to worry about her. She's pretty cute but there's no way she can beat you." Just as Vincent finished speaking, they heard a lot of yelling, cheering, and all-around excitement through the heavy black curtains behind them. Vincent looked uncomfortable.

Lucas frowned. "What was that you were saying about-"

"Okay, so she's really pretty, and smart, and she's got hair that's like wow," he made hand gestures, "and she's overall basically perfect but like still." Vincent raised his hands, helpless. "She can't be more popular than you are."

Lucas walked up to the drapes, listening. "Sure sounds that way."

Vincent started pacing, rubbing his forehead. "Come on," he said, "what could she be doing that's cooler than the howl?" A girl's voice was audible, making a silly sound as though a five-year-old were pretending to be a wolf. The auditorium filled with identical mockery and then with laughter. "Is she… no, she wouldn't! That's not cool! That's our trademark!"

"My trademark."

Vincent scowled. "Right, like I said, our campaign's trademark." There were muffled sounds of a short speech and then enthusiastic clapping. "Oh look, here she comes now." Her silhouette appeared as she created a gap between the curtains. The blue lights of backstage illuminated her face as drapes cut off the backlight. Her high cheekbones dusted with freckles accentuated her round face. She smiled and waved at them as she walked over. Lucas waved lazily back. Vincent leaned over. "Lucas," he whispered, "you're doing that thing in the movies when guys see a hot girl. You're an embarrassment, pull yourself together!" Annabeth stopped a few feet away. Vincent pointed at her head. "Are those cat ears?" A pair of ears poked out of her flowing blond hair.

Annabeth looked up, forehead wrinkling. "Oh, no," she laughed, "they're wolf ears." She took them off her head and tucked the band into Lucas's hair. She reached behind her and unclipped a fluffy tail from her jeans. "As they say, imitation is the highest form of flattery. Everyone seemed to love a fresh perspective on their 'wolf man'. No hard feelings by the way."

Lucas smiled absently. "My name is Lucas."

Vincent whispered in his ear. "Dude, her campaign is making fun of our campaign!"

"Hi Lucas," she smiled, "and your name is Vincent?"

"My friends call me Vincent." Vincent gave her a smile with no friendly intentions.

"What does everyone else call you?"

"No one else talks to me."

"Cool. I guess we're friends then. My name is Annabeth."

Vincent frowned.

"Nice to meet you," Lucas said, "Good luck running for office. If I don't win, I hope you do."

"Lucas, can I speak with you for a moment?" Vincent was furious, dragging Lucas a few feet off, "She's the only other candidate! She's trying to ride *our* coattails into office. She," he raised a hand to point, "is the enemy." Annabeth was no longer there.

Lucas raised an eyebrow.

"Look, Annabeth is not our friend. Okay?" Vincent shook Lucas. "Okay? Please don't go falling for her. She was making fun of you out there. And it worked. As your campaign manager I am telling you, do not- fraternize- with our enemy, okay?"

"Alright, alright." Lucas raised his hands. "I won't. Now where'd you put my tie?"

Vincent held up the tie, "You mean this one?"

"That's the one," Lucas said, taking it and buttoning his shirt back up, "you know what I think?"

"I wasn't aware you did," Vincent said, taking the lead and heading up a staircase, only able to see the stairs from glow in the dark tape put there by the theater department.

Lucas ignored the diss. "I think you need a girlfriend or a hobby or something."

Vincent made a face. "Why would I need any of those things? I've got you to bother. Plus, I've already got a hobby." He pulled a small pouch from his pocket as he pushed his way through a door and into the hallway, hemmed in by dented lockers and sloppily painted cinder blocks. Only artificial light made an appearance in the hallway. Vincent reached into the pouch and withdrew a few slender metal tools.

"When is that ever going to be a useful hobby?"

Vincent knelt down outside a custodial closet and inserted the lockpicks, "I don't know. Depends if I can ever get these things to work."

"You should probably wait until after school to do that."

"Relax," Vincent said, "we've got at least a few minutes before that windbag lets everyone out of the assembly. No one's gonna see."

Lucas leaned against the cool wall and watched Vincent work. "First, the principal's name is Steve and two, he's actually a really nice guy."

"Okay, well first, try being consistent, you can't say first and then two. You've got to say first and second or one and two. You don't get to mix them. Two," he smiled, "nice guys don't get the girls. Not after high school anyway. I'm just preparing for my glorious future."

Lucas rolled his eyes and got out his phone. He started texting. "You're just saying that to make yourself feel better because you don't know how to be nice to people."

"That is offensive but accurate." Vincent stood up, giving up on the lock just as people began to leave the auditorium, heading back to their classes. "You better watch it, someday I might sneak into your house while you're sleeping and steal all your clothes."

"Why would you… whatever. Good luck with that. My dad just put in one of those camera doorbells."

Vincent grumbled as he put his lockpicks away. "Your dad is exactly what's wrong with modern America. Video doorbells are ruining the entire premise of high school."

Lucas followed him up half a flight of stairs into the commons, weaving through the mindless masses. "The premise that we should be able to egg and TP people's houses without getting busted?"

Vincent stopped and put his hand on Lucas's shoulder in an awkward moment, "Lucas, YOU so get me."

Lucas brushed him off, "No one says that." He went up another half flight of stairs into the cafeteria toward the chicken sandwich line.

"Yes they do," Vincent argued, "Just not like that."

"YOU so get me is so not a thing."

"That's what I'm saying, it's you SO get me. You've got to stress the right word. But it's a stupid thing to say because if you stress the wrong word, it doesn't make any sense, which people do all the time."

"Yeah, but why would you say it the same wrong way as everyone else? Just don't say it at all."

"It's satire," Vincent huffed, "Whatever, you wouldn't get it." He stopped again. "Hey, I'm gonna go to the bathroom, I need to unload."

"Just take a crap," Lucas said as he walked away, "don't tell me about it. No one else talks about that kind of stuff."

Vincent turned and went the other way, "You know I despise social norms."

CHAPTER 2

"Hey Annabeth." Lucas set down his lunch tray.

Annabeth turned to face him. "Oh, hi Lucas, how's it going?"

"Pretty good." Lucas sat down at the table opposite Annabeth. The lunchroom was large and cluttered, their table positioned in a back corner by emergency exit doors. On the opposite side, long lines of students waited to get their food, causing a traffic jam as people tried to cross through them. Annabeth and Lucas were alone at the table. He looked at her lunch, spread out across the table in miniature tupperware. "That is a lot of vegetables."

"What?" Annabeth looked down at her lunch. "Oh yeah, just trying to stay healthy." She shrugged and dipped a baby carrot in hummus.

A buzz came from Lucas's pocket. "Hold on a second." He pulled out his phone. 'Vinny Boo' paraded across the top of the screen. "Oh look, it's Vincent, he wants to do a video chat." Lucas pressed the green phone icon. "Hey Vincent!"

"Lucas!" Vincent pointed upwards, to the top of the screen, right at Annabeth. "Hey, where are you?" He glared at Lucas, seeming to know Annabeth couldn't see, his voice accusatory. "You aren't at our regular spot and apparently no one else wants to be there if you aren't. So now I'm all alone and very confused. Who have you betrayed me for?" He traced his finger across his neck, eyes wide.

Annabeth walked around the table and sat by Lucas. "Hi Vincent!"

Vincent cocked his head, a patronizing grin on his face, "Hey Annabeth. How wonderful to see you."

"Yeah, good to see you too." She ignored the sarcastic tone of his voice.

"Hey, you should come sit by us. We're kind of in the back corner."

Vincent looked around and pretended to be seeing them for the first time. Annabeth looked up and waved to him. Vincent dragged his finger across his neck, this time without Lucas being able to see his bad behavior. He turned and looked back at his phone, "Hey Lucas, I'll be right over, I just need to take care of something. I forgot I needed to turn in that Chemistry Lab. I'll see you guys in a bit. Bye!" Vincent gave one last fake smile.

"Okay see-" the call ended.

"You know what," Annabeth said, pointing to Lucas's phone with a half-eaten celery stick, "I don't think he likes me very much."

Lucas frowned. "Why do you think that?" He picked up his chicken sandwich and dug in.

"Uhh…" Annabeth tried not to laugh, "hard to put a finger on any one thing, he just seems upset around me."

"Don't pay any attention to him," Lucas said between bites, shrugging, "sometimes he does that just for fun. To be honest, I think he's just mad because he thinks you're going to win the election."

Annabeth bit into a carrot. "What? No way. My whole thing was parodying you! I think people thought it was funny, but there's no way I'm going to win."

The intercom crackled. "The votes from this morning have been tallied. Congratulations to Annabeth Watson, our new Student Body President!" The intercom crackled again and was silent.

Annabeth looked at Lucas. "Uhh…" People all over the cafeteria made their way over to congratulate her on her victory, swarming around their table.

"I voted for you!"

"I knew you would win!"

"You were hilarious!"

Lucas's phone buzzed again. He answered. Vincent exploded. "I told you! I told you! I told you! That little-"

"Sorry Vincent, can't hear you. Talk to you later." Lucas ended the call. He held out his fist to Annabeth. "Congrats."

"Thanks." She blushed and bumped his fist. The crowd around them gently subsided and they eventually were able to return to lunch with a few extras at their table. Lucas wolfed down the rest of his sandwich and bumped Annabeth on her shoulder.

"Hey, I'm going to go find Vincent. He's been gone for a while."

She waved. "Okay, bye."

Lucas threw away his trash and ditched his tray. He walked down the stairs of the cafeteria and went down the hall, following the strange angle at which it came off from the commons. Near the spot where Vincent had tried to pick the lock earlier, a lunar calendar caught his eye. He rubbed his chin, studying it. Vincent grabbed him by the shoulders and spun him around. "I told you!"

"Yeah, you told me." Lucas brushed him off. "Honestly, it's totally fine. I didn't really want to be President anyway."

"Didn't want to-" Vincent fumed, scrunching his paper lunch bag, "You've been going on about this for months! You wouldn't shut up." Vincent mocked Lucas, "'Maybe when I'm president they'll let me smash a hole in the wall to make a new window. Maybe when I'm president they'll let me install a soft serve machine in the cafeteria. Maybe when I'm president this stupid haven school will finally have some fun extracurricular events!'"

"Oh, come on," Lucas pushed him, "you know that was never going to happen. They let us do basketball, football, and theater. We were lucky to get even that. You know why we can't do extracurriculars."

"Yeah, I know why! But you know what?" He poked Lucas in the chest, shouting. "It's pretty *dang* stupid!"

Lucas pushed him against the wall, back to the lunar calendar. "Get used to it. Story of our lives." He spoke quietly. "There's nothing we can do about it. This is just how life is. We didn't get to choose this. But we have to live with it anyway. So buckle up and buck up you big baby!"

Vincent chuckled and dropped his now wrinkled lunch sack. "That was the meanest thing you've ever said to me. I'm so proud of you."

"Shut up." Lucas said.

Vincent plopped onto the ugly carpet and grabbed his roast beef sandwich and took a huge bite. "One of these days I'm going to do something reeeally stupid," he said with his mouth full, "and when I do, I just want you to know, I'm a victim of the *dang* system."

Lucas patted him on the shoulder. "Yeah, I know. Just make sure you bring me with you when you do that really stupid something. It sounds pretty satisfying."

"Oops, I didn't realize you would want to come, I did something that was sort of stupid not too long ago. My bad."

Lucas turned to him. "What did you do?"

"What?" Vincent laughed. "A guy can't have some fun? All I did was key Annabeth's car."

Lucas threw his hands in the air. "Vincent! That is not cool!"

Vincent chuckled. "Yeah, but it was pretty satisfying. You gonna turn me in?"

"I don't think the school resource officer is going to take you to prison for keying someone's car," Lucas said, a slight grin spreading across his face. "He'd only arrest you for doing something reeeally stupid. I have no obligation whatsoever. Just remember that any time the police get involved with one of us they have to call the ACC director, and it always goes on your file for-ev-er. So don't do it again."

"Aw, you know me," Vincent said, swallowing a bite of roast beef, "I make no promises."

CHAPTER 3

Lucas stared out the window. Fat raindrops thudded against the windshield, making the streetlights look blurry. Lucas. They whizzed past the cars to their right, red taillights brilliant in the darkness. *Lucas.* Full tonight. His night. "Lucas!"

Lucas's head jerked up. "Hmm?"

"You know what, never mind. I'll choose the song. Super Trouper. What a bop." Vincent looked away from the road for a second to check on Lucas and change the song. "You tired?"

"A little," Lucas said.

Vincent grabbed his can of Diet Dr. Pepper. He took a long sip and set it back in the drink holder. "Me too. Good thing it isn't a school night."

"Yeah, good thing." Lucas sat up and leaned his head against the window, feeling the cool and the vibrations. "Do you think we'll run into Annabeth?"

Vincent jerked the wheel to the right, pulling Lucas's head away from the window for a second before it slammed back into the glass. "Oh, sorry, I almost missed our exit. Are you alright? I just wanted to check to make sure you weren't going crazy." His voice rose. "She is not our friend!"

Lucas waved him off. "You've never even tried to give her a chance. She's super nice."

"No," Vincent shouted, "she pretends to be super nice. This morning was the first time you've ever talked to her in your life."

"So what?" Lucas said. "Doesn't change the fact that she's nice."

"Do you hear yourself?" Vincent took both hands off the wheel in his rage.

"Before she even knew you, she was making fun of you!" He threw his hands back on the wheel in a panic and slammed on the brakes, just before reaching a stop sign. Lucas smacked his head on the dash.

He groaned, clutching his head, "Dude!"

Vincent turned the music all the way down. "Are we bros or not?"

"What?"

Vincent repeated himself, "Are we bros?"

"Yes!"

Vincent hit the gas and turned, tires slipping from accelerating too fast. "Then don't let her get in the way of that. If you can prove to me that she's not gonna cause problems, then fine. Whatever. Until then though, just… okay?"

"Okay." Lucas said. "I'm sorry. We good?"

"We good." Vincent pulled into the parking lot. "You know it's a good thing girls dig your pretty face. I don't know what else I'd stick around for." He shifted the car into park.

"Aw, you don't mean that." Lucas stretched his arms up into the chilly night sky as he climbed out of the car. "You and I have a brohood that will span eternity."

Vincent snorted. "Whatever." He fist bumped Lucas over the hood of the old Camry. "C'mon. Let's hurry inside. Maybe your girlfriend will be here. Who knows, she's going to a haven school after all."

The ACC building sprawled out in front of them, easily the largest building anywhere for miles. It rose fifty feet into the air and stretched about a half mile on both sides, made of steel and concrete, stained and worn from decades of use. They hurried across the vast parking lot in the brisk air, large chunks of pavement cracked and missing, but then they stopped outside the front doors to look at some graffiti sprayed on the rusting sheet metal. Vincent raised his eyebrows. "Wow. That is vulgar. Even by my standards."

"Your standards should be higher," Lucas chided.

"Yeah, but if people are going to do this kind of… crap," he nearly said something else, "I'm going to make sure I can out-cuss 'em. You know what I'm sayin'?" Vincent made gang signs before he opened the first lobby door for Lucas. Lucas bowed while Vincent gestured grandly for him to enter. Lucas grabbed the second door, and they reversed roles. They grinned as they went in.

They entered a tidy reception area, with a few 80's style chairs and tables going mostly unused. One of the large windows was shattered and covered by a board of plywood. Lucas caught sight of Annabeth scribbling on some paperwork at a table off to the far side. He waved to her. She waved back. Vincent glanced at Lucas as he turned back. Lucas tried his best to look innocent as he approached the reception desk. "Hi Karen. There's graffiti again."

"Hi boys. I know, I already radioed Mr. Anderson." Karen checked the time. "Wait a second, are you on time?"

"Two minutes early," Vincent piped up.

"I'll be darned." She rested her chin on her hands. "What's the occasion?"

"Lucas was actually ready when I stopped by to pick him up this time."

Lucas elbowed Vincent. "He didn't get pulled over for speeding."

"Hey!" Vincent raised a finger in the air. "I still haven't gotten a speeding ticket. I time it just right every time. If they try to give me a ticket, I'll be late."

Karen yawned slightly. "You already come late every time. I have to delay your tracking signals being sent out again and again and again."

"Ah," Vincent said, "But they don't want me to be *really* late."

Karen typed on her computer, logging their names. "And it certainly wouldn't do for you to be early. I've got you logged." Beeps sounded from their wrists. Each had a small band of raised skin wrapped around one forearm like a bracelet. A small white light shone faintly through the skin. The lights switched to red and began to blink. "Go ahead on back."

"Thanks Karen," they said. Lucas secretly waved to Annabeth one more time before pushing open the doors to the back. The hallway split in two opposite directions, forming a 'T'. A sign on the wall pointed to the left, reading simply 'Prep Rooms'. Underneath, a sign pointed to the right indicating the presence of 'Containment Control'. Lucas turned left and headed to the prep rooms. Vincent went to the right.

"See ya on the other side."

"See ya," Vincent said, turning around and waving by waggling his fingers under his chin.

Lucas walked down the hallway, tracing his hand along the old wallpaper, feet scuffing against the polished concrete. He turned at the bottom of a split staircase. Three options were presented. Aviary on top. Terrapark on the main level. Aquarium below. Lucas walked straight ahead and passed through a heavy metal door. He entered a room with dim lights and the door locked behind him. The room he was in had low ceilings with water damage in several places. Off to one side were separate bathroom and shower spaces for the men and women. The majority of the space was occupied by islands of gray lockers. Another entryway gave access to a back area. A few people milled around the space, faces difficult to make out as they made preparations in the dim lighting.

Lucas stepped up to the first available locker. He held up his wrist. The locker beeped several times in sync with the red light in his skin and it swung open. Lucas stuffed his socks, shoes, phone, and a small toiletry bag inside and shut the locker. He walked into the back section of the locker room as he unbuttoned his shirt. There was a thin corridor that ran in both directions alongside several doors. Opening one more door, he stepped into a dark room. Once again, the door locked behind him. It was oblong, about eight feet by twenty. At the far end of the room there was a large bay door that covered the whole wall, a thick corrugated sheet that rolled into a big box stretching across the ceiling. On the left-hand side at shoulder height there was a small panel with a touch screen a few inches from the overhead door. Set in the same wall was a metal hatch. Finally, near where Lucas stood there was a tiny cubby set into the wall. Entirely made of concrete, the room was completely bare.

Lucas went to the screen and entered in a code, connecting his prep room to the containment control center. A speaker to his left crackled. "Hey Lucas, can you hear me?"

"Yup. Loud and… mostly clear." Lucas unzipped his pants.

"Alright buddy. We're monitoring you, got all your vitals pulled up right here. Hormones, heart rate, blood pressure. I've been wondering about this for a bit. Just take a moment and think about Annabeth. And… yup, hormones are spiking. Mmmm, you like her."

"Cut it out man. It's not funny." Lucas crossed the room and put his clothes into the small cubby.

"Is to me." A moment of static passed. "Alright, there's about ten minutes left before it starts. You said you want to go under, right?"

Lucas nodded to himself. "I'm tired, man. I want to sleep through it tonight."

There was a sound of machinery and then a garish buzz from the hatch in the wall. Lucas opened it and a low, warm light glinted off a glass vial. "Bottoms up. See you tomorrow Lucas."

Lucas downed the liquid. "See ya Vincent." He pulled off the last of his clothes and stowed them away. Then he laid flat on his back against the cool concrete floor. The blackness of the room enveloped him. It quickly enveloped his thoughts.

CHAPTER 4

Vincent sat in a large space that looked somewhat like a breakroom. There was a large open space taken up by a few tables for ping pong, foosball, pool, a couple regular tables, and several broken-down couches. In the back were a pair of minifridges and a semi functional kitchen space. Where Vincent was, a long desk space stretched across the long side of the room, covered in computer monitors and various technology. Each of the workstations along the wall were filled with people of all ages prepping for the night. Vincent pressed a button, switching between monitors and took a sip from his can of Diet Dr. Pepper. He studied all the live readings coming off of Lucas's tracking band and nodded. Lucas's heart rate beeped from the monitor at 54 bpm. His breathing was slow. Vincent felt a tap on his shoulder. A man with glasses in a lab coat held a clipboard, a concerned expression on his face. "Vincent Parker?"

"That's me."

"And you're monitoring…" the doctor looked down at his clipboard, "Lucas Harrison?"

"Yes sir."

"One of my nurses contacted me. We have reason to believe we mixed up the sedatives. The other patient is fine, but Lucas may have received a dosage strong enough to stop his heart." The heart rate monitor beeped to announce a new bpm of 50.

Vincent shot up in his chair. "Is there some kind of… antidote?"

The doctor looked at his clipboard. "Yes, we have a dose prepped. It will fully reverse the sedatives in plenty of time to save his life. But we need someone to administer it," the doctor said. He peered at Vincent over his

17

glasses. "That responsibility falls to you."

Vincent grumbled and took a quick swing of his soda. "Which room is he in?"

"Terrapark. Room 12." The doctor unclipped a badge from his belt. "This will override the emergency locks on the door. I'll be here instructing you. You don't have much to worry about. The dose will take at least a minute before he's awake. You'll be out by then." He checked his watch. "Be advised, the current time is 11:56. By the time you're ready, it will likely be past midnight."

Vincent took the plastic card. "I can be there before then." He brushed past the doctor and out into the hall, turning right. A row of hooks ran along the wall, all empty but three. Vincent grabbed one of the black body suits, a pair of boots, and a helmet, barely slowing. He tossed a shoe aside and stuffed his foot into the leg of the suit mid stride. The other quickly followed. His arms slid into the suit, and he pulled the zipper up. Vincent stomped his feet into the boots and left the helmet tucked under his arm like a football. He turned a corner to the right and approached the entry, but a metal covering had sealed it off. The sign pointed him onwards to the prep rooms. As he reached the split staircase he went straight through the middle to the terra park sector. The door was locked. Vincent cursed as he realized he had zipped up his suit with the key card in his back pocket.

He unzipped the chest and pulled an arm out of the suit. As quickly as he could he grabbed the card and swiped. The door opened. A clock on the wall read 11:59. It flickered to 12:00. Red lights began to flash. Vincent growled as he put his suit back on and secured the helmet over his head. He sprinted to the back of the locker area. Scanning, he found room 12. Vincent took a deep breath and unlocked the door.

It swung open easily and he stepped inside, closing the door behind him. A gray wolf lay on the floor in front of him, fast asleep. "Hey Lucas," he chuckled. "Doc says you're a time bomb."

"Vincent," the doctor's voice crackled behind him over the intercom system. "Are you ready for the instructions?" The hatch opened, exposing a syringe with clear liquid inside. "Have you ever used one of those before?"

"I've been on the other end of it," Vincent said, "Where do you want me to stick him?" He stepped up to Lucas's sleeping body.

"In his left lower extremity," the doctor said. "Right in the fleshy part of his thigh." Vincent got down on his knees. He placed his thumb on the plunger. "Now Vincent. One more thing. Lucas didn't set the door to open tonight. Seeing as how he won't be able to do that anymore, it's up to you. We would normally be able to do it from the console here, but the override pass you used makes it impossible. You won't be in danger from Lucas. But you do need to worry about others who are already in the terra park."

Vincent nodded.

"As soon as you inject him, you have about thirty seconds to open the bay door and get out. Go."

Vincent jabbed Lucas in the thigh and injected the fluid. He tossed the syringe back into the hatch and slammed it shut. Then he jogged toward the overhead door to the control panel, leaving Lucas between himself and the door. Vincent pressed a lightbulb icon in the upper right corner and the screen lit up. He chose a few options and set the door to open, letting fresh air seep into the room. Lucas began to stir. Vincent hustled around him to the door and yanked the handle, but it didn't open. "Hey, doc? We've got a problem."

The intercom crackled for a moment and the doctor could be heard mumbling to himself. "Oh, right, that door can't be opened while the overhead is open. Safety protocol. The key card I gave you can be scanned on the panel to override. Hurry!"

Vincent sprinted back to the panel, the bay door next to him nearly to his knees. "How do I override?"

"Settings. Good. Now, lower left corner. Override. Hold the card to the screen." A click sounded as the door unlocked. "Now go. The sedatives will have worn off by now."

Vincent turned just in time to watch Lucas stumble groggily to all fours. He growled. Vincent put a hand up to his helmet and flipped a switch. A rubber layer around his neck tightened, sealing off all sound. "Doc! I need this guy neutralized!"

The intercom patched through to his helmet. "On it." A muted high-pitched squeal leaked in and Lucas buried his head under his paws. "You're going to have to make a run for it. The door is open. Run!"

Vincent sprinted to the door. Lucas jumped. Vincent slid and Lucas sailed over him. The bay door was halfway open. The helmet muffled a roar that came from a grizzly bear as it tried to squeeze through the widening gap. Vincent grabbed the door handle. Suddenly, his right leg slid from underneath him, Lucas biting into the thick fabric of the suit.

"Doc! Helmet's coming off!" The squeal stopped as Vincent tore the helmet off his head. Lucas jumped at his throat as Vincent swung the helmet. "Aw shoot!" Crack.

Lucas crumpled to the floor as the grizzly bear slid under the opening. Vincent jumped to his feet and ripped the door open. He jumped through and kicked the door, hitting the grizzly in the face as it thundered toward him. The door bounced back open but Vincent body slammed it, forcing it shut.

The deadlock engaged.

He collapsed and lay panting on the floor for several seconds before getting to his feet. "Sorry bud, you might have a bit of a headache in the morning." He checked his leg for bites or scratches. There were none. Vincent let out a long breath. "I swear, next time, I'm letting you die in there."

CHAPTER 5

Vincent slumped into his chair back at the monitoring center, wiping away sweat, still in his protective suit. His computer monitor showed the now empty room where he and Lucas had just been. Dozens of people all around the room stopped what they were doing to stare at him. A handful of people in one corner whispered, putting away the video they had taken over the doctor's shoulder of Vincent's near escape. Even the ones who were seated at the computers were watching Vincent. The doctor stood beside him. "That was a close call. I'm sorry, I should have warned you. I should have known that would happen."

Vincent yawned and took a drink of his Diet Dr. Pepper. "It's fine Doc. I didn't die." He slid the keycard across the desk, back to the doctor. "Worst case scenario, you'd've had to find someone else to keep an eye on Lucas for the night." He pressed a few buttons on the computer. Tucked behind the computer was a small wrist gauntlet, plugged in to charge. Its touchpad lit up as the computer shut down and a plastic card slid out of a port in the computer. "Now that he's out there, I just can't sit in here anymore, now can I?" Vincent put the card between his teeth to slide on the gauntlet and tighten the leather straps.

As it turned on a mechanical voice announced itself. "Hello. Now tracking, Lucas A. Harrison."

Vincent stood and patted the doctor on the back and then saluted to the gaping bystanders. "As you were." He walked into the hall, this time turning left.

A sign indicated the direction to 'The Skywalk'. Vincent followed it without more than a glance. He took a flight of stairs with two landings before reaching a glass door with two-way hinges. Pushing the door open he entered the armory. The walls were covered with rows of modified rifles and handguns, each with a sleek air tank and altered magazine port. One section held dozens of protective suits. A rack of tactical vests hung on the back wall above trays filled with magazines and tranquilizer darts. There was a locked display case with powerful laser pointers on the top. Inside were vials of clear liquid. Vincent grabbed a tranq gun and two extra magazines. He slid a camo vest over his suit and stashed the magazines in a pocket. Using his fingerprint, he unlocked the case and grabbed a small vial and a laser, putting them into his vest pocket as he pushed through the door. Vincent walked back into the hall, tucking the gun into a sash on the back of the vest. He turned left and swiped his keycard to walk through another glass door.

A blast of humid air woke him up. The cold and the smell of forest were electrifying. Vincent turned on a flashlight to reveal a network of metal catwalks thirty feet high spanning a massive enclosure, the large jungle canopy blocking out much of the light. Easily a half mile on both sides, the massive Terrapark sprawled outward showing patches of curated mini biomes, each separated by unclimbable walls.

Forests of several kinds, coniferous, tropical, deciduous, all set next to each other near the center, tall trees reaching up to the glass ceiling, branches brushing against massive flood lights that hurled imitation sunlight downward. A frigid tundra with rusting fans blowing snow down into icy caves where polar bears settled down for naps and ponds where penguins dove for fish. An ocean of dunes spotted with cacti, camels, and sturdy grass, teeming with more animal life than any natural desert. Wide grasslands occupied by small herds of bison and giraffes mingling with twice as many dairy cows was a sight found only in other ACC buildings. The catwalks had cage-like structures around them in the forest biomes, all the branches hacked off a few feet from the metal railings, with rolls of razor wire wrapping around the spots where the cage ended so nothing could climb past and onto the catwalks.

Roars, howls and twittering filled the air all around. Vincent craned his neck to see the aviary above him. A huge mesh enveloped the top half of the enclosure, wrapping around tree trunks, the only entrance a large opening near the top of the wall, almost fifty feet from the ground. Hundreds of birds flew every which way, letting out a cacophony of sound. Across one side of the enclosure the Terrapark dipped underwater into the Aquarium. A glass barrier separated the two sections where a pod of dolphins played, and a sperm whale swam slow steady laps down and back in the limited space. A large underwater tunnel served as both entrance and exit for the area. Another large body of water drove into the center of the Terrapark, home to freshwater fish and other aquatic animals. All around the Terrapark going into each of the biomes were large metal doors of which about half were open, revealing prep rooms like where Vincent had nearly been bitten earlier. The rest contained transformed but sleeping Anthropes.

Vincent began walking along the catwalk and he activated the tracking systems on his wrist gauntlet. He began a light jog, following the blip on the screen that told him where to find Lucas. The blip led him to the water line.

There he was. Lucas was lapping up water with his tongue along the river. A glass barrier had been placed a few feet offshore from him to keep land animals out. On the opposite side there was a metal dividing wall a few feet from shore, separating it from other biomes and making that area isolated and inaccessible except for animals already in the river. The river was much deeper in the middle, the bottom dropping off rapidly. All kinds of fish swam around, and an otter paddled past, stopping to take a rest on the isolated bank. In the distance other guardians wandered around on the catwalks, each following an anthrope down on the ground.

Vincent rested his arms on the railing and watched Lucas. "I'm guessing after I woke you up, you had a lot of energy," he said to Lucas. Lucas couldn't hear him, but Vincent grinned, keeping himself entertained. "You usually just hang out in the trees and sniff around, but you haven't stopped moving since you woke up. Whatever I gave you must have been zesty."

Lucas pawed his head. "Hurts, huh?" Vincent smirked, "Well, if I hadn't done that I'd be out there playing with you, but then who would keep an eye on us?" Vincent glanced down at a metal container welded to the railing. A box of latex gloves sat on top. He put a glove on one hand and reached into the container, pulling out a slab of raw beef. "Hungry bud?" He tossed the meat down, hitting Lucas on the side. "Sorry!" Vincent called out. Lucas looked up, seeming to glare at Vincent before wolfing down the meat.

"Mind if I join you?"

Vincent turned around and saw Annabeth walking over to him. "Annabeth?"

"Hi Vincent." She waved. "May I?"

Vincent turned around and looked at Lucas again. "Free country. Do whatever you want. Why are you here?"

Annabeth stood next to him. She pointed over the railing. "That's my friend over there. Kenzie." A grizzly bear walked out of the woods and began to drink from the water several paces away from the gray wolf. "Is that Lucas?"

"Yeah," Vincent cocked his head, "Kenzie didn't by chance try to get into one of the prep rooms while it was opening, did she?"

"Actually yeah, it's the one Lucas came out of."

Vincent frowned, "I was in there."

"Wait, really?"

Vincent nodded, "He wanted to sleep through tonight, but they gave him the wrong sedatives. They mixed his up with another dose that was strong enough to stop his heart. I had to go in there, give him… whatever to wake him up, and then open the enclosure from the inside. Lucas almost bit me and then Kenzie nearly ate me."

"Woah." Annabeth said. "You must have been really brave to do that. I think Kenzie might have gotten his sedatives."

Vincent did a double take. "Wait really?"

She nodded. "Yeah. She wanted to sleep tonight too but the sedatives took longer than usual to work. Usually it drops her like a rock. That's when I said something to the anesthesiologist. Then after midnight she woke up, so we let her out and now she's here. She's kinda groggy, there's still a bit in her system, but not enough to knock her out."

Vincent laughed. "That's crazy." His laugh died out and he turned away from her.

She looked at him, suspicious. "What's wrong?"

Vincent shook his head, "Nothing."

Annabeth nudged him. "Come on, you can tell me. Is it about the election this morning? Or well, yesterday morning?"

Vincent looked over at her, "That wasn't very cool," he said, "You made fun of my best friend and you used that to win," Vincent looked away, "But that's not it."

Annabeth rested one elbow on the railing and faced him. "What?"

Vincent sighed and said something under his breath, then stood there for a moment in silence before finally asking, "Do you know why I wanted to be Lucas's campaign manager?"

"Umm," she said, "wasn't it because you wanted to ride his coattails or something?"

He shook his head, "No, that's not why. I did it because I was afraid I would lose my best friend."

"But-"

Vincent put his finger up to her mouth. "Let me talk. You asked for this." She nodded and he dropped his finger. "Lucas and I have been best friends since long before he was the wolf man, and neither of us really had friends back then. Just each other. The two of us were out in the woods, camping. We heard a noise outside and went to check it out. So, we unzipped the tent and this wolf jumps out and bites Lucas on the arm. Then he… well he turned into a wolf. And the two of them ran off. The guy that bit him was arrested. When we finally found Lucas that next morning, he'd already been all over the news. That year when school started, he basically became famous, and I was still just his friend. And ever since then he's been… the wolf man. Last year he ran for junior class president and he won in a landslide. I was happy for him, but it took up a ton of his time. And I was pretty lonely."

"But-"

"Hush. I'm getting there. This year he told me he was going to run again. And I panicked at first. But then I realized, maybe if I was more involved in the whole thing, I'd get to hang out with him more. So, I told him I wanted to be his campaign manager."

Annabeth interrupted him. "I don't see what any of this has to do with me. Why do *you* hate *me*?"

Vincent exploded. "Because you represent everything unfair about it!"

Annabeth froze. "What do you mean?"

He looked at her. "Everything is so easy for Lucas." He counted on his fingers. "Friends, fame, girls…" He looked back up. "Guys like me, don't end up with girls like you because of guys like Lucas. They're too irresistible."

Annabeth looked down. "That's not always true."

"What's that supposed to mean?" Vincent asked, eyes piercing.

Annabeth floundered. "Well… what I'm trying to say is… there's lots of girls who…" She turned red.

"Kenzie is leaving," Vincent pointed without breaking eye contact, "You should go."

"Vincent, I-"

He turned around and took hold of the railing, knuckles white. The sound of boots on metal faded behind him. Vincent huffed. Lucas looked up at him from below, head tilted curiously. Vincent shook his head and tossed another slab of beef.

CHAPTER 6

Darkness.

"Hey Lucas."

Lucas opened his eyes, back in the prep room. "Hmm? Hey Vincent." He sat up. "How'd I do last night?"

Vincent spoke into the microphone. "Well, you tried to eat me and you almost died, but other than that… pretty alright." He took a sip of his Diet Dr. Pepper.

"I almost died?" Lucas grabbed his underclothes from the wall cubby.

"Yeah," Vincent said, swirling his drink around in the can, "and you also kind of tried to eat me but, hey, who am I to judge? Not a big deal."

"Sorry," Lucas said. "What happened?"

"So, there was this girl named Kenzie-"

Lucas put on his underclothes. "Kenzie? Kenzie Wallace?"

"Yeah, her." The intercom crackled. "You decent?"

"Yeah." Lucas said.

The door swung open and Vincent stepped inside, already in his normal clothes. He tossed Lucas his shoes with his socks and phone stuffed inside. Lucas pulled on his pants. Vincent sat on the concrete floor. "So, Kenzie, apparently she's a… oh what's the word… Arkoanthrope."

"A bear?"

"Yup. So apparently, they mixed up your sedatives and hers weren't strong enough, so they realized something was wrong and I guess they figured out they mixed you two up. So, they sent me down here and basically I had to give you some kind of reverse sedative and then I had to let you out, but the door wasn't opening so then you woke up and tried to eat me. And then when the overhead door opened Kenzie the bear tried to eat me."

Lucas pulled his shirt over his head. "Sounds like a pretty wild night."

Vincent nodded. "Oh, and one other thing," he said, "Annabeth was here." He took another drink.

Lucas perked up, pretending to be surprised, "She was?"

"Yup," he said, "she's paired up with Kenzie."

"But I thought Kenzie already had a partner." Lucas sat next to Vincent and put his shoes on.

Vincent shook his head. "Nah, her mom was coming to keep an eye on her."

"You going to be fine with her being here at the same time as you and everything?"

Vincent shrugged. "Last night was fine." He said. "She kept her distance."

Lucas eyed him. "What did you do?"

"What?"

"You've got that look in your eye."

Vincent tossed his hands in the air, nearly sloshing his Diet Dr. Pepper everywhere. "I didn't do anything. Just because my normal face looks mischievous doesn't mean I'm always up to mischief. For goodness' sake, I'm not some kind of satanic leprechaun."

"Okay, okay." Lucas stood up. "Let's get out of here. I'm hungry."

"You ate so much last night."

"And I want to eat more now. C'mon. Let's go to Mickey D's." Lucas walked out of the prep room and Vincent followed, passing through the locker room where dozens of guardians waited for their partners to wake up and get dressed. They walked out to the lobby and waved goodbye to Karen before walking all the way out to the car. Vincent hopped in the driver's seat and turned on the engine.

"You know what," Vincent said, sipping his Diet Dr. Pepper, "you don't have many talents, but at least you wake up pretty fast. Means we can beat the rush out of here." Vincent clicked his seat belt on, and the tires screeched as they whipped out of the parking lot and pulled onto the interstate. Lucas turned on the radio and the two jammed out on the way to McDonald's. They finally pulled off at their exit and turned into the parking lot. Vincent got his wallet out as they walked through the door, the smell of fries washing over them. He handed the cashier, a groggy middle-aged woman with red hair, a five and a one. "Hi, I'm going to get a Double Quarter Pounder. How are you doing?"

She shrugged, "Pretty good. You?"

"I'm doing alright," Vincent said, shoving his hands in his pockets, "You can keep the change."

The lady smiled and took Lucas's order. They filled their cups and sat down at a booth, the leather seats worn with holes on the corners. Lucas checked his social media and found a few dozen posts from yesterday with his face in them. "Hey, check this out," he said, "this was so crazy, in English this one dude brought beer goggles into class and had the teacher try them on." Lucas showed him a selfie with the English teacher wearing a funky pair of glasses.

Vincent blinked a few times. "Those aren't beer goggles."

"Aren't beer goggles just glasses that distort your vision like you're drunk?"

"No," Vincent shook his head, "not even close."

Lucas cocked his head, "Then what are beer goggles?"

After taking a long breath, Vincent took a sip of his soda and looked at Lucas. "Beer goggles are when you get drunk and you start to think people are hotter than they are. So, I think it's pretty safe to say your English teacher didn't have beer goggles with the students."

"Oh," Lucas said, "well shoot. I have about a hundred likes on that post."

Vincent shrugged as their food was brought over. "Eh, people don't expect much out of you. Much less to know what beer goggles are." He smiled his thanks to the worker before saying a quick prayer over his food and then dug in.

"It's not like you would even know," Lucas complained, "you aren't even on social media."

Vincent pointed to Lucas with his burger, "And you know why?"

Lucas rolled his eyes, "It isn't all fake."

"No," Vincent said, "some of your posts are genuinely idiotic. It's just the rest of it that's fake. This is why I have superior mental health to everyone else. It's because I don't put poison into my body."

Lucas flicked Vincent's can of Diet Dr. Pepper and it fell over, empty. "And that poison?" He went back to scrolling through posts.

"Different," Vincent muttered, brow furrowing, "I can stop. Either way, the point still stands. I am far and away happier than the average high school student and way more stable."

Lucas lifted his camera, "Smile."

Vincent's face didn't budge, "I don't believe in smiling, and definitely not for your posts. I'd rather keep all the happiness inside instead of wasting it on all the miserable plebeians at Weber."

Lucas typed out a quick sentence. "Alright, it's time for Weber to answer that question. Who is happier, Vincent Parker or the average high schooler?" He pressed the screen and posted it.

"I'm going to win in a landslide. People like to complain about how hard their lives are," Vincent shrugged, "Basic high school sheep mentality."

Lucas huffed at the first comment that complained that even someone depressed probably was happier than the average high schooler. Vincent shoved the last third of his hamburger into his mouth. "I found this new band last night that's pretty dope."

"What're they called?"

"The Monkees. They're from the sixties. They did a ton of good music, and a few of their songs you probably know."

"Like what?" Lucas said, munching on a fry dipped in ketchup and mayo.

Vincent swallowed. "I'm A Believer."

"By Neil Diamond?"

"Yeah, he wrote it for them. Low key like their version better."

"Huh," Lucas said, distracted by something outside. "Look who it is."

Vincent glanced out the window and saw Annabeth and Kenzie walking up to the door. "Did you post where we are?"

Lucas checked his phone. "Uhhh… yes. It's probably just a coincidence, though, it was only a minute ago." Annabeth and Kenzie walked in and Lucas waved to them. "Annabeth! Kenzie!"

They waved and went to the front to order. After getting their drinks they joined Lucas and Vincent at the booth, Annabeth sitting next to Lucas. Kenzie took her seat next to Vincent. She had brown hair that fell past her shoulders, splayed out around a sports jacket. She had a narrow face with a curved scar on the left side. A handful of dark freckles were scattered across her face. "Sup dudes," she said in a low voice.

Vincent blinked a few times and looked at her.

Lucas had a similar reaction to hearing her talk, pausing for a second before responding, "Not much, you?"

"Nothin'."

Vincent got out his phone and texted Lucas discreetly, *Serious man voice.* Lucas sent back a laughing crying emoji and went back to scrolling, showing Annabeth his favorite posts he'd seen that week. Vincent ate a couple of fries and then pulled a pen out of his pocket and doodled a hangman game on a napkin, with the noose already included and six empty spots. He slid it over in front of Kenzie. "Wanna play?"

"E."

Vincent shook his head and drew a line with a bend in it from the bottom of the noose. "Nope. No E."

"Hey, bro," Kenzie complained in her man voice, "that's against the rules, that's the noose, you have to draw the head."

Vincent looked up innocently, "What rules?"

"The rules of hangman, dude."

"What rules?" Vincent's eyebrows crept upward.

"The rules every dude plays by."

"No such thing," Vincent said, "there are no codified hangman rules. And since I started the game, we can play by my rules."

Annabeth stopped watching Lucas scroll through his feed and looked over at the hangman game. "Hey, she only guessed one letter and there's already three body parts there."

"Nah sis, there's two," Kenzie said, "the head and the body."

"There's a leg there," Annabeth pointed to where the body bent, "Next wrong letter he'll add another leg at that bend and then he'll probably draw both arms at once. That's only three wrong guesses. That's dirty."

Vincent settled back into his seat and smirked. "Perfectly legal," he said to Kenzie without looking at Annabeth, "Morally wrong, but legal."

"Dang," Kenzie said, "alright, 'T'."

"There is no T," Vincent said, drawing the second leg like Annabeth had predicted. "One more guess."

Lucas put his phone away and gave a good hard look at the game. "Oh, I know this one, it's O. He always does this."

Vincent looked at Kenzie, his face perfectly neutral. "What'll it be?"

"Don't play his mind games," Lucas said, "just say O."

"O."

Vincent wrote the letter O in the second, third, fifth, and sixth spots. "One more guess."

"Broooo, what's the next letter?" Kenzie asked Lucas.

Lucas shrugged. "This is the farthest I've ever been able to make it. There's so many possibilities, I never guess the right one."

Annabeth squinted at the napkin, "You really do play dirty."

Vincent nodded. "The dirtiest."

"This is unwinnable."

Vincent nodded, "No one has ever guessed the right answer."

"No, what I'm saying is that you can just change it," Annabeth said, "even if you get the O's on the first try, there's too many possibilities to guess everything before running out of guesses, so you can just change the answer to whatever isn't guessed. Voodoo, booboo, googoo, I wouldn't put poopoo past you. And I'm assuming you think onomatopoeia is fine."

"Of course it is."

"So, you can just change the answer if they guess the word you chose."

Vincent propped his head up with his hands and feigned innocence, "I suppose I could do that if I wanted."

"Start a new one," Annabeth said, "you have to write the answer down on the back of the napkin."

Vincent gave Annabeth a withering look before flipping over the paper and writing something down secretly. He turned the paper back over and drew another six-letter hangman, noose included. "As you wish. Go ahead. You still won't win."

"O," Kenzie said.

Vincent chuckled and wrote O by the hangman and drew the body and a leg. "Oh, come on, I'm not going to give you the same word."

"Dude," Kenzie nudged Lucas, "what are his favorite hangman words?"

Lucas shrugged. "He really likes the O one, and jazz. He likes jazz."

"Ya like jazz?" Vincent asked. "Sorry, I had to."

"Jazz is only four letters but jazzed is six," Annabeth said, "I'd be comfortable guessing an A."

"A," Kenzie guessed.

Vincent put his hand to his mouth, pretending to stifle laughter. He wrote an A next to the hangman and drew the second leg. "One more guess."

"Okay, we need a vowel," Lucas said, "so e, i, and u."

"Or y," Kenzie added.

"E is too obvious," Annabeth said, "y is classic, u is too obviously unobvious. It's got to be i."

"*I* can get behind that," Lucas said, winking.

Vincent groaned. "Is that what you're guessing?"

Kenzie nodded. "Yeah man."

"That is just too bad," Vincent said, smiling as he ended the life of a stickman, "The word was fluffs. Better luck next time."

Annabeth folded her arms. "Do another one."

"Much obliged." Vincent made another hangman, complete with six letters and a noose. Annabeth shortly failed to correctly guess the word doodoo. After several more games undefeated, Vincent announced it was time to go home to take a nap, clicking his pen and sticking it in his pocket.

After Vincent was out the door Lucas glanced around. "Wait, all my stuff is in his car!" He stood up just in time to hear Vincent's tires squeal as he sped away. "Dang it, I guess I'm gonna need a ride…"

CHAPTER 7

Vincent dug his finger under the pop tab and yanked up. "Mmm… I love that sound." He took a swing of his drink.

They sat in the basement of Lucas's house. The soft beige carpet paired well with the cream-colored walls and white trim. There were three couches set around a large TV in an adjacent space. They were seated at a square game table with a red felt top and drink holders. A ping pong table was stowed against the wall to the left. A minifridge that Vincent had claimed for his favorite beverage was under a marble countertop with a sink. Two hallways went off in separate directions toward bedrooms.

"Vincent," Lucas said, "ya know, just because it's diet doesn't mean it's healthy to drink those so much."

Vincent wiped his mouth with the back of his hand. "Dude, my metabolism can keep up with it, I want to drink it, so I'm going to drink it."

"Fine, whatever, just pick up your cards." Lucas tossed Vincent a pair of cards.

Vincent picked them up. Two of clubs and seven of hearts. "Screw it," he muttered.

Lucas placed one chip in the middle of the table. "I didn't hear that. I'm not letting you get inside my head. Your mind games aren't going to work today." Vincent put two chips in the middle. Lucas laid down another chip.

Vincent's phone rang. "Hey, give me a second," He walked off into the hall, "Hello?" He grumbled under his breath.

"Yo, Vincent, everything alright?"

Vincent held up a finger. "We had to leave our protective suits at the ACC the last time… We'll be fine without them… Tell them to bring tranq pistols… I still didn't get reimbursed from the last time I bought darts… No, tell them to go home, they'll just get in the way… It doesn't take that many people to catch a… what? Yeah, tell whoever it is we've got this, that's why they're paying us. Whatever." He grumbled again.

Lucas got up from the table and went into his bedroom. Vincent heard him rummaging around his closet. "Lucas!"

"What?"

"It's a rabbit!"

Lucas stuck his head out the door. "A rabbit? Do we know anyone that-"

"Not that I can think of. But they said it was in our area."

Lucas tossed him a black hoodie. He put on a camo jacket with thick fabric. "This should be good enough for a rabbit, don't you think?"

Vincent shrugged as he stuffed his head into the hoodie. "It'll have to be," he said, voice muffled. They ran upstairs to a brightly lit space right in the entryway. A beeping noise sounded and Lucas unlocked the door.

"Is that the fire alarm?" Lucas's mother shouted.

"No mom. ACC alarm. We're dealing with it. Nothing dangerous, just a rabbit. Keep the doors locked."

"You boys be careful!"

"We will, love you mom!" Lucas shut the front door behind him, turning the deadbolt with a key. With the clouds blocking out the moon, he could only see Vincent by the light that peeked around the curtains in the windows. "Where are we going?"

Vincent turned on his phone and pulled up a map, squinting at the bright screen in the darkness. "Right there." A ping showed up on the map.

"The thicket?" Lucas asked.

"Yeah." Vincent tossed him the keys. "You drive." They hurried down the front steps to Vincent's car parked along the curb. Lucas climbed in the driver's seat and slammed the gas pedal the instant the car was on and in gear.

"Where do we want to ditch the car?"

"Drive toward five hundred," Vincent said, "We'll go past the fire station and through the nature park. They're heading that way." Lucas nodded and turned right onto 4300 North. Vincent kept a close eye on the tracker. "Wait," he said, "wait stop!" A massive rabbit burst out of the trees next to the road. Lucas slammed the brakes. The squealing tires were deafening. They skidded to a stop. The rabbit slammed into the side of the car and ran off down the street, shadow enormous in the headlights. Vincent opened the door and jumped out of the car. "Call me and keep following. I'll do better on foot. Go!" He slammed the door and took off after the rabbit, sprinting full out down the street.

Lucas hit the gas while he dialed Vincent's number. "Vincent, look at that rabbit! It's bigger than a cat! Goodness, why couldn't it have been a cat?"

"You know I don't get along well with-" static noise overtook Vincent. "That's one massive-" Static. "Screw it, it's going back into the thicket. Park the car!" Vincent hung up.

Vincent sprinted after it into the woods.

Lucas pulled to the side of the road, popping a tire onto the curb as he stopped. He threw himself out of the car and chased after Vincent into the trees down a wood chip trail. "Vincent! Be careful! Don't let it bite you!" He crashed into the woods, only a few seconds behind.

"Well duh but I still have to catch-" Vincent fell silent mid-sentence with a crack, followed by a pair of thuds.

Lucas skidded to a stop. He turned in every direction, seeing only the dark woods. "Vincent? Vincent!" He turned on his phone's light and took off again, following Vincent's footmarks in the wood chip trail.

Lucas saw Vincent on the ground motionless, and a girl with a scar down the side of her face rubbing her head, getting to her feet next to him. "Kenzie? Is that you?"

"Who- Lucas?"

"Kenzie, what are you doing out here?"

Kenzie held up her phone. A map with a small blip moving away from them appeared on the screen. "Annabeth, man." She was breathing hard, head in obvious pain. "We were supposed to go in tonight, but she didn't come home when she was supposed to. I called the ACC peeps and they sent me her tracker." She started to get up, rubbing her head gingerly. "Took too long to find her though. I've been chasing her for twenty minutes. I almost had her but then Vincent came racing out of the bushes like some crazed stoner on a bad trip and then-"

"Woah, chill out. Sit down, you hit your heads together pretty hard." Lucas knelt down next to Vincent. "Vincent. Vincent, you okay?"

Vincent groaned. "Head hurts." He started to get up grunting. "The trail's all wet and it's soaking through my-"

"Stay down. You ran into Kenzie." Lucas said, cutting him off. "The rabbit. It's Annabeth."

"I knew that girl was bad news." Vincent put his hand over his face. "I told you. Goodness, I'm starting to get sick of being right."

"Not cool dude," Kenzie protested, "This is not her fault!"

"What are you even doing out here besides trying to break open my skull?"

Vincent yelled.

"I'm trynna to keep peeps safe by catching Annabeth."

"Yeah," Vincent said, "well good job, that was really safe back there. Good going! This is why I told them on the phone to send you home!"

"Vincent!" Lucas said. "Shut up! While you're arguing, Annabeth is getting away! Give me your phone, stay here, you might have a concussion." He took Vincent's phone and started jogging off. "Stay there." He went around the corner. "Wait a second, the tracker says-"

"Rabbit!" Vincent yelled.

Lucas sprinted back only to see the rabbit lunge at Vincent. Vincent grabbed the rabbit, trying to hold it back. Kenzie screamed. Vincent threw the rabbit off him. It ran off into the trees.

"That rabbit," Vincent panted, "is the fattest rabbit I've ever seen in my life."

"Yo dude…" Kenzie said, "that blood on your hand?"

Vincent sat up and looked at his hand and saw a smear of crimson on the backside. He closed his eyes. "Crap." He began to writhe in pain, his ears growing up past the top of his head. His pupils exploded and his body shrank into his hoodie.

Lucas lunged forward and pinned Vincent inside the hoodie. Vincent squirmed around for a few seconds before falling still. Lucas looked up at Kenzie. "Kenzie, you need to take him. I'll chase down Annabeth, but we can't have him running off too." He picked up the hoodie, careful to not let bunny Vincent wiggle out. Kenzie took the bundle, cradling it in her arms.

"Sure?" Kenzie asked. "She's fast. You're probably too slow to catch her on your own."

Lucas nodded, ignoring the diss. "I have to try. And you have to keep *him* from getting away." Lucas picked up the phone and began to walk away.

"Wait, dude," Kenzie said, "you'll want this." She held out a tranq gun.

Lucas looked down at the gun. "Where'd you get this?"

"Bought it. Never been a guardian until last month and I wanted to be prepared." She offered it to him again.

Lucas took the gun. "Thanks." He jogged off into the woods. The tracker showed Annabeth was moving away from him. North. Deeper into the thicket. Lucas heard approaching sirens. "Thank goodness." He followed the trail.

The tracker beeped. Annabeth had stopped. Lucas kept jogging until she was just a few paces to the right. He peered into the foliage, trying to make anything out. It was pitch black. He took off his shoes and slipped into the leaves. His socks were silent on the ground but quickly soaked through, causing them to squelch. He heard a rustle to his right. Right where Annabeth's tracker was. He squinted and could just make out the outline of an oversized rabbit.

As quietly as he could, he lifted the tranq gun. His finger tightened around the trigger. A blast of air and a scuffle. Annabeth thrashed around trying to knock the dart out of her neck. Little by little, she stopped moving. Lucas reached deep into the underbrush and poked Annabeth. She didn't move.

Lucas scooped her up and crawled out of the foliage, carrying the bunny like a big baby. He jogged down the path a ways before he came across with a man in a protective suit. It was Mr. Anderson, the ACC's odd job man. He wore a tranq rifle slung over his back and carried a metal rod with a loop at the end of it. "Hey Lucas. Is that the girl?"

Lucas nodded. "This is the biggest rabbit I have ever seen." He handed Annabeth over to the man.

"Apparently she's a Flemish Giant, which is supposedly the largest kind of rabbit."

"Huh. Who'd've thought."

They walked out of the thicket. An ACC truck was parked outside, lights flashing. It was shaped like an ambulance with the back section converted into a holding space for rogue anthropes. Kenzie rushed up to them, still holding a hand to her head. "Dudes, did you get her?"

Mr. Anderson held up Annabeth.

"Thanks man. I thought I was sooo scooby dooed."

"Wasn't me." Anderson pointed to Lucas. "It was him."

Kenzie gave him a fist bump. "Thanks dude," she said.

"Yeah, no problem… dude," he shifted awkwardly. "Uh, is Vincent alright?"

She nodded. "Yup, in the truck."

Lucas walked over to the truck. He opened the passenger door and climbed inside. A door to the back was shut. Lucas peered into the hatch and saw Vincent on the floor, sniffing at the air. "Hey buddy. How ya doing?"

Mr. Anderson knocked on the door. Lucas pushed it open and Mr. Anderson handed Annabeth up. Lucas cracked open the door to the back of the truck and pushed Annabeth inside. Vincent hopped over to her and sniffed. He nudged her with his nose. "See buddy, she isn't so bad. She's just like us. And you're just like her." He winked at the huge rabbits.

Anderson climbed into the driver's seat. "Hey, we're going to take these two back to the compound. Is that your car over there?"

Lucas shook his head. "No, it's my buddy Vincent's but I've got the keys."

"Good. By law there needs to be at least one guardian in the truck, so the girl will come with me in here, but you need to bring the car with you so you guys can get back home."

Lucas nodded and stepped out of the truck. Kenzie stood outside patiently. Lucas held the door open for her. "I'll see you there," he said.

Kenzie got into the truck, and he walked over to the car. He put the key in the ignition and started it. He followed the ACC truck all the way to the compound. The truck pulled around to a side parking lot and backed into a loading dock. The driver got out of the truck and pressed a button on the side. The back end of the truck opened up. Lucas and Kenzie followed Mr. Anderson through a door. They entered what was basically an all-concrete hallway with a metal cage dividing the walkway in two, one for people, the other for transformed anthropes. A closed metal door connected the parallel walkways. The overhead door was at the end of the anthrope side. Anderson pressed another button that opened up the exterior wall, connecting the truck to the passageway.

Vincent hopped through and went down the passage, leaving Annabeth unconscious in the truck. Lucas turned to Mr. Anderson. "Do we need to get her out of the truck?"

Anderson smiled. He held up a remote and pointed it at the truck. A piston activated and the floor began to rise on one end, making the sleeping Annabeth slide out and into the building, then he shut the bay door. "Let's get these two separated for the night and we can figure out what we need to do in the morning. Are you two good to do that?"

Kenzie and Lucas nodded.

"Good. They're harmless, so one of you can go to the other side and carry her to the holding rooms. I need to go file some paperwork and give my report on this. You two do your thing." He walked off down the hall, leaving them with rabbit Annabeth. Vincent had already followed the enclosure around the corner up ahead.

"Vincent is going to be so mad when he wakes up." Lucas laughed, opening the connecting door and stepping over to Annabeth. "C'mon, we should hurry and then check in with the director."

CHAPTER 8

Lucas and Vincent sat in the ACC Director's office. The director was a short and friendly grandma who kept a jar of red and white mints on her desk. She wore a blue corduroy vest over a knitted sweater and her gray hair was tied back into a loose ponytail that stuck to the back of her vest. The walls were filled with pictures of her kids and grandkids. The whole room smelled like cookies. A wide couch from several decades ago was pushed up against the wall. Lucas and Vincent sat on opposite ends. Vincent rubbed his forehead. "My mom is going to *kill* me."

"Well, good thing it's only permanent the first time an anthrope bites you. Otherwise, I'd have like seven anthropes and have to show up here twice a week. Your anthrope is still the same as before even though you transformed last night. You don't have to change your lunar schedule. And neither do I."

"Try explaining that to my mom. She's still going to flip."

"So let me get this straight," the director said as she peered over her massive glasses. She pointed to Lucas with a pencil. "You were chasing the rabbit through the woods, and you hit your head on the rabbit's guardian's head." She pointed to Vincent. "And then you kept going." She pointed back to Lucas. "And then while you were still on the ground you were bitten or scratched by the rabbit?"

"No," Lucas said, "it was the other way around."

"Oh, sorry, excuse me. I'm getting old." The director laughed and bopped herself on the forehead. She flipped the pencil over and erased their names. As she talked to them, she wrote the names down exactly as they were before. "So then, you caught *him*," she pointed to Lucas, "And this young lady… uh…"

"Annabeth."

"Annabeth. Yes. I knew an Annabeth when I was younger." She wrote the name down on the paper. "She had these big, long pigtails and in second grade our teacher, oh she was a witch, she cut off her pigtails in class with a pair of scissors. And then Annabeth's mother came in very upset about the whole thing and demanded the teacher apologize if she didn't want the county sheriff involved."

Lucas scooted forward on the couch, engaged. "What happened?"

The director frowned and tapped her chin with the pencil. "Hmm… I don't remember. But either way, it was very interesting. Poor Annabeth."

The door handle turned and Kenzie walked into the room, followed by Annabeth. Annabeth didn't look up from the floor. She wore a set of generic blue clothes the ACC kept on hand. Vincent and Lucas slid over to the ends of the couch, making room for the girls in the middle. Annabeth sat down next to Lucas and Kenzie next to Vincent.

"Which one of you is Annabeth?" The director asked.

"Me." Annabeth still didn't look up.

"Hello Annabeth," the director said, "so help me understand, what exactly happened?"

Annabeth didn't say anything.

"Sweetie, I can't help you if you don't talk to me." The director slid forward the jar of mints. "Here, take a candy. All of you take one." The teenagers all obediently took a mint from the jar. "Now, Annabeth, dear, please tell me what happened."

Lucas noticed something fall from Annabeth's eye. He looked down at her knee and saw a tear glistening on her pant leg. He leaned forward and grabbed a tissue off the desk and handed it to Annabeth. As he settled back into his seat he paused. He raised his arm slightly but then stopped. Lucas leaned back into the seat. Kenzie put her arm around Annabeth. "Hey, dude, it's alright. It's not your fault. Just tell the director what happened and everything will be alright."

Annabeth looked up teary eyed. "I was out hiking in the woods. There's this path up in the mountains. So, I was up there, and I decided to go exploring a little bit off the trail. But I got lost and I didn't know where I was and then my phone died, and I could tell it was getting pretty late and I knew I was far out. So, I started looking for the trail and it took me a couple hours. The sun had been down for at least three hours by the time I found the trail again. So, I tried to run back but I…"

The director nodded. "It got too late."

Annabeth nodded and buried her face in her hands. "I'm sorry," she whispered, "it was an accident."

"That's alright," the director said, "accidents happen. Lucas, best of luck explaining to your mother."

"Uhh, thank you," Vincent said. "I hope everything goes over alright."

"Well," the director said, standing up, "you can go now. I'm sure you are all very tired. You've had a long night." She opened the door for them.

Vincent stood and walked out of the room. Kenzie followed him. Lucas stood but waited. Annabeth didn't get up for nearly a full minute. Lucas reached out to touch her on the shoulder, but hesitated. The director nodded to him. He rested his hand gently on her warm shoulder. "Annabeth, she said we can go."

Annabeth let out a shaky breath. "I'm not in trouble?"

"No sweetie," the director shook her head, "you aren't in any trouble. Accidents happen. Lucas signed paperwork saying he wouldn't press charges if something like this happened. It was part of his extended contract as an emergency guardian. So did Vincent here. Right?"

"Yup," Lucas said, trying to suppress his smile over her mistake, "it's okay Annabeth. It's not your fault. Come on, let's get you home. You must be tired."

She nodded and let him help her up. "Thank you," she said to the director. She followed Lucas out the door and he went right. She stopped. "Lucas, where's the car?"

He turned around and pointed over his shoulder with his thumb. "It's parked out back."

"Oh, I thought it was the other way." She followed him side by side down the hall and out the door by the loading dock into the early morning, the sky still dark.

Vincent and Kenzie sat against the hood of the car, waiting for Lucas to bring the keys. Instead of walking over, Lucas turned to Annabeth, looking into her eyes in the dim light of the lamp posts. "You doing okay?"

"Not really. I feel so stressed." Annabeth folded her arms and shivered.

Lucas noticed and pulled off his sweater. "Well, you can relax now. Sleep if you want while we drive." He held the sweater out to Annabeth. "Here. You look cold."

She nodded gratefully. "Thank you." She put it on. They walked to the car in silence. The chirps of crickets in the early morning enveloped them as the first glimmers of light began to peek over the far-off mountains. Vincent and Kenzie were talking quietly by the car. Lucas opened the backseat door for Annabeth, and she sat down. Lucas closed the door and handed Vincent the keys. He walked around to the other side of the car and climbed in next to

Annabeth. Annabeth rested her head on the seat and closed her eyes. Vincent put the car in gear and pulled out going slow, and he maintained a speed five miles per hour under. They drove all the way to the freeway entrance without a word passing between them.

Vincent was the first to break the silence. "Hey Annabeth, where do you-"

"Shh," Lucas held a finger up to his lips, "She's asleep."

"I know her address," Kenzie said. "I think it's actually pretty close to where you live, Lucas."

"Cool," Vincent said as he merged onto the interstate. "And where do you live Kenzie?"

"I live just south of the school."

"Alright, I'll drop you off first."

Lucas looked over at Annabeth. He brushed some of her loose hair out of her face. She looked peaceful. Lucas looked up to the front and saw Vincent watching him in the rear-view mirror with a blank expression on his face. Vincent held his gaze.

Lucas looked away first. He glanced back up a second later and Vincent had his eyes trained on the road, once again expressionless. Lucas looked back over to Annabeth for a moment and then closed his eyes, twenty-four hours since he had last slept.

The ACC director opened up the mini fridge in the back of her office. She poured water out of a pitcher into a glass. After a few drinks to clear her head, she sat down at the desk again. The top of her computer read 'Annabeth L. Watson Tracker'. The director picked up a pencil and used it to press a few keys on the computer. A map popped up on the screen showing the ACC and the surrounding cities.

A blip on the screen indicated Annabeth's current location. She mumbled to herself as she pecked out keys, "And zoom in…" the director punched a few more keys and read a few lines at the side bar, "good, she's at home, sleeping it looks like." She selected an option at the bottom of the screen. "Now let's see where you *were*." The screen reset to display Annabeth's location from the day before. The indicator traced a path from Annabeth's house into the woods, indicating the time of the display to be five o'clock. The blip wandered out along a mostly straight path near the mountains before taking a sharp turn. It proceeded a quarter mile before stopping in place. "That's strange."

The director activated satellite mode and trees dotted the screen. But the area around the tracker was cleared. A thin trail led from the main path down to the clearing. The tracker stopped moving. The director used her pencil to speed up the tracking.

Suddenly the blip zipped away and stopped at the ACC. "Oops, too fast." The director rewound the recording and watched again slower, seeing Annabeth's tracker leave the clearing around midnight, move around in the forest, and then be driven to the ACC. "Either the signal on the tracker cut out, or that girl didn't get lost." She picked up a radio on her desk and pressed down a button on the top. "Anderson, are you there?"

A voice crackled through. "Director?"

"Hi, I'm going to forward you the location of that uncontained anthrope from earlier. Make sure you pick up her clothes and things. If they aren't there, radio me first chance you get."

"Sure thing boss. Out."

"Anderson wait-"

Static. "Boss?"

The director tapped the end of her pencil on the desk. "While you're there, it's a little clearing in the woods, can you look around for anything out of place?"

"Sure can do. Think something is up?"

"No, maybe, her tracker stopped moving and it doesn't match up with her story. I just want to make sure it was her tracker cutting out and not something else. You know they can be a little wacky up in those mountains."

"Will do."

The director poured herself another glass of water. "Do you remember that lycan a year or two ago that attacked that kid in the woods? It took us hours to find him. Poor kid. He was one of the kids who helped track down the girl actually. For now, I'm going to flag Annabeth's file just in case. Anything unusual will be reported. If she gets pulled over, or applies for a job, or even uses her credit card we'll know. We just want to keep an eye on her for now."

"Uh, hey boss," Anderson interrupted, "I'm pulling out right now, so I should probably focus on driving, but do you think you could send me that location?"

"Yes," she said, sending the tracking log to him, "it's done. Good luck out there."

"Thanks boss." Anderson's line went dead. The director unpaused her game of sudoku.

CHAPTER 9

In Vincent's basement all the walls were so faintly blue they looked white depending on how much sunlight came through the window wells. Most of the space was carpeted except for the workout station. Next to it was the library, which although small was unusually large for a home library. A couch and two reading chairs were positioned facing away from the home gym with shelves filling the walls on three sides. In the center was a chestnut coffee table with a can of Vincent's favorite beverage and a blue book open near the middle. Vincent closed the book, showing the gold lettering on the cover. He flipped around on the couch, resting his arms on the backrest and his chin on his arms. He watched Lucas struggle on the bench. "Are you sure you want just the two of us to go together?"

Lucas did one last rep on the bench press before sitting up. "Vincent, look," Lucas said, "we could take people to go with us, but it's the big game. Weber against Fremont. We need to be fully invested in the game, we can't have any distractions."

Vincent shrugged and drank some Diet Dr. Pepper. "Alright, fine. I'm pretty sure Annabeth would be a huge distraction anyway." Vincent walked over and took Lucas's place on the bench.

Lucas eyed Vincent. "Annabeth? I thought you said-"

"She's proven herself worthy." Vincent shrugged and lifted the bar. "Just don't expect me to talk to her."

"Are you messing with me or are you serious?"

"Look at my face," Vincent said, cranking out reps, "do I look serious?"

Lucas rolled his eyes. "You always look serious."

"That I do." Vincent grinned as he sat up. He grabbed his soda and took a drink. "But seriously though, I'm cool with it. Have her bring Kenzie though so I'm not bored the whole time."

Lucas whipped his phone out of his pocket. "That's very mature of you."

"Don't make me regret it." Vincent slid more weights onto the bar. "Come on, twenty more and then you're done."

"Agh, my arms already feel like noodles," Lucas flopped his arms around, "do we really have to add weight?"

Vincent reached toward the weight rack. "We can do more if you'd like."

Lucas pushed him aside and laid down on the bench. "Nope, I'm good." He did ten reps and then stopped, holding the bar up in the air. Breathing heavily, he did three more reps.

Vincent put his hand under the bar.

"Nope, I've got this. Just taking a little rest." Lucas did three more reps.

"Okay, four more. Go."

"Arms," Lucas did a rep, "are," he did another, "noodles", another rep, "hate," last rep, "everything!" Lucas practically dropped the bar back into place. "Man, that stinks."

"Yeah, but your veins are popping," Vincent said, pointing to his arms, "You'll be thanking me later."

"Yup…" Lucas was already distracted sending a text to Annabeth. "I will…" He typed a quick message and pressed send, "Sorry, what did you say?"

Vincent rolled his eyes, "Whatever. Not important. Did she say yes?"

Lucas nodded, "Annabeth is coming. Waiting to hear from Kenzie," His thumbs flew over the keypad and pressed send again, "Kenzie's coming too. We're going to pick them up at six."

"Six?" Vincent checked his phone.

"Yeah. What's wrong with that?"

"Dude," Vincent smacked his forehead, "it's five right now. I need to take a shower! Plus, the game doesn't even start until six thirty."

"I want good seats. You'll have plenty of time to shower."

Vincent shook his head. He grabbed a fistful of his thick curly hair. "Do you have any idea how long my hair takes to dry? If I want it to look good, it needs to air dry. We are going with girls. And they are cute girls! Even Annabeth. I can't be around cute girls in public with my hair looking like a poof ball! I need to be suave."

Lucas laughed. "Just stick your head out the window while we're driving to pick them up. That'll work right?"

"No," Vincent growled, "that does not work! It just makes my hair frizz."

"Oh no," Lucas mocked, "my hair! It's frizzy! I'm gonna die!"

Vincent walked into his bedroom. He walked back out with a towel around his neck. "Yeah, as much as that helps, I need to get in the shower now so I can let it dry. You know where the door is." He walked down the hall and into the bathroom.

Lucas laughed and walked up the stairs. "Alright, see you in an hour," he called out.

"Yeah, whatever, see you in an hour!" The shower turned on.

Lucas left and walked out to his car. He opened the door and turned it on. "Oh no! My hair!" He rolled down the window. Shifting into gear, he drove out of the neighborhood.

His phone buzzed in his pocket. Annabeth was calling him. He pinched the phone between his head and his shoulder. "Hey! What's up?"

"Is he really okay with us coming?"

"Yeah," Lucas said, turning a corner, "he actually suggested it."

"Uh huh. Really."

"No really," Lucas waved to a neighbor out for a jog, "He asked me if I really wanted to go with just him and then he suggested you and Kenzie come with us."

"That's kinda strange. He usually can't stand me."

"It's not that… he…"

"Lucas," Annabeth cut in, "He doesn't like me at all."

"Okay," Lucas admitted, "maybe, but I think he's coming around."

"Whatever you say, 'wolf man'. What were you two doing anyway?"

"Uh," Lucas hesitated and eased off on the gas as he passed a radar speed limit sign, "we were working out."

Annabeth snickered on the other end.

"No, really!" He protested. "We were!"

"Yeah, since when did you work out? Your arms are twigs."

"Yesterday." Lucas said defensively as he turned into his street. "This was the second time."

"How was it?"

"Ummm… I don't know. Awful? We ran about a mile. Then we did like forty squats with some weights. And we lifted the bench press bar twenty times and then traded off three times."

"How much did you lift?"

Lucas lied reflexively. "I'm not really sure, I wasn't paying attention."

"Oh, come on," Annabeth said, "you know how much it was. I can tell by your voice."

"It was like a hundred pounds." Annabeth said nothing as Lucas pulled into his driveway. "I know, I'm a wimp. Go ahead and say it."

"No, that's good for your second time. Really good."

Lucas climbed out of his car and locked it, "Well thanks. My arms don't feel very good though," he said as he walked in the front door, "If you don't mind, I need to take a shower. I smell awful."

"Well then in that case, definitely take a shower." Annabeth said. "I don't want you around if you're stinky."

"Okay bye."

"Bye!" Annabeth hung up. Lucas hurried up the stairs to his room to get in the shower. He turned on his speaker and cranked up the volume on 'I Believe in a Thing Called Love' by The Darkness. As the grainy electric guitar started, he hopped into the steamy stream of water, flipping his hair and drenching the ceiling as he belted out the words.

A few miles away, Benny Anderson sat atop a riding mower, using his knee to steer while playing the air guitar along with his headphones. He'd nearly finished the two-acre property, which hadn't taken long this being the first time he had to mow that year. His dark hair was cropped short on the sides, fading down into his light brown skin, sprinkled with sweat droplets. He wore jeans with holes at the knees and permanent dirt, grass, and motor oil stains with a rugged button up shirt he'd cut the sleeves off of.

While his palms were calloused, his fingertips were even more so from the hours he spent each day with the guitar. While he usually played very tenderly, he was also solidly built with a broad chest and strong arms. The music on his headphones cut out and he stopped the mower to answer a phone call.

"Hey Dad, yeah, I'm just finishing the lawn right now… I'm going to the basketball game later today… Of course I won't get in any fights, but those guys deserved it. They should've gone to prison for what they did." He nodded. "Alright, I solemnly swear to use my words and not my fists." He started up the mower again. "Okay, I just need to finish this one spot in the back and then I've got to go to get things set up. Talk to you later. Bye!" Benny finished mowing the lawn and took only a brief moment to brush the dust off himself before getting his car and driving to the school.

About an hour later, Lucas turned the wheel, going around a corner in a neighborhood under construction. "Hey Vincent, can you text Annabeth and tell her we're almost here?"

"What?" Vincent had his head sticking out the window, trying desperately to dry his hair. "I can't hear you!"

"Text Annabeth!"

Vincent pulled his head back into the car. "Big fan of meth?"

"What? No, I said to text Annabeth to let her know we're almost to her house."

"Oh, well, I couldn't hear you very well and I don't have her number." Vincent said.

"Why don't you have her number?"

"It's not like I'm going to ask her for it," Vincent shrugged.

"Whatever, just use my phone," Lucas tossed his phone into Vincent's lap.

Vincent doubled over with a clenched groan of pain. "Next time," he grunted, "aim for anywhere but there." He grabbed the phone and put in the password. "Where're your contacts?"

"Lower le-"

"Never mind," Vincent said, tapping the screen, "found it." He swiped up. "Uh, Lucas, I only found one Annabeth and there's a heart next to her name. Did you put her under a different name or…"

Lucas didn't look at Vincent. "That's the one," Lucas said through gritted teeth.

"Oh, my mistake." Vincent began to type, mumbling the words. "Almost at your house. Be ready. Kissy face. And send!"

"Dude!"

"Chill, just kidding." Vincent slipped the phone into his pocket as Lucas pulled up to Annabeth's house. It was a normal sized house with two thin stone pillars and a red door. Most of the house was made of red brick. Annabeth walked out of the open garage, tripping over a clutter of half unpacked boxes.

She opened the door to the backseat and slid into the car. "Hey guys!"

"Hi Annabeth! How are you?"

"Doing good, you guys?"

"I'm doing great," Lucas said. Vincent was silent. "Are you ready to win?"

"I think so." Annabeth said. "I know the Fremont team is pretty good, but are we better than them?"

Vincent finally piped up. "There's no question. Weber Warriors are a thousand times better than those Fremont-" They went over a pothole.

"Our basketball teams are pretty close," Lucas explained, "but we do really well at away games. I think we'll win. I'm definitely excited either way." Lucas lifted a window switch and Vincent's window began to roll up.

Vincent pressed the switch on his side and the window stopped closing. "Hey, I need that open!"

Lucas lifted the switch again and the window closed all the way. He pressed a button, locking the windows in place. "I wanna listen to music. It's too loud. And I'm driving." Lucas turned on the radio. Vincent pressed the switch, but his window didn't budge. He folded his arms and sat back in his seat. A piano riff played out of the speakers. "Awww yeah," Lucas yelled, "I love this song!"

Annabeth yelled over the blasting music. "Isn't this song about LSD?"

"What?" Lucas shouted, "No! It's about a really nice road called Lake Shore Drive, LSD is just the acronym! Listen to the words." He started singing along. "See? Lake Shore Drive! It's just a road!" He swayed his head and shoulders in opposite directions, trying to dance to the jazzy piano. "Vincent, come on, you know the words!"

"No." Vincent turned away. "Open the window, you'll still be able to hear the music."

Lucas turned on the AC full blast. "Compromise."

Vincent looked at Lucas, an eyebrow raised. He swayed to the music and pretended to play the piano riff on the dashboard. When the chorus came, he sang with all his heart.

"What about right here," Annabeth asked, "it said he was slipping on LSD!"

Lucas shrugged. "Look, all I know is that it's about a road and not drugs! I looked it up!" He turned down the music. "Is this Kenzie's house?"

Benny strode down the hallway of Fremont wearing his student officer jacket over his clothes. It weighed easily five pounds and was practically made of carpet, but he was required to wear it to every school event regardless. Fremont was a much newer and nicer school than Weber. The walls were made of fiberglass and there were lots of windows everywhere, letting beautiful natural light in. The carpet was a clean gray with blue highlights. The lockers were new and clean, without any dents in them.

Benny made his way to the gym and stopped before reaching the entrance. There two women and a brunette girl he'd seen at school were getting a concession stand ready. He walked closer and spotted Peanut M&Ms. "Hi, how's it going?"

"Good," the girl said, "how are you?"

"I'm doing great," Benny said, "question for you, how much are the Peanut M&Ms?"

"Buck fifty."

Benny dug two dollars out of his pocket and handed them over. "We have a class together, don't we?"

The girl handed him the M&M's and dug through the cashbox for quarters. "Yeah, we're in US History together. I'm Claire."

Benny snapped his fingers. "That's it. How's it going?"

"Still good." She handed him two quarters. "There's your change."

"Thanks! Are you going to be watching the game, or will you be here?"

"I'm just helping set up, then I'm gonna go watch."

"That's great, I'm going to be over in the student section if you want to come. See ya!" He walked off opening the M&M's.

The gym was packed for the rivalry game, bleachers filled with people wearing either blue or red. The students began to yell, building from a low rumble. One of the Fremont players dribbled the ball twice at the free-throw line. He made a clean shot that sailed into the basket, only brushing the net. The Fremont section cheered. Lucas groaned. "Ten points in the third quarter? There is no way we're winning this game." His stomach growled. "Hey Annabeth, I'm going to go get some snacks, wanna come?"

She nodded. "Sure." They squeezed out of the bleachers and walked up the steps and out into the hall. Annabeth looked around, a concessions table was situated to the left. "Can I go to the bathroom first?"

"Yeah, I guess I'll go right now too. I wonder where they are."

Annabeth pointed down the hall. "Boys bathrooms are over there, around the corner. Girls are the other way."

"Oh yeah, I forgot you used to go here. Alright, see you in a minute." Lucas walked down the hallway and turned the corner. The lights were off but flickered on as the sensors activated. Lucas found the bathroom and opened the door.

Back in the gym, Vincent leaned over to Kenzie and yelled over all the noise. "I know we're making a comeback right now but I've gotta, uh, take care of business. I'll be back." He worked his way out of the crowded bleachers and into the hall.

A concessions lady to his left waved to him. "Hi! Can I get you anything?"

Vincent smiled awkwardly, not a buck on him, "Bathrooms?"

"Around that corner," She pointed.

"Thank you." A trio of boys with boots and cowboy hats walked around the corner a ways in front of him. He followed them.

Lucas zipped up his pants and flushed the urinal. He walked over to the sink and started washing his hands. The bathroom was nice for a high school, there were even dividers between the urinals. The white tile floor and backsplash were kept pristine, and the mirror didn't have a spot on it. Lucas used the water on his hands to fix his hair. The tracker bracelet under his skin flashed softly just as a trio of boys walked into the bathroom. He shook the water from his hands. One of the boys, wearing a cowboy hat with a massive belt buckle, stepped forward and grabbed his wrist. The other two stood in front of the door. "What's that?"

Lucas looked down. His tracker flashed. He twisted his hand out of Belt Buckle's grip. "I'm sure you know." He tried to step past him, but the boy shifted, blocking his path.

"Why don't you tell me, freak?" Belt Buckle eyed Lucas's hands twitching by his side.

Lucas sighed. "Know what subepidermal means?"

Belt Buckle took off his hat, revealing a mullet. "Under your skin?"

"Exactly." Lucas said, chuckling softly under his breath while looking down at Belt Buckle's belt buckle. "That's what you're doing right now. Getting under my skin." Lucas met his eyes, daring him to back down. "So why don't you just bugger off and pee already like you came in here to do? Sound good cowboy?"

One of the boys who stood at the door peeled away and stepped up to Lucas, massive height and girth imposing. "We ain't cowboys." Behind him the door jerked. Lucas heard someone grumble on the other side.

"Vincent?" Lucas whispered. He looked up at the one who was 'not a cowboy'. "Then what exactly are you?"

"This is Fremont. We're the hunters." Not A. Cowboy said. "That's our mascot. 'Cause we hunt scared little animals like you."

"Is that so?" Lucas nodded absently. "Well, happy hunting. I'll be on my way. I'll tell the others to look out."

The door shook. Vincent yelled, pounding. "What's going on in there? Open the do-" The boy standing at the door kicked behind him just as it began to open and there was a thump from the other side.

"That's a good idea," Belt Buckle said, handing off his hat to Not A. Cowboy, "Go tell everyone. Here's a better idea though. You can show them." Belt Buckle slugged Lucas in the jaw. Lucas snapped around and fell to the floor.

Belt Buckle kicked him in the side and in the leg. Lucas groaned. Two voices shouted from the hall. "Open the door!"

Lucas rolled over on the dirty floor. He spat blood and stood up, favoring one leg and reaching into his back pocket. "You don't want to do this."

"Why not, freak?" Belt Buckle held his fists up, ready.

"Because if you don't leave me alone, I'm going to drink this." Lucas held up a vial filled with clear liquid. He shook it and it lit up blue. "Do you know what this is?" The three boys turned white. Lucas nodded in satisfaction. "We keep these for emergencies, so punks like you three leave us alone. And you're going to leave me alone, or I will drink this, and I'm hungry. Ever met a hungry wolf? That's right. Gray wolf. So you're going to walk out of here, right now." Lucas popped the plastic top off with his thumb. "Three..."

The door rattled violently. The door guard began to sweat.

"Two... one-"

Belt Buckle launched himself at Lucas, pinning him to the ground. Lucas tried to drink the vial, but Belt Buckle held his arm down. The door burst open and Vincent and a boy with a Fremont jacket rushed in. Vincent pounded Belt Buckle in the head and the other boy threw himself at Not A. Cowboy. Lucas took a deep breath as Belt Buckle fell limp on top of him, bending his leg at an awkward angle. He shoved the boy off of him and put the cap back on the mostly spilled vial. The door guard ran off into the hall.

Vincent punched Not A. Cowboy across the jaw, and he fell to the ground. He didn't move. Lucas's other defender kept an eye on him. Vincent picked Lucas up. "You alright?"

Lucas touched his jaw and winced. "A little out of breath and my jaw might be dislocated or something. Bruised maybe? He hit me pretty hard. My leg got twisted too. I might need a little help to walk."

"Well," Vincent said, looking at Belt Buckle slumped on the ground, "I think I hit him harder." He shook his hand as though it were wet. "Yeah, a lot harder."

The other boy walked up to them. He had broad shoulders but was an otherwise normal size. His short hair was dark, creeping into the edges of a rough face that was handsome enough when it wore a smile. His tan skin came from his mother's Chilean ancestors. He folded his arms across his chest, popping veins indicating familiarity with hard work. "You okay?"

"Yeah. I think I'm good."

The boy looked at the near empty vial in Lucas's hand. "Is that…"

Lucas followed his eyes to the vial. "Oh, goodness no. If I had one of those that would be super illegal. This is just a fake. We carry them to scare off anyone who might pick a fight. It's come in handy more than once."

"Oh," the boy said, "my dad works at the ACC, so I've heard of the serum, but I guess those fakes must be a secret or something. Name's Benny by the way." He stuck out his hand.

"Lucas." They shook, Lucas wincing slightly at the tight grip. "Thanks. If you hadn't showed up, I might not be standing."

"Don't mention it. Let's get you out of here." Benny and Vincent helped Lucas hobble out of the bathroom and down the hall. As they rounded the corner Annabeth spotted them. Seeing Lucas, she rushed over to them in a panic.

"Lucas! What happened?"

"Annabeth?"

Annabeth looked at Benny. "Benny?"

"What are you doing here?" Benny asked, "Do you know these guys?"

She nodded. "Yeah, they're my… they're my friends."

Benny frowned. "Ah, you sound sure about that. How have you been?"

"Good," she said, "Weber has been good. I won the election for SBO president next year." Benny nodded and fell silent. Lucas coughed, breaking the awkward tension. "Oh, right, Lucas. We've got to get you some help. I think there's a doctor here just in case for the game. I'll go find them." She ran into the gym.

Benny and Vincent helped Lucas sit down on the ground. Benny looked over at Lucas. "So, are you her boyfriend?"

Lucas looked up. "Hmm? Oh, uhh, no? She's not, I mean-"

"You then?" Benny pointed at Vincent.

"Me?" Vincent laughed. "Goodness no! I'd rather die. Why? Do you think one of us…"

"Well, Annabeth always has a boyfriend." Benny shook his head. "I would know. Experience."

"Oh," Vincent mumbled, "awkward."

"What happened?" Lucas asked. "Did you two break up?"

"You might not have noticed, but this school is a bad place for an anthrope. There's a reason there's a haven school so close. Annabeth moved into our boundaries a few years ago and went to school here. She had this bracelet she wore every day to cover the tracker you guys have. She had to keep it secret but eventually people found out. I had known for a while, but I didn't care. She was pretty popular and an officer here but once people found out, things got ugly. Her and her dad ended up living in a hotel for two weeks. She thought the best thing to do was to switch schools. We fought about it, broke up, and she moved out of her old neighborhood to get away from it all."

Annabeth jogged into the hall with a doctor. "I found help." The doctor hurried over and began checking Lucas over.

"What exactly happened to you?" The medic asked.

"Fight," Vincent answered for him, "In the bathroom. There were three of them. Two of them are unconscious. The other's probably long gone."

The medic nodded, "You his girlfriend?"

Annabeth looked at him, "Me? No."

"Got a phone?"

"Yeah."

"Call the police." The medic turned back to Lucas. "Can you open your jaw for me?" Lucas nodded and swung his jaw open. Annabeth dialed 911.

"Hello? I'm at Fremont High School. There was a fight in the bathroom." She paused. "My friend has a hurt jaw and leg."

"And a concussion." The medic said.

"And he's got a concussion. Two of the boys that attacked him are unconscious. I think the other is gone." Annabeth nodded. "Ok, I'll just hand the phone off, this is his best friend. If you need anything else, he can tell you." She gave the phone to Vincent. "Here. They're on their way. She's just going to stay on the line."

Lucas chuckled. "What do you think my mom will say about me getting in a fight?" He started to giggle. "I've never been in a fight before."

Benny muttered something about his dad.

Vincent rubbed his forehead and sighed. He looked at Annabeth. "Don't you just love concussed people?"

"Have you ever talked to someone that was concussed before?" She asked.

"My dad crashed the car once and hit his head. I was in the passenger seat. He laughed for ten minutes about insurance before the ambulance came." He grimaced. "It was weird. Lucas, we're going to have to explain this to your mom tonight. Do you want to tell her you fell?"

Lucas nodded drowsily and gave a thumbs up. "I fell super hard."

Vincent looked around and saw Annabeth and Benny off to the side arguing. There was a lot of pointing and hand waving. "If there's one thing more annoying to listen to than someone with a concussion," he muttered, "it's a pair of exes." He rolled his eyes and sat back against the concrete wall. "I need new friends."

His phone buzzed in his pocket. Kenzie was calling him. "Hey. What's up?"

"Dude, where are you guys? You've been gone forever. We're winning now by the way."

"Lucas got in a fight."

"Oh. I'll come find you. In the meantime, tell him not to do that again." The line went dead.

The ACC director tapped her fingers on her desk. An empty vial sat in front of her, the cap missing. She shook it lightly, but the residue had all dried up. Picking up her radio, she pressed down the transmit button. "Anderson?"

"Boss?"

"So you're telling me you found this vial in her clothes up in the mountains?"

"Yeah, it was in the back right pocket."

The director nodded. "Did that Annabeth girl look hurt to you?"

"Kinda hard to tell, she was a rabbit. Do you think she was attacked?"

The director spun in her chair. "I think so. Her story just doesn't make sense. Why wouldn't she tell us if she was attacked? She's scared of someone. We need to figure out who it is. Can you keep track of her? If her tracker leaves a fifteen-mile radius or goes anywhere out of the ordinary, let me know and keep an eye on her."

"Got it. I just need you to send me her tracker code."

"Sure thing," the director said. She sent the code in an email.

"Came through. Thanks. See ya boss." The radio crackled briefly before cutting out.

The director tapped the desk again. Suddenly, the phone rang. She picked it up. "Hello?" A pause. "Hi Officer… There was a fight with three anthropes? What are their names? Those kids again?"

CHAPTER 10

Annabeth sat down on the couch next to Lucas in his basement, facing the TV. Vincent and Kenzie scooted over to make more room. Vincent picked up the remote and pressed play. Lucas reached over to the wall and flipped off the lights, leaving the screen as the only light source. Annabeth leaned over to Lucas. She whispered over the music, "how's your head?"

"Way worse than my leg." He stretched it out, running his toes through the carpet. "My leg feels pretty much normal, but my head is terrible. How's yours?"

"I'm not the one who got a concussion last night," she said.

"So pretty good then?"

Annabeth rolled her eyes. "Yeah, pretty awesome."

Lucas nodded. He stretched upward, eyeing the cushion behind Annabeth. His arm drifted down behind her until he noticed Vincent watching him. Lucas put his hands in his lap, then leaned over to Annabeth. "I think we should have a joint prom."

"What?"

"A joint prom. Us and Fremont."

"Lucas, are you crazy?" She turned to face him. "Do you remember last night?"

"Yes, I do," he said, looking her in the eyes, only a few inches away, "that's exactly why we need to do it. They hate us because they're afraid. In the Middle Ages, people were burned alive just because people thought they were werewolves. The government would put people on trial and burn them to death. Now the government is on our side, they're protecting us, but people are still afraid. If we can show them that we're just like them, things will get better. It's just xenophobia, right? You said Benny was an officer, he's on our side, he understands. If we work together with him, we can make it happen."

"Lucas, this is crazy, what if it turns into a brawl?"

"Dudes," Kenzie said, "shut up."

Lucas whispered into Annabeth's ear. "We bring the police. I don't know. But we can do it."

"No, we aren't going to do that."

"Annabeth, I don't need you to like it, I just need you to understand."

"Why are you even asking me? I'm not the student body president yet. You don't need my permission."

"No, I just need you to sell Benny on it."

Lucas walked through the labyrinth of Weber High. There was a scent of musty carpet in the stale air. Random hallways jutted off here and there. As he walked Annabeth caught his eye. He grabbed her arm. "Can I talk to you for a minute?"

"Sure."

"Okay first," Lucas said, "those are huge textbooks, what are they for?"

Annabeth fingered the textbooks under her arm. "AP chemistry, AP biology, and this one is for AP calculus."

"Do you need a hobby? That sounds like all kinds of not fun."

She laughed. "I've always been interested in bio chem. My dad is a chemical engineer, so he taught me a little bit. I know most of the stuff already, so it's really just college credits."

Lucas blinked. "Okay, yeah, you need a hobby."

"It is my hobby! Really, if you want to come over sometime I could show you. I'm free tonight if you want."

"Did you just ask me out?"

She shrugged with just one shoulder. "Maybe I did, maybe I didn't. But you still haven't answered."

"I'll be there. What time?"

She bit her lip. "My dad is working late tonight, but he should be back before seven."

Lucas nodded. "Okay, seven." He paused. "Oh, right, I wanted to talk to you because I brought up the joint prom in student government and explained things to everyone, and everyone is on board with the idea, but they want to hear from Fremont. I know you don't like the idea, but-"

"I think it's a good idea."

"Really? What changed?"

"Well," she sighed, "it's got to get better somehow. Might as well try now. I'll talk to Benny. I think he'll go for it."

Lucas smiled. "Thank you."

Lucas knocked on the door. He heard someone moving around inside. The door swung open and a lanky man with messy hair wearing a button up shirt and aviator glasses opened the door. "Hello, you must be Lucas. Come on in." Lucas stepped inside to the small entryway. "How are you?"

"I'm doing well. You?"

"A little tired, long day at work. But other than that, I guess I'm doing well as well." He smiled.

"Annabeth told me you're a chemical engineer. What's that like?"

Annabeth's dad leaned against one of many stacks of boxes. "Chemical engineering is a bit different for everyone since it's so broad. I mostly research different compounds in various medicines and supplemental products. My main area of research is in hormonal medicine."

"Oh cool," Lucas said, "hormonal stuff like the transformation serum we use at the ACC?"

"No, but I had a professor in college who was on the team that developed the serum. He wasn't supposed to, but he occasionally slipped and gave us tiny hints about how they made it in class. I never could piece together just how they made it, but maybe if I had a sample it'd be possible. Although it's pretty hard to get your hands on that stuff, the ACC keeps track of the vials they have." He paused for a second. "What was I saying? Oh yeah, in my lab I mostly work on pregnancy products."

Annabeth walked out of a room and into the hall, a white coat on. "Hey Lucas, sorry, I was in the middle of something. You can come in if you want and check it out."

"It was nice talking to you Mr. Watson." Lucas followed Annabeth into the room. A countertop ran around the room, and it was covered in glass and chemicals. A beaker boiled with a yellowish liquid in it next to the open window. The curtain had been rigged up with an old wire hanger to extend over the beaker, venting the steam outside. The bed in the middle seemed more like an afterthought than the primary function of the room. "Woah, what's all this?"

"It's my hobby. This is what I do for fun." She hesitated. "Do you want to see something cool?"

"Sure?"

"Come here." Annabeth walked over to a corner. She opened a pill bottle and set two pills on the counter. Twisting the top back on, she opened another bottle and grabbed two gel capsules. She handed Lucas one from each and took the others. "Take these."

"Are you sure? Isn't it dangerous to share medicine?"

She shook her head and popped the pills into her mouth. "Not medicine." She swallowed. "I made these myself. Trust me, just eat them."

"Okay." Lucas popped the pills into his mouth and forced himself to swallow the dry lumps. "So what exactly was that just now?"

Annabeth walked across the room to a white board. She picked up a marker and began drawing out an equation. "Have you ever mixed baking soda and vinegar together?"

"Yeah."

"Same idea." She wrote out $C_2H_4O_2$. "This is the formula for acetic acid, which is basically vinegar. Vinegar just has extra water to thin out the acid." The marker flew across the whiteboard. $NaHCO_3$. "That's baking soda. When they mix together, they make three new chemicals, first is water, H_2O. Then there's carbon dioxide, which is a gas." She wrote out the chemical formulas, and one extra, $NaC_2H_3O_2$. "That last one is sodium acetate, sometimes used as a food additive, but it's also in concrete and a few other things. It's perfectly harmless. One of the pills I just gave you had concentrated acetic acid, the other had baking soda. There was just enough of each to make sure all the chemicals got used up. The real trick was stopping the vinegar from dissolving the capsule."

"So, nothing is going to happen?"

Annabeth smiled deviously. "No, carbon dioxide is a gas. Those pills are going to give you gas."

Lucas squinted. "Why would you make that?"

"I don't know." She tossed her hands up in the air. "It seemed like a good idea when I made them. Now that I think about it, it's pretty much useless. The only time anyone would ever need it is for a prank or something." Annabeth smiled with a devious glint in her eyes. "Next time Vincent goes on a date you have to sneak those into his food." She chuckled.

Lucas grinned. "If Vincent ever goes on a date, I'll let you know. Just don't change your phone number for the next ten years."

Annabeth laughed and looked at her watch. "Well, the pills are in our stomachs now. They'll have dissolved in about thirty to forty-five minutes and then our stomachs will be doing science."

Lucas stood up and wandered over to a series of glass instruments all connected together in a clump. Next to it was a rack filled with tiny vials. "What's all this for?"

"Well, after the other night, I figured maybe it wouldn't hurt to have a few extra of those fake serums. So… I made this." She picked up a vial and shook it. It lit up blue. "I made a few dozen of them, the rest are in that cupboard. If you need another one you can have one."

"Thanks," Lucas said, taking one, "I spilled mine and I hadn't gotten around to swinging by the ACC for another." They stood there in silence. "Well, what now?"

"In thirty minutes," Annabeth said, taking a step closer, "we're not going to be feeling up to this, so maybe now is a good time to…"

"To what?

She paused. "Never mind." She looked at her watch again. "Do you want to watch a movie or something?"

"No really, tell me. Good time to what?"

"Good time to watch a movie," Annabeth insisted, "come on. We just got our projector set up last night on some empty boxes."

Lucas agreed by following her into the hall, a frustrated expression on his face.

<h1 style="text-align:center">CHAPTER 11</h1>

Annabeth shivered in the cold and folded her arms across her chest. Her breath made gray clouds in the air, faintly visible against the looming wall of the ACC building. The back door swung open, shining brightly into the night. Lucas smiled, already wearing a protective suit, a helmet under his arm. "Hey."

Annabeth brushed past him quickly, hurrying to get inside. "Goodness it's cold out there. Thanks for hurrying."

"Sorry, Karen, the receptionist was talking, and I had to ditch Vincent." Lucas led her down the hallway. Metal bars divided the hall in half. "You know, last time I was here, you and Vincent were rabbits."

"I'm still mad about that."

Lucas stopped and turned to face her. "Because they sent me and Vincent to catch you?"

"Yes," she said, "that was so embarrassing. That's so weird."

"It's not that weird." Lucas said.

"Not that weird?" Annabeth brushed her hair out of her face. "Not that weird? So just to be clear, chasing some girl you just barely met around in the woods while she was a bunny rabbit wasn't weird?" She raised an eyebrow. "Because it was weird for me to hear I had been shot and drugged by a boy I just barely met and then taken hostage as a rabbit overnight. That's not exactly a good impression when you're starting to get to know someone." She flipped her hair and walked past him.

"Annabeth!" Lucas went after her.

She ignored him.

"Annabeth, come on, that isn't fair. It's my job!"

Still no response.

"Annabeth!"

She whirled around. "I'm not really mad, I'm just messing around. But you can't deny I'm right. Wouldn't that be weird for you?"

Lucas rocked his head from side to side, "I guess you're right."

"Yes I am." She started walking again for a moment but then turned back to him. "I don't actually know where this hallway goes, by the way, you go in front."

Lucas walked up to her and took her hand, making her blush. "Just keep your head down. No one's going to realize anything, but let's just avoid drawing attention to you." They walked out a door and found themselves in the main hallway of the ACC, just below the armory. A trickle of people walked past them and up several flights of stairs. "Vincent said he's going out tonight, so we'll need to head up top. That'll be better anyway, more spread out, less other people to run into."

Annabeth nodded and followed him up the stairs. Lucas held out his wrist gauntlet and opened up the tracking system. "Did you get that earlier?"

"Well... yes?"

"So that's why I was waiting out in the cold for so long?"

"I had to get everything ready." Lucas said defensively. "Plus, I didn't want you to have to wait for me to pick it up later."

"No," Annabeth nodded, "I just had to wait for you to pick it up while I was outside in the cold."

"I'm sorry, I didn't think about it."

"It's alright," she punched him in the shoulder.

"Ow!" Lucas rubbed his shoulder. "It doesn't feel alright." He put on his helmet and made a few system adjustments to the wrist gauntlet. "Well, we've got about ten minutes before we need to be out there, let's hurry." He pushed open the door to the armory. Annabeth followed him in and they each grabbed a tranq pistol and a few extra magazines. Annabeth quickly pulled on a protective suit, matching Lucas. They synced their helmet comms.

Lucas handed Annabeth a flashlight and grabbed one for himself. Annabeth used a finger scanner to unlock a bulletproof glass case full of vials, grabbing three and giving one to Lucas. She put the other two in her back pocket. They slid vests over their heads and went back into the hall.

Lucas swiped an ID card and opened the door. Humid air washed over them. They walked out onto the metal catwalks and surveyed the darkened Terrapark. Annabeth whistled and turned on her flashlight. "It's always so dark at this entrance."

"Yeah," Lucas said, flicking his light on, "but it's the main habitat they're using for this group. The animals using the Terrapark right now are animals like dogs, cats, a few kinds of monkeys, horses, and there's actually a few elephants too. What makes my job easy is that there's only one kind of predator on Vincent's night."

"What's that?"

"Lions. There's two prides of 'em."

"And the best habitat is this?"

Lucas looked at the habitat and shrugged, "I don't call the shots here. Apparently, some big brain decided this is the best sector for all those species to be in so they don't have to do maintenance in the other sectors." Dense jungle trees rose all around them, the tops reaching up past the walkways and blocking out most of the light in the Terrapark. A metal cage enclosed the top of the walkway so nothing could get in except a few vines that dangled through the bars. Every couple dozen feet, a cage door was placed on each side of the catwalk. When opened they led to small semi-circle extensions from which guardians could have better vantage points, but with no cage. Far off on the opposite side of the enclosure, lights began to flash and alarms went off. Annabeth and Lucas sprinted down the walkway for a full minute before they reached the entry point. Dozens of people were spread out along the walkway, each watching one out of a long row of massive bay doors. Each had a large number painted on it in yellow.

Just as they arrived, about half the doors began to open. Dogs and cats rushed out immediately and their guardians ran after them. A dozen monkeys scraped under the doors next, their guardians peeling away to follow them as they vanished into the trees. Annabeth looked over to Lucas. He shook his head, eyes on the gauntlet. "Vincent's still in there."

A wave of lions and horses ran out next, the two groups steering away from each other. Their guardians carried larger tranq rifles slung over their backs. The doors were nearly open all the way. Only seven others remained on the catwalk with them. Seven elephants lumbered out into the jungle. Lucas pushed a few buttons on the wrist gauntlet. "It says he's still in that one right there." He pointed at one of the open bay doors.

Annabeth squinted, shining her flashlight. "I think I can see him moving around in there. Here he comes."

Vincent walked out of the door wearing a stretchy tank top that read, 'I'm A Good Boy' on the back. He carried a bone in his mouth. His shaggy golden hair stuck out in tufts at the edges of the shirt. His eyes sparkled with excitement. Lucas smiled. "That's my Vincent."

Annabeth gasped. "He's so cute! You didn't say he was a golden retriever! That's my favorite kind of dog!"

"Really?"

"Yes really! That's so weird. He's the grumpiest person alive but right now he's absolutely adorable." Vincent trotted toward the elephants and began to weave between their legs as if trying to show them his wonderful treat. Annabeth walked along the catwalk, following Vincent. Lucas adjusted his wrist gauntlet and followed her. Annabeth looked back at him, "Does he usually do this?"

"You mean follow the elephants?"

"Yeah."

"Yeah," Lucas said, "he doesn't really like to hang out with the other dogs. Not really sure why. That's just kinda how he is."

"Is there ever any trouble with this group?"

Lucas shrugged. "I mentioned there were two prides earlier, I think. Occasionally if one of the male lions doesn't show up, the other pride tries to take the lionesses and there's a bit of a turf war. That can get a little rough, but most of the others know to stay out of their way when that happens. And their guardians have special training so they can deal with that kind of thing. They usually let everything play out and only use the guns if things get really nasty."

"How often does that happen?"

"Not super often. I've only seen it maybe once or twice. The male lions both come out most of the time, they'll only sleep maybe twice a year. And even then, it's not that bad."

Annabeth nodded before falling silent beside him. The elephant guardians walked several paces in front of them, occasionally glancing back at them. "Lucas," she whispered, "do you think they know I'm not supposed to be here?"

"I don't know," Lucas whispered back, "they probably can't see you anyway, it's too dark. Just play it cool. Maybe they'll ignore us." Down below Vincent wandered off. A proximity alert beeped on the wrist gauntlet. "Vincent is splitting off, we don't need to worry about them." Lucas and Annabeth followed Vincent. Vincent wandered through the jungle toward a large rock.

A loud clang startled them. They looked up, shining their flashlights to see an orangutan saying hello. It waved, sticking a hand through the bars. Annabeth started to reach up to the orangutan before Lucas stopped her. "I wouldn't do that. Just in case. An orangutan could rip your arm off without even trying."

"Oh, bye orangutan!" Annabeth and Lucas kept following Vincent. A large cluster of people stood on the walkway up ahead, all pointing their flashlights down below. They carried massive rifles. Lion guardians. The voices became audible as Annabeth and Lucas approached. Their words were hard to make out, but clearly upset. Another group of lion guardians were walking over slowly. "Lucas, what's going on?"

"I don't know, I'll ask them." Lucas took his helmet off and clipped it to his back. He walked up to the guardians. "Hey guys, what's going on?"

One of them, a man, addressed Lucas in a rough voice. "That one yours?" He pointed to Vincent.

"Yes."

"Get him out of here. One of the males is gone. The other pride is trying to take over. The lionesses aren't going to care who's who, they're just going to fight until there's no one left to fight. Anyone in the way is going to be collateral damage."

Lucas looked down and saw the lions snarling as the other group approached. He frowned and waved Annabeth over. Using his ID badge, he unlocked and opened one of the doors on the catwalk. They stepped out into an unprotected half circle. Pulling out a laser pointer, he shone a bright green beam down in front of Vincent, grabbing his attention. Lucas called out to Vincent. "Vincent, come here boy!" Vincent followed the green dot and Lucas guided him. Upon reaching Lucas, Vincent sat underneath them and wagged his tail. "Hey buddy," Lucas called, "over there!" He tried to point the laser away from the lions. Vincent just turned his head, looking confused.

"Vincent!" Annabeth yelled, leaning way over the railing, "Get away from the lions!" She pointed away. "Go!" One of the lionesses looked over and saw Vincent. She hissed. "Vincent! Go! Run!" The lioness stalked toward Vincent. Annabeth drew her tranquilizer pistol and unloaded a magazine of tiny darts into the lioness. The lioness snarled and sprinted toward Vincent. The door behind them swung open and a lion guardian burst out. He slammed his gun down on the rail and fired at the lioness, bumping into Annabeth. Annabeth screamed as she fell over the rail. She grabbed the bottom lip of the walkway. "Lucas! Help!"

Lucas tried to reach through and grab her hand, but the bars were too narrow. "I can't reach! Hold on!" He swung a leg over the railing, looking warily at the ground below. The lioness collapsed unconscious next to a very confused Vincent. Lucas pulled his other leg over the railing and grabbed the top of the rail tightly.

The guardian shouted at Lucas. "Idiot! Get back!" Two more lionesses moved in the dim light toward Vincent. Vincent started barking at Annabeth.

Annabeth held on with one hand, the other reaching up toward Lucas.

"Don't let me fall!"

Lucas grabbed her hand. "Never!" He pulled and Annabeth rose slightly, but his hand on the rail was too sweaty and he fell. Annabeth braced herself to catch him, but he was too heavy. He fell to the ground, landing awkwardly on his leg. Vincent was on him in an instant, licking his face.

"Lucas!" Annabeth screamed.

"Protocol 3!" The lion guardian bellowed. "Protocol 3!" Sirens began to wail and red lights flashed. A pair of lionesses jumped at Lucas with darts in their necks. Already feeling the tranquilizers, they landed awkwardly to his side and fell unconscious. All around they heard discharges of air as the guardians began to tranq the anthropes. The two prides began to run away in different directions, evading the guardians and their darts. Annabeth swung back and forth before letting go of the catwalk. She fell a couple of feet before hitting a tree. Grabbing on tightly, she climbed down as quickly as she could. Lucas groaned and she hurried to his side. Vincent dropped his bone next to her. She picked it up and threw it as far as she could. "Run away Vincent! Get out of here!" Vincent ran off.

Annabeth reached into her vest and grabbed a knife, biting it between her teeth. She rolled up the fabric of Lucas's pants. Lucas lifted his head, still in the helmet. "How bad is it?"

Annabeth pushed his head down, knife still in her mouth. "Relax, it's actually fine. You probably just sprained it."

"Protocol 3 is failing!" Two guardians stood above them on the catwalk, one already jumping to the tree. "The lions are escaping! We need to do an emergency evacuation!" The first guardian jumped from the tree and onto the ground, immediately scanning the perimeter for approaching anthropes, rifle drawn. The other guardian jumped from the platform above onto the tree.

"Lucas, they're gonna keep us safe until the lions are down but we need to move you to somewhere safer."

"I can go wolf. I don't know if I'll be able to walk."

Annabeth shook her head. "Too risky. There's still lions loose, we can't just leave you here unconscious. Anything could happen."

The two lion guardians shouted, and Annabeth turned to see a lioness jump out of the trees. She ran toward Lucas and Annabeth, but the guardians managed to hit her with a dart. Trying to claw at them, she stumbled and fell to the ground unconscious mere feet from where Lucas lay defenseless.

Lucas breathed in relief and then grimaced in pain. "Ok, how are we getting out of here?"

They could hear more rustling in the trees behind them as the rest of the pride approached. Up above several guardians fired off tranq rounds and the lions ran past them through the clearing, not even noticing them. The guardians kept running, still in pursuit. One lioness stumbled into the clearing, falling asleep on the ground.

One of the guardians ran to them, the other still scanned the trees for threats. Annabeth grabbed Lucas's hand and held it tightly. "Don't worry, we have help."

The first guardian took off her helmet and clipped it onto her back, assessing the situation. Annabeth looked up at her. "Do either of you have medical training?" The guardian shook her head. The other, a stocky man in his forties, took off his helmet, came over, and helped Lucas stand up. Lucas wrapped his arm around the man's shoulders and hopped on one foot to adjust his weight. Annabeth helped hold him up on the other side.

The first guardian, a slim woman in her thirties circled around them. She held up her wrist gauntlet, surveying a map of all the anthropes. They were surrounded with dots all throughout the enclosure. She pressed a few more buttons and most dots turned gray, showing them to be unconscious. The woman squinted at the screen, then whipped around drawing her gun. "It looks like there's one moving straight toward us." Her voice had a slight drawl. A thud came from behind them.

Annabeth turned her head and saw the friendly orangutan from before. The female guardian shot it on sight. Sedatives still not taking effect, it took a few steps forward, knuckles on the ground. The orangutan smiled, showing its teeth. The male guardian tried to raise his rifle with his free arm. The orangutan looked at him and screamed. It grabbed the gun and hit the man in the side, knocking him down, Lucas and Annabeth going down with him. The woman fired another shot at the orangutan. It shied away and scampered into the trees, already drooping. A guardian passed by them on the catwalk ahead, flashlight beam bouncing all over as they ran after the orangutan.

Annabeth climbed off of Lucas, accidentally jostling his leg and making him gasp in pain. The woman checked the man over and tried to help him up.

"Are you alright?" The woman asked.

"Yeah," the man nodded, holding his side, "I'm good." He climbed to his feet and put his helmet back on. The man tapped the side of his helmet. Lucas and Annabeth took the hint, putting their helmets on and syncing comms together. The man's voice came through. "Hey, I'm Jarron. This is Synthia with me, are you both okay?"

"I'm Lucas and I'm alright," Lucas said, "Annabeth thinks I sprained my ankle."

"That doesn't sound alright honey," Synthia drawled, "not with a pack of lions nearby."

"As long as we get somewhere safe soon, I'll be okay. What do we do?"

"If those lions were down, they could send people in to pick us up, but it might be a while before that can happen. It looks like most of the lions are still loose. There's an emergency exit door on the far side of the forest," Jarron said. "If we can make it over there we can get out."

"How far is it?" Annabeth asked.

"A couple hundred yards." Jarron said, scoping out the area around them.

"That may be a problem," Lucas said, "I doubt I could hobble much farther, plus, who knows when something else might stop by."

"We only need to worry about the lions and the monkeys," Synthia said, looking at her gauntlet, "The lions are in the northern corner, they shouldn't give us trouble for a while. The monkeys might be a problem if they get too close."

"Wait," Annabeth looked at Lucas, "didn't you say there were horses in here?"

"Yes, but they aren't domesticated. And they're probably mostly unconscious by now."

"Not an option, hon," Synthia agreed. "What are your anthropes?"

"Wolf," Lucas said, "won't help."

"Rabbit."

"I'm a polar bear," Jarron added, "not helpful either."

"I'm a fish." Synthia chuckled. "What did you say your name was hon?"

"Me? Annabeth."

"Annabeth, we're going to need you to switch over to your anthrope and bite Lucas. A rabbit can be carried. Our best option is for you and Lucas to become rabbits so Jarron and I can carry you two out of here safely. Lucas hon, is that alright with you?"

Lucas nodded. "Just be careful while you're carrying me."

"We will."

Annabeth took off her helmet. Lucas removed his. Annabeth locked eyes with him. "Are you sure about this?"

He shook his head. "No, but what other choice do we have?"

She looked down. "None." She took his hand as she grabbed the tiny vial from her pocket. She opened it and looked at Lucas. "You know how you can never remember those last couple moments before you go anthrope?"

"Yeah?"

"I- I've been wanting to- I mean, I've been trying to work up the courage to-" She looked down at the vial in her hand. "What I mean is-" she downed the vial. "I like you Lucas. A lot." She kissed him.

Lucas stammered. "I-"

"I'm not going to remember this, so just say it."

Lucas met her eyes. "I like you too."

Annabeth smiled. "See you on the other side, Lucas." She fell down in the grass. Her ears grew up through her hair. Annabeth's cheeks bulged and a huge pair of teeth shot out of her mouth. Her hair shrank into her head as fur grew all over her body. The protective suit she wore deflated all around her as she fully transformed into a bunny. She hopped out of the pile of clothes, wiggling her nose.

"Mmm… we just kissed. Nice." He held his arm out and used Annabeth's paw to scratch his arm. "I hope I don't forget that." A bead of blood formed on his arm. His vision went dark and he collapsed on the ground. Jarron and Synthia stepped up to the pair of rabbits on the ground.

"I hope we never have to talk to these kids again," Synthia said, "I don't want to remember anything about tonight." She put her gun on her back and picked up the rabbits. "Come on, let's go."

CHAPTER 12

Annabeth and Lucas plopped down on the couch next to each other. Lucas was rubbing his ankle in amazement. "Well," he said to Annabeth, "I guess that rabbits must have some kind of quick healing power because it's barely sore." Vincent was sleeping with his whole body draped over one of the couch's arms. Lucas poked Vincent. "Hey buddy, what's up?"

Vincent moved a tiny bit and his eyes drifted open. "Hey Lucas." He saw Annabeth sitting next to Lucas and he raised an eyebrow. "What are you doing here?"

The director spoke up, peering over her massive horn-rimmed glasses. "That is a great question young lady. What are you doing here?"

Lucas spoke up. "It wasn't her fault. I asked her to come with me."

"Hush," the director said, "Annabeth, this is the second time you've been in my office in less than two weeks. This had better not become a habit. Now tell me, what were you doing here?"

"Lucas asked me if I wanted to come with him tonight," she said, "I didn't think it would be a big deal."

The director shook her head. "It wouldn't have been a big deal if nothing had happened. That being said, the two of you were so distracted with whatever it was you were doing that your friend here was almost eaten by lions." Vincent stiffened on the couch, glaring at Lucas. The director continued. "And if that wasn't already enough, you fell into the enclosure and were almost eaten yourself. The other two guardians in there with you were put in danger and one of them has several broken ribs."

Annabeth hung her head.

"I understand it was an accident that Lucas fell into the enclosure trying to help you but jumping in after him was the worst thing you could have done."

"But-"

"Young man," the director yelled, "if you interrupt me one more time, I will see to it you personally scoop out every last piece of animal waste in the entire Terrapark!"

Lucas withered and sank into the couch.

Annabeth's voice quivered, "I couldn't leave him down there."

"That is what you are required to do." The director sighed and rubbed her forehead, leaning back in her chair. "Set off an alarm on the gauntlet, everyone tranqs the anthrope in their charge. Someone keeps an eye on whoever fell in from above and once we're sure all the anthropes are incapacitated, we send a team into the enclosure to pick them up. It's simple, it's safe, and it's effective. We couldn't operate that protocol because the lions went into a frenzy and ran off after you dropped into the enclosure. It took nearly half an hour to get them all knocked out."

Vincent stood up. "Can I go?"

The director gestured to the door. "You may. Sorry for the trouble." Vincent walked out of the room, kicking Lucas's good ankle as he did. Vincent closed the door behind him. "You two are going to need to make some serious apologies. To your friend and to Synthia and Jarron. Tomorrow is a new moon, everyone will be here, you might run into them. You can make your apologies then." She looked straight at Annabeth. "Young lady, one more time in my office and there are going to be serious consequences. Do you understand?"

Annabeth nodded.

"Good," the director said, "now get out of my office."

Annabeth and Lucas walked out of the room. Lucas turned to Annabeth, "Can you drive me home? Vincent was my ride. Again." Annabeth nodded and closed the door.

The director waited a few moments and then picked up her radio. "Anderson, Anderson, are you there?"

A spurt of static announced Anderson. "Yeah boss?"

"Did you check that girl's belongings?"

"Yeah, I found an extra vial in her back pocket. I dropped it by your office earlier. You were gone."

"Thank you, where did you put it?"

"Ummm…" Anderson paused. "I think I set it next to that flowerpot."

The director spun around in her chair and spotted the small vial next to a pair of fake foxglove flowers. "Found it." She picked it up and shook it, it gave off a faint blue glow. "Thanks. How's your family doing?"

"Umm, my boy Benny is alright, he's enjoying school, doing well, went through a breakup a while ago. He's still a little cranky about it but he just met a girl he seems to like, so we'll see how that goes. And my wife is pregnant with our second."

"Oh really? That's wonderful, you two have been trying for a while, haven't you?"

"Yeah, we have. Well, I should head home, I need some sleep."

"Alright, and remember, you have tomorrow night off. New moon, training day."

"Thanks boss. Bye."

"Bye." The director opened up her computer and wrote a note for herself. *Annabeth L. Watson was discovered attempting to steal hormonal activation serum last night, possibly for the second time. I believe it's for protection. Watch carefully. Do not intervene. Be ready to protect her.*

Lucas stared at his phone screen, breathing slowly. It was nighttime. Annabeth glanced over at him while she was driving. "Still nothing?"

Lucas closed his eyes. "Nothing. I've been trying all day. I even called his mom. Straight to voicemail."

"I don't get it." Kenzie said from the backseat. "Why does he care if you two wanted to make out?"

"Kenzie," Annabeth gritted her teeth, "that's not what we were doing."

"Well, objectively, sure, you weren't trying to suck each other's lips off, but that doesn't mean he doesn't see it that way. I just don't get why he's mad you two are into each other."

Lucas squirmed. "That's not why he's upset, and like Annabeth said, we weren't doing that. He's upset because he almost died, and it was our fault. Well, it was my fault."

"It wasn't your fault, it was my fault, I shouldn't have been there. I was just distracting you."

"Yeah," Kenzie mumbled, "distracting."

"No," Lucas said, not hearing Kenzie, "it was my fault. I asked you to come with me and you wouldn't have come if I didn't ask."

Annabeth rolled her eyes, "oh please! Who cares? I should have realized it was a bad idea."

"It was my idea!"

"I said yes!"

"Just kiss already!" Annabeth and Lucas looked back at Kenzie. She looked back at them expectantly. "Also don't hit that car."

Annabeth turned back to the road and swerved to avoid a car. "Kenzie-"

"Seriously, you two keep going back and forth, it's my fault, no my fault, what?" She mocked. "No, it's my fault, I wanna make out, we sound like an old married couple. Pull over and get it over with."

Lucas and Annabeth fell silent.

"Not necessary? Good, then drive. And you'd better get it all out before we go home because I will cause an accident if that's what it takes to make it stop." There was no more conversation.

Annabeth pulled off the freeway onto the exit and slowed down. She took a few turns into the ACC parking lot. All the parking spots were filled as well as most of the nearby vacant lot. Annabeth parked the car, and everyone got out. Kenzie walked past them, feet crunching on the gravel, and hurried into the building. Lucas looked at Annabeth and sat down on the hood of her car. "Do you remember last night down in the Terrapark..."

Annabeth laughed and sat down next to him, looking up at the stars. "Of course, how could I forget?"

"Right, I could never..." he trailed off, "just to be clear, you're remembering..."

"How we almost died. Like five times."

Lucas rubbed his arm. "Yeah, I was thinking about something else." He paused. "There was a moment there when I totally thought we were dead, actually a few. And I remember thinking that if I wanted to be about to die with anybody..." he blinked a few times, looking down at the ground, "I don't think that came out right."

"No, I get it," Annabeth said, glancing at him, "I remember feeling that way too. I felt like... I guess I don't know how to describe it, but I remember wanting to tell you something. I can't remember what happened, but I've been wondering all day-" she looked at Lucas.

Her breath caught as they met eyes. He looked back, searching for something. "Don't worry," he said, "I didn't forget." He leaned in. She closed her eyes and kissed him.

After a second, she pulled back. "Was it like that?"

Lucas nodded. "Yeah, except this is even better."

She smiled and kissed him again. "Lucas Harrison, you're like a dream." She slid off the car hood and held her hand out. "Did we hold hands last night too?"

Lucas got off the car and took her hand. "Last night was too rushed."

"That's alright, we started over today with more time."

Lucas smiled and they walked toward the huge building. He let go of her hand to open the door for her and they blinked as their eyes adjusted to the light. They found two lines of people on opposite sides of the lobby. A table on each side had colored strips of cloth. Karen the receptionist and the ACC director manned the tables, handing out blue and green bands respectively. Kenzie stood in the green line. Across the room Lucas spotted Vincent standing in the blue line. Lucas nudged Annabeth. "I don't want to talk to the director right now, let's get in Karen's line."

Vincent looked up from his phone to see Annabeth and Lucas get in his line. Glaring, he moved across the room and stood behind Kenzie in the green line. They started talking and glancing over toward Annabeth and Lucas.

Annabeth turned her back to them. "Just ignore them." Lucas nodded and faced forward. They worked their way to the front of the line.

Karen tied a blue armband tightly around their wrists, covering their tracking bracelets. "Good luck out there."

"What's going on?"

"You'll find out pretty soon. Just head down to the Terrapark locker rooms." She winked. Lucas and Annabeth walked out of the room and followed the signs. A trickle of blue bands headed the same way. People wearing green went the other way to the control rooms.

Annabeth leaned over to Lucas, "what are we doing?"

"I don't know, must be some kind of training exercise."

"Do you think they're going to make us go anthrope?"

"Maybe," Lucas shrugged, "we'll see."

They walked around a staircase and went into the Terrapark locker room. Hundreds of people stood around, not sure what to do. A handful of people wandered into the room after them, followed by the ACC director. She closed the door behind her and stood up on a bench.

"I guess you're all wondering what we're doing tonight. I've been asking my boss for a while to do this but he's a real stickler. Fortunately, he got promoted and my new boss did give me permission. So tonight, we're going to be playing a game I've decided to call Hide and Seek: ACC Edition. The green team is suiting up with paintball guns. You, the blue team, are now moving targets." A chuckle spread through the crowd. "Here's how the game works. You and one person from the green team will be tracking each other using linked tracking gauntlets. They will be trying to shoot you with a paintball. Whoever goes longest without getting shot wins. If you're shot, get out and go home. We'll post the rankings just for fun tomorrow night. Next time we'll switch teams and do it again.

"If you want, you may give yourself an edge and, as I understand you all like to say, go anthrope." People started talking immediately. "Wait wait wait! Hold on, there are rules. Carnivores, out. Anything smaller than a cat, out. Birds, out. Water species, out. Anything large and slow, I wouldn't recommend it. If your anthrope is in any way dangerous or at risk with other anthropes, out. These rules will be followed, and we will be checking. This is for your safety, and it will not be compromised. If you meet these guidelines, meet me out in the hall and I'll give you a hormonal activation serum. I think we already took care of this but anyone who isn't physically up to this, head down to the shooting range and fire off a couple dozen paintball rounds and you're free to go home.

"One last thing, we've randomly assigned people to be your 'guardians' and as I said, they have tracking gauntlets to find you. However, we reconfigured the gauntlets for the green team, so their trackers don't work normally. You all on the other hand, will have precise, real-time access to their location. Just try to wipe any paint off the gauntlets so we don't have to spend too long cleaning them. If you are hit, we've instructed them to call out your name, which they'll see on their gauntlet. If you are hit but your name isn't called then it doesn't count, so keep moving. Questions?"

Annabeth raised her hand. "Rabbits?"

The director shook her head. "Too small. Anyone else?"

"Where are the protective suits?"

The director smiled. "I knew I was forgetting something. We put them in the morph rooms. The closest one is open and that's where we put all the suits. Those of you who would like to 'go anthrope', feel free to use the other morph rooms. Now, all of you, hurry and get out there. The green team can't go into the catwalk for another half hour, so you'll have a head start, but that time will pass quickly. Stay safe, have fun, and don't get shot. Oh, and by the way, we've lowered the barriers between biomes, so you have free reign of the Terrapark." The director stepped down from the bench and walked out of the locker room as everyone began to applaud. People began to file to the back of the room to head out into the Terrapark. A couple dozen people walked out into the hall to get the serum from the director. Lucas looked over to Annabeth. He took her hand, and they went to find the protective suits.

CHAPTER 13

Vincent leaned against the wall just inside the armory, gun strapped to his back, appearing indifferent to everything going on around him. He used tape to attach a flashlight to the side of his helmet on the off chance it would serve him better than the helmet's night vision, ears listening intently as people picked up their tracking gauntlets from a table at the end of the armory. A jumble of computerized voices said their hellos and announced who they were tracking. His ear perked up. "Hello. Now tracking, Lucas A. Harrison." His eyes flicked up. Kenzie was strapping the gauntlet on her wrist. Vincent walked up to her.

"Can I have that one?"

She looked up, surprised to see him. "They're supposed to be random."

"I know." He didn't move.

Kenzie looked at him for several seconds. "Alright," she said, pulling off the tracking gauntlet. "Here you go."

Vincent grabbed the gauntlet and strapped it to his wrist. "Thanks Kenz." He walked out of the armory, joining a large group of people all waiting for the door to be opened. Karen the receptionist stood at the door with her radio ready, waiting for the signal. She raised the radio to her ear and nodded.

Clipping the radio on to the back of her pants, she pushed open the door and stood out of the way. Everyone shuffled forward toward the door. As the guardians passed through, they broke into a run, heading after their charges, eyes straining to pierce the darkness into the jungle through the cage that covered the catwalk. Vincent pressed a button on the side of his helmet to activate the night vision. He stood a while in the open air, watching Lucas move around on the tracking gauntlet. Lucas was near the center of the enclosure, nearly a quarter mile away. Vincent broke into a jog, heading in the general direction. A handful of people ran around underneath him, all wearing protective suits. A flash of light caught Vincent's eye, and he stopped.

Vincent could make out a man wandering around the enclosure in the darkness, he was looking down at a wrist gauntlet as he walked, completely unaware of everything around him. Vincent pointed his flashlight at the man and rubbed his chin. "His gauntlet is tracking someone. He's got a blue band so he's not a guardian. Could he be…" He looked down at his gauntlet. The little dot that showed Lucas's location was moving straight toward him. "No, it can't be… why would he come toward me? Unless…" He broke into a sprint.

Vincent didn't take his eyes off the tracker until Lucas was right under him. He stuck his head over the railing. There was a clearing right underneath him, but no Lucas. Vincent whispered to himself. "The tracker isn't working. And if he's tracking me, he would go the opposite way… the tracker is backwards." Vincent pressed a few buttons, and a control panel appeared. Inverted tracking was enabled. Vincent shut it off and the screen flipped around, showing him exactly where Lucas was. "There you are you little-"

A paintball struck him in the shoulder. A twelve-year-old boy ducked down a different catwalk and hid behind the railing. Vincent lifted his gun and peered down the scope. He pulled back the trigger twice and grunted in satisfaction as the kid yelped at the paint splattering on his back. Vincent scoffed and started moving again.

Lucas walked through the forest, eyes up, watching the people up above and keeping to the shadows. The jungle canopy didn't let much light in, but the shrubs were small in that spot, so they had no trouble navigating. Lucas's ankle twinged. Annabeth walked behind him, eyes down toward the tracker, the display dimmed as much as possible. "Looks like whoever is tracking me is going the opposite way. You?"

Lucas looked down at his tracking gauntlet. "They were coming straight toward us for a while but then they stopped for a bit. It looks like they're headed back toward us though. We should be fine for a few more minutes." Lucas fell silent. He wiped his forehead and took a deep breath of the humid jungle air. "Do you think we're tracking the gauntlets, or the wrist bands?"

Annabeth looked up at him. "What?"

Lucas shrugged. "Well, I was just thinking, we have trackers and we're tracking them, and they have trackers and they're kind of tracking us, right?"

"Yeah."

"So," Lucas said, "how did they make sure we're tracking each other? I think they must have linked the gauntlets in pairs. Like, they're not tracking our wristbands, just the gauntlet. When you have access to someone's wristband you can see their location, personal information, vitals, where they work and anything else you might need to track down and contain a rogue anthrope. Basically, all the information the government has on a person is in there, although that's not necessarily useful to us right now. What I'm trying to say is that we had to sign in to our gauntlets, so they must not be tracking our wristbands, because otherwise they'd already have our information automatically. But we don't know who's tracking us."

"I don't think I follow." Annabeth said. "You think the tracking gauntlets are linked together, but not to our wristbands?"

"Yeah? I guess that's what I'm saying."

Annabeth stopped him and put her hand on his shoulder. "Can I be honest with you?"

"Sure."

"I don't have a clue why that's even relevant," Annabeth shook her head, "Like not even an idea." She started walking ahead of him.

"Wait, no," Lucas protested, nearly tripping over a root as he tried to catch up to her, "you didn't let me finish though, don't you think it would be easier to link two gauntlets together than to link our wristbands to their gauntlets and then their gauntlets to ours? As soon as we logged in on the gauntlets, we were tracking the green team."

"Okay," Annabeth shrugged, "I'm just going to take your word for it because I'm super confused and I don't know what you're talking about."

Lucas brushed aside a fern. "But it matters though, because the director said they can track us, but it's somehow reconfigured to not work correctly. But if they figure out how it's reconfigured, they could just change it back and figure out where we are."

"What does this have to do with anything?"

"You aren't letting me finish."

Annabeth shrugged again. "You talk too much. You never get to the point."

"Annabeth, come on, this is important. Look, if they're tracking our gauntlets, we could just ditch them somewhere, and then they won't be able to find us because they aren't connected to our tracking bands."

Annabeth stopped. She looked at Lucas. "Look at you, Einstein. That just might work."

"Might?" Lucas raised an eyebrow.

Annabeth punched him in the shoulder, gently this time. "I'm just teasing. That's a really good idea. But how will we know if it works?"

"We could test it. Leave our gauntlets somewhere out in the middle of nowhere and watch and see if someone comes and finds them. But then they would know…" Lucas trailed off as something rustled in the bushes behind them. A massive St. Bernard padded out of the shrubbery and sat down in front of them. Lucas's face lit up and he started petting the dog. "Hey buddy. How are you? Who's a good dog? You are. Yes you are."

Annabeth knelt down next to him and strapped her gauntlet around the dog's leg. "Strap your tracker on. This will give them a moving target to follow. It'll be a lot longer before they realize anything is going on."

Lucas smiled. "You're a genius."

"Just borrowing an idea," She elbowed him, "And making it a little better."

Lucas strapped his tracker onto the dog and stood up. "Bye bye. Time to go." The dog wagged its tail and barked. "Come on, go," Lucas commanded, "Get out of here." The dog didn't move. "Well, I guess we'll just have to hope our new friend doesn't follow us." He turned and walked into the trees. Annabeth followed him.

Vincent looked down into the clearing. A St. Bernard looked up at him, wagging its tail with its tongue hanging out. He looked back at his tracking gauntlet. "He's supposed to be right here." His eyes skimmed the clearing. Nothing. "Wait, is that…" A pair of tracking gauntlets were strapped to the dog's legs. "I'm going to kill him." Vincent looked around and found a tree next to the catwalk. He climbed over the railing and jumped onto the tree. Within seconds he was down on the ground.

"Hey boy." Vincent crouched and looked down. "Hey girl. Where'd you get these from? These trackers? Can you show me?" The St. Bernard barked and trotted into the woods. Vincent grinned and followed. The dog led him through the trees and into a small clearing.

Several boot prints showed in the mud. "Is this where they were?" The dog barked. "Can you find them? Can you take me to them?" The dog barked again and sniffed. Vincent looked around. The boot prints went a few paces into the trees but faded as the path went over firmer ground. The St. Bernard walked past him, following the trail. Vincent swung his gun around and held it up in front of him. He followed.

Lucas heard a crack from behind him. Annabeth grimaced. "Sorry, my bad. That was a stick."

"You're fine. I'm just a little too tense. What if we're walking around like everything is fine when they can still track us?"

"Don't worry about that," she nudged him, "Your idea is pretty clever. I'm mostly pretty sure it works."

"And that's super comforting. 'Mostly' could be as little as 51 percent. 'Pretty sure' is less than 100 percent. 51 percent times less than 100 percent is probably less than fifty percent. So that could mean you think more likely than not, it doesn't work."

Annabeth hesitated and then smiled. "Okay, technically, that is true. But it's not what I meant."

"Uh huh. I'm sure."

A crack came from behind them. "This time," Annabeth said, wincing, "it wasn't me." They stepped to the side and hid behind some trees. Annabeth whispered to Lucas. "If someone is after us, wouldn't they be up on the catwalk?"

The St. Bernard from before walked out of the trees and into view. "The dog?"

"That's pretty weird." Annabeth walked up to the dog and knelt down. "You can't follow us girl, that defeats the purpose." There was a popping sound.

"Hey Annabeth," Lucas said.

"Yeah?"

Lucas pointed to a yellow splotch on a tree next to his head. "Is it just me or is this paintball splatter new? Because I swear I just heard it hit."

She looked at him and nodded. "I would say, maybe we should run." She shot up and started sprinting into the woods. Lucas followed her, hobbling slightly on his ankle. Vincent tumbled out of a bush behind them.

"Crap! It's Vincent!" Lucas grabbed a branch as he ran by it, Vincent close behind. Lucas let go.

"Get back here you little-" Smack. Vincent stumbled backwards and shouted nonsense. He put his hand to his face, feeling the angry red stings left behind from the tree branch. He fired several shots at Lucas and Annabeth. They dove into the jungle around them. The St. Bernard rushed past Vincent chasing after them. Vincent followed, leading with the paint gun.

Suddenly, the dog stopped. Vincent skidded to a stop and looked at the dog. Lucas jumped out of the trees, knocking Vincent to the ground. They rolled, wrestling for control of the gun. "Vincent, I'm really sorry about last night! Will you please stop trying to shoot me?"

"No!" Vincent ripped the gun out of Lucas's hands and jammed his forearm into Lucas's neck, pinning him. He put a knee on Lucas's stomach and smiled as he pressed the barrel of the gun into Lucas's chest.

"Vin-"

Vincent shot him. Lucas groaned, part in pain, part in defeat. Annabeth stepped out of the woods as Vincent stood up triumphant.

Lucas raised a hand, out of breath. "There. You shot me. Can I please just have one minute to talk while you listen?"

Vincent rocked his head. He lifted his gun and shot Lucas again. "Two minutes. Then I'm leaving and ignoring you." He pressed some buttons on the wrist gauntlet and sat down on a fallen log, looking down at Lucas on the ground. "Go. Time starts now."

Lucas looked at Annabeth. "Can I talk to him alone?" She nodded and walked back into the trees. Lucas turned to his best friend. "Look, Vincent-"

"You're down fifteen seconds already."

"I'm sorry," Lucas said, "I know what I did was wrong, and I shouldn't have. I let how much I like Annabeth get in the way of my best friend even after you warned me, and you almost died. So, if you don't trust me and never want to talk to me again, I understand, you have every right. But please know that I'm sorry."

Vincent sniffed. "Can I tell you something? I think you might actually be a pretty good friend again once you get your hormones under control." He scratched his nose. "Plus, I literally have no friends so I can't not accept this terrible apology. Happy?"

Lucas stood up and spread his arms. He raised his eyebrows.

"Nope. You know how I feel about hugs. Not gonna ha-" Lucas bear hugged him, knocking the wind out of him. "You're a-" Lucas squeezed him tighter, cutting him off before he could say something naughty. Vincent groaned in complaint, "I was going to say terrible hugger."

Lucas stepped back. "Says you. When was the last time you hugged anyone other than your mom?"

Vincent held up a finger to point at himself. "I give my mom a hug every night because I love my mother." He raised his eyebrows in vindication. "So you can stuff it."

"So," Lucas said, ignoring the retort, "how much longer do I have before your timer goes off and you go romping off into the jungle?"

Vincent laughed, "I never set a timer."

"Does this mean I can come back now?"

Lucas looked into the trees. "How long have you been listening in?"

Annabeth stepped out of the shadows. "Not long. A little less than two minutes I would guess," She winked at him, "I guess you two need to go. I'll see you later. Do you mind taking the dog with you? He's blowing my cover." Vincent and Lucas walked into the jungle, calling out to the dog so it would follow. Annabeth sat down on a log and sighed. She put her head in her hands.

CHAPTER 14

A stocky man wearing a Hawaiian shirt under a leather jacket and cargo shorts walked into a bank. Over his shoulder he slung a duffel bag. His olive-green crocs squeaked slightly on the polished marble floors. Large stone columns supported the immense building. Two dozen people were scattered throughout the main area. He walked up to a free teller. "Hi, I need money."

She looked up at him from her computer. "Hi. You'd like to make a withdrawal? I'll need your bank account number first."

"No no no," he waved his hands as if she had said something foolish, "I need money. Everything you have under your desk. Cash."

"Sir, I can't just give you the money."

The man sighed. "I notice you've got one of those tracking bands on your wrist there. I used to have one too." He held up his wrist and revealed two scars, one old and faded, the other fresh and raw as though it had been opened with a kitchen knife. "I'm going to grab a few things from my bag here." The teller turned white. "Don't worry, it's perfectly harmless. To you." He unzipped the bag and secured a gas mask over his face. Then he removed his leather jacket and stowed it in the bag, replacing it with a white lab coat. With a small effort he picked up a propane tank and set it on the table. "This isn't propane." He unscrewed the valve.

A bluish gas shot out of the nozzle, quickly filling the air. The teller began to spasm and fell on the floor behind her desk, the man turned and walked toward the exit. A pair of security guards ran over to him, pointing their guns at him. "Hands up! On the ground!"

He knelt on the ground just next to the revolving door. Whispers filled the room, and everyone watched. The guards began checking him over for weapons. He had none. The pale blue gas drifted over toward them. One guard inhaled the gas. "Woah, that gas is filling up this place, cover your-" He began to shake and collapsed to the ground.

The other guard pulled out handcuffs, while trying to cover his face with his shirt. "What is this gas? What did you do?" He locked one of the man's wrists into the cuffs.

"A shirt isn't going to protect you. I would know. I made this stuff."

The guard's eyes grew wide, and he collapsed to the floor, shaking. The man stood up, a pair of handcuffs dangling from his wrist. He picked up the gun from the ground. Everyone in the room had moved to the edges. He pointed the gun at them and lifted his gas mask to talk to them. "If you come out this door, I'll shoot you. Don't come out this door. But run because there are eleven anthropes in the building and they'll kill you. Good luck." A cougar leapt on top of the teller's desk. The man put his mask back on and left, gas still filling the room. The guards picked themselves up off the floor, a bear and a crocodile.

The people in the bank screamed and ran. One woman fell to the floor, thrashing. A snake slithered out of her clothes. Her husband ran away into a hall, snake in pursuit. A golden retriever padded alongside a young woman with red hair, leading her away from the lobby. Another teller held his shirt over his nose, holding his breath for as long as he could. He dialed 911 on his phone. A woman picked up on the other end. "911, what's your emergency?"

The man took a deep breath and uncovered his face. "Attack at the bank. Gas. Anthropes are-"

"Sir? Are you still there? Are you alright?"

The only other sound from the other end was snarling.

Outside the man with the gas mask tossed aside a can of spray paint. Then he posed in front of security cameras, showing off his face, his clothes, he read his license plate and the serial number of the stolen gun out loud. He walked over to his car, parked along the curb. He opened the door and climbed into the driver's seat. Tossing the mask and the gun out the window, he shifted into drive and sped off down the street.

The ACC director called Anderson and Karen into her office. "I just got a memo from my boss."

"What about?"

"There was a terrorist attack in Chicago. A man dressed in a Hawaiian shirt, leather jacket, cargo pants, and crocs walked into a bank and demanded money. The teller said she couldn't just give him money, so he pulled out a gas mask and a propane tank. The tank was full of a gas form of the hormonal activation serum we use. Two tellers, three customers, and all five security guards in the building were carnivorous anthropes. Another anthrope was a golden retriever who helped her sister get out, lucky girl. The rest of the people in the building ran and hid until the police arrived. It took them thirty minutes to clear the building of anthropes. A man was bitten and died from poison. Another is in the hospital after getting mauled. The terrorist drove away after making sure he was caught on camera outside the building. He was an anthrope."

Karen covered her mouth. "Why would he do that?"

"Not sure. He never took any money. He spray painted on the wall of the bank, 'HOW LONG CAN YOU IGNORE THE PROBLEM?'"

Karen frowned. "What problem?"

Anderson rubbed his forehead. "More important question, how did he get that much serum?"

"He didn't get it." The director said. "He made it. But the question is still the same. How? My boss wants us to identify all possible security threats, any way he could have gotten his hands on the serum or the formula. I think that Annabeth girl might be involved. She must have had a run in with him or someone he was working with. They threatened her or asked her to bring them the serum or something. That would explain why she snuck in the other day and grabbed an extra vial."

"So, what do we do?" Karen asked. "Do we call the feds?"

"We'll have to." The director picked up her phone. "We need to know what happened out there in the woods. She might be able to help us catch this guy. Maybe even stop another attack."

Anderson frowned. "Do you think there's going to be another attack?"

"A person like this who can cause that kind of chaos, a person who seems to have no motivation, certainly hasn't had enough. There will be more until he either gets what he wants, or we stop him. And if he's threatening someone here, we might be next." The director made the call.

There was a knock at the front door of the Watson house. Mr. Watson answered it. "Hello officers. Can I help you?"

One of the three officers stepped forward, taking off his blue patrol hat. "Is your daughter Annabeth home?"

"She's in her room," Mr. Watson answered, "Is she in trouble?"

A blonde woman with short hair in a black suit stepped forward, pushing between the officers. A tracker band under her wrist flashed softly. If she hadn't been wearing a suit she might have looked like a teenager. She showed an FBI badge. "We have reason to believe she is being threatened by a terrorist. We need to ask her some questions."

Mr. Watson nodded emphatically, turning to go run for her, "I'll go get her."

The agent grabbed his arm and shook her head. "No, you're under protective custody now. You aren't leaving our sight. Everything in your house is now evidence. Follow us but don't touch anything. We need to search your house. Your daughter is a victim, but there's no room for slip ups in such a high priority case. I'm sure you've heard about the attack at the bank in Chicago?"

The officers rushed into the house. Mr. Watson stepped back and put his hand to his forehead. "How did my daughter get mixed up in this?"

The agent stepped past him and walked into the house. "We aren't sure sir. You'll know when we know. Is this her room?" Mr. Watson nodded. The agent opened the door and stepped into the room. Annabeth was in the middle of a titration, wearing a lab coat and some protective goggles. Liquids fizzed in a beaker in front of her. "Annabeth Watson?"

Annabeth stepped back. "Yes?"

"Are you alone in this room?"

"Yes?"

Mr. Watson stepped into the room behind the agent and sat on a chair. The agent gestured to the bed. "Have a seat. My name is Agent O'Hara. I need to ask you some questions. Please don't touch anything." She paced around the room looking at all the vials, beakers, and test tubes. She narrowed her eyes, "What's all this?"

Annabeth seemed confused but set down her things and sat on the bed. "Just some chemistry things."

One of the officers stuck his head in the room. "The house is clear."

"Good. Just wait outside the room if you don't mind." Agent O'Hara picked up a small vial sitting on the countertop. She shook it and it lit up blue. O'Hara took a step toward Annabeth, staring her down, "What is this?"

Annabeth backed away, glancing nervously at O'Hara's gun. "Dummy serum, I swear. It's a fake. We use them for self-defense. I've been making them. There's more in that cupboard over there."

Agent O'Hara opened the cupboard and pulled out several dozen more vials on a rack, popping a lid open and sniffing the liquid inside. "They look real."

"They aren't, I swear," Annabeth said, pushing her goggles up to her forehead, revealing red lines around her eyes from the goggles, "I don't know how to make real serums, no one does."

Agent O'Hara opened the door and handed the vials to an officer. "These are going to a lab for testing," She closed the door and turned back to Annabeth, "Are you aware of the terrorist attack that happened this week in Chicago?"

Annabeth nodded, biting her lip.

"Then you know that somehow the secret is out and someone does know how to make them. The local ACC director called me in last night. She said they've been keeping an eye on you for a while. First you failed to report to the ACC at the appropriate time and had to be chased down by your guardian and two young men, one of whom was bitten."

Mr. Watson stood up. "Annabeth, is that true? You never told me one of them was bitten."

"Sir, please don't interrupt me." Mr. Watson sat back down, and the agent continued. "The young man who was bitten was already an anthrope, there were no lasting effects. When reviewing your tracking log, the director found your story didn't match up with your tracker. They found your spent dummy serum. Then there was the incident at the ACC with the two young men from before. You were found carrying a second vial. There's no reason to do so. After the attack in Chicago the director was asked to notify us of any security threats. She gave us your name. So right now, I'm going to give you one chance to answer me honestly. What do you know?"

Annabeth looked at her, then her dad, then back to Agent O'Hara. "I was on a hike. This guy came up to me. He had a gun. I tried to scare him off with the dummy serum, but he knew it was fake. He was an anthrope." She started to cry. "He told me that if I didn't bring him some of the serum, he would shoot my dad. I didn't know what to do, he told me not to call the police or tell anyone."

"So you gave in to his demands?"

Annabeth nodded.

Agent O'Hara suppressed a groan, "Can you give us a description?" She got out a pad of paper and a pen, "Do you think it was this terrorist or was it someone else?"

Annabeth shook her head. "He was wearing a mask. The build was different though. This guy was a little bigger."

"Do you know his name?"

"No." She shook her head again, wiping away tears.

"Do you know anything that could help us track him down?"

"I know when he was going to come back. He wanted me to meet him back there this Saturday at noon in the same place. He said to bring the serum."

"So you never even gave him the serum?"

"No, that was supposed to be this Saturday."

"So how did he figure out the formula without the serum?"

Annabeth shrugged. "I don't know." She hesitated. "Maybe he got it some other way. And maybe he couldn't even figure out the formula. I could probably think of a way to multiply one vial enough to fill a propane tank. He might have stolen just one. That's probably why he asked me to steal another. I mean, he clearly never needed what I stole for him for that attack, so he must need more for something else."

Agent O'Hara paced across the room. "Well, if you never show up to give him the vial, he's got no chance of doing another attack. Unless he's got other people stealing the serum for him. In which case if you don't go then we'd miss the chance to set a trap for him." Agent O'Hara leaned against the countertop and thought. "But what if he does have the formula? He might not even show up."

Annabeth shrugged. "He must want that vial for something."

O'Hara nodded. "Okay, so we'll set up an ambush. Do you have the serum?"

"No," Annabeth said, "that's why I was making the fakes. I tried to steal the serum, but I couldn't get it. So, I tried to make some fakes. I hoped he wouldn't know the difference."

"Is there anything else you can tell us?"

Annabeth thought for a second. "I don't know anything else."

Agent O'Hara squinted. "What makes you so special that he came looking for you? An ambush in the mountains? He must have been following you for quite some time, he must have been interested in you for some reason."

"He uh…" Annabeth looked down and pointed to a framed certificate on the wall, "he said he saw me on TV. I won the national chemistry Olympiad last year."

O'Hara went over to the wall and looked at the paper. "You won ten thousand dollars? So, you're some kind of chemistry prodigy?"

"Well…"

"Yes," Mr. Watson cut in, "she's a genius. She paid for all this equipment with the prize money."

Agent O'Hara put her hands on her hips. "That's quite impressive. I can see why he came looking for you then." Agent O'Hara looked around the room again. "Do you have a computer?"

"It's over there in the corner."

"We're going to search your computer." Agent O'Hara picked it up and carried it back over. "We want to look for any messages they may have sent you. They may have sent you spam that had a virus in it. They could be monitoring you. What's your password?"

"It's password."

Agent O'Hara cracked a smile. "When this is all over, you might want to change that. For now we're going to keep it so we can get in easier. Okay?" Agent O'Hara handed the computer to the officers in the hallway. "This is going to evidence." She closed the door again. "One last thing before we leave. This man has threatened you and your father. We need to protect you, but if he sees you're in protective custody, this man will run. The best we can do for you is station an undercover officer in your house. When you go places, we can send an officer to tail you. Both of you will have at least one law enforcement officer everywhere you go. The three officers with me now are going to take shifts guarding you. Do you have any concerns?"

Mr. Watson spoke up. "My workplace is a secure facility, I have to use an ID to get into work every day."

"We can coordinate with your employer." Agent O'Hara said. "I'm sure there won't be an issue. My number one priority is your safety. A close second is catching this terrorist. Now, if you'll excuse me, I need to go back to the police station to review everything. I'll leave two of the officers here. You two will be perfectly safe." Agent O'Hara stood and walked out of the room.

The police officers stepped through the door. The tallest one smiled at them. "Hi. Where do you want us?"

CHAPTER 15

Agent O'Hara typed on her computer in a small windowless office at the police station. The room was bare except for the desk where she sat. A police officer stuck his head in the door. "Excuse me, Agent O'Hara?"

"Yeah? What is it?"

"We went through the computer. We didn't find anything. No alternate accounts, no suspicious emails, no viruses. It's all clean."

She nodded. "Thank you. We're going to keep it until this is over. Keep checking on it every so often."

The officer nodded and closed the door. Agent O'Hara started a video. A female news anchor began to talk. "On Monday morning this week, David Mitson, a biochemical engineer with an IQ of 170 who recently quit his job, entered a bank in Chicago. When his demands for money went unanswered, he put on a gas mask and released a gaseous form of the top-secret hormonal activation serum used in Anthropomorphic Containment Centers across the nation. Both of the tellers and all five guards on duty that day, along with four customers, were anthropes. According to those familiar with the matter, all anthropes in the building transformed and attacked the others. There was one casualty, and another individual is hospitalized who is now in critical condition. We wish them a speedy recovery." The video cut to security footage.

Mitson posed outside of the building. "David Mitson made sure he was seen by cameras and provided his name, license plate, and even the serial number of a gun he had taken from one of the guards. He then spray painted a message on the wall. 'HOW LONG CAN YOU IGNORE THE PROBLEM?' Authorities entered his house later that day. Mitson was gone, but he left a warning." A picture of his living room appeared. A red circle was spray painted on the floor, and a small pile of papers sat in the middle. "A pile of plane tickets on the floor. The tickets were for an hour after the attack. Departing from O'Hare Airport in Chicago, each led to a major airport across the US. Hartsfield-Jackson Atlanta, Los Angeles, Dallas, Denver, and twenty others. By the time these tickets were found, David Mitson could have been anywhere in the United States and possibly the world." The camera switched back to the news anchor. "The Federal Bureau of Investigation asks that any citizens with information regarding the whereabouts of David Mitson step forward to help combat this violent terrorist."

A video of protestors appeared on the screen. The anchor continued. "In the face of this horrible attack, more victims have emerged. Those classified as anthropes, those with unstable genetic states are being called upon as responsible. We're now taking you to Simon Johnson on the scene."

A man with slicked back hair in a blue suit held a microphone. "Thanks Carol. I'm in Chicago at the bank where the attack occurred. People here seem to be very upset. It's fairly interesting. This is a phenomenon that happens often after something tragic. Anyone associated with the responsible individuals are also blamed. People here are protesting the anthrope community."

A woman holding a baby appeared on screen. Simon held up the microphone. Protesters rallied in the background. "These were-people are responsible for this attack. If it weren't for them, this wouldn't have been possible."

"Don't you think that's an unfair statement? There are many anthropes at home who think this is just as horrible as you do. They weren't in the bank."

She shook her head and shifted her baby to her hip. "The anthropes have been compromising our safety for years. The programs to make things convenient for them is a drain on government funds that the American people have to pay for. The magic potion that terrorist used was created by these government programs. There's no place in our country for people that take away from our safety and freedoms. I won't tolerate them anymore and I don't think anyone else should either."

"Are you aware that the government funds to provide these programs are being paid for by special taxes on the anthrope population?"

"If the anthropes are all paying for it," she growled, "then explain why I've had to mortgage my home? The government is raising our taxes to accommodate for these people, and I won't have it. We need to get rid of them."

Simon paused. "You're talking about an entire group of people. That's like saying we need to get rid of the lower class just because the government helps provide for them.”

“This is different, these people-”

“I’m sorry miss,” Simon interrupted, “that’s all the time we have for now. Back to you Carol.”

The video went back to Carol. “Thanks Simon. These protesters aren’t the only ones. Across the nation, people are calling for something to be done about the anthrope community. This only widens the gap between the anthrope community and the general public. Tensions and prejudices between the groups seem to be growing worse by the day. And despite how many people believe something must be done, one question remains unanswered. What do we do with all the anthropes?

“David Mitson, who is calling himself ‘the Anthrope’, sent a prerecorded video to news organizations shortly after the attack,” Carol continued, “Let’s see what else he had to say.”

A video played of Mitson standing in front of the Empire State Building. “I’m sure by now you’ve all heard of me, the Anthrope. I just wanted to tell you a little bit about the special event over at the Stanton Bank. Some people might call it a terrorist attack, but if you really think about it, I’m doing the same thing that everyone else is doing to the anthropes. How long can you ignore the problem?”

The video went back to Carol. “He says he’s doing the same thing everyone else does, referring to widespread discrimination against anthropes. You can see pretty quickly that it’s not true. People around the anthropes are the only ones getting hurt here. None of the anthropes were ever in any real danger in this attack. This is the reason by the way that so many of us have hard feelings against the anthropes. Not because we hate them, but simply because they are a danger to society.”

Agent O’Hara closed her computer. She tapped her finger on the hardwood desk. “Loose ends. There have to be other loose ends. This guy can’t be perfect.” She picked up her phone and dialed a number. It rang for a few seconds. The other end picked up. “Officer Edwards?”

Officer Edwards set down a bag full of food. The smell of burritos and tacos drifted up to him. “Yeah?”

“This is Agent O’Hara. Is everything going smoothly?”

Officer Edwards nodded as Annabeth grabbed her burrito, on the phone herself. “Yup. Everything is going great. Just picked up some food for everyone.”

“Good. I need to talk to Annabeth. Can you get her for me?”

“Yeah sure.” He held out the phone. “Agent O’Hara wants to talk to you.”

Annabeth looked up from opening the foil bowl. She set her plastic fork down and quickly finished her phone call, "Hey Benny, thanks for being willing. I need to go." She hung up and took the phone from Officer Edwards. "Hello?"

"This is Agent O'Hara. I just want to review a few things. You said he wanted to meet again tomorrow at noon in the same place as last time, right?"

"Yeah," Annabeth said, cutting into her burrito, "that's what he told me."

"And you can't remember anything that might help us identify this person?"

Annabeth shook her head, "I wish." She took a bite.

"Okay, Annabeth, I'm going to be honest here, I'm worried about tomorrow. This guy is probably going to be watching for you. He's probably going to be making sure you aren't followed. We're going to have to send you in alone, we'll follow from a distance, but we can't let him see us. This all really boils down to one question I have for you."

"What?"

"Well," Agent O'Hara sighed, "how well can you use a gun?"

CHAPTER 16

Annabeth frowned. She wore her running shorts and a neon pink shirt. Her running shoes were tight on her feet, and she wore short white socks. She held a Glock in her right hand as she looked herself up and down. "Where the heck am I supposed to hide this?"

Agent O'Hara called out. "Annabeth, are you ready?"

"Uh…" The car door slammed. "Yeah!" Annabeth scrambled around the car and presented herself to Agent O'Hara, hands empty. They stood on a gravel access road near the base of the mountains. A short path went into the trees and connected to a hiking trail, the same one Annabeth had been on the last time.

"Alright, we'll be in contact with you the whole time. Don't say anything out loud to us, just scratch your ear to let us know you're still there and that you're safe. As soon as you see him, that's when you cough. After you cough, we'll come right away, we've got ATV's so we should be able to get there in about two minutes. Just keep stalling until we get there. Got it?"

Annabeth nodded.

"Alright. Go ahead. We'll be waiting." Agent O'Hara cocked her gun and Annabeth jogged over to the trail in and into the forest. She gripped a dummy serum in her hand. The path was narrow, passing through trees that blocked the sun. Roots and rocks littered the trail. Agent O'Hara's voice filled her ear. "Alright Annabeth, you're making good progress, go ahead and slow down a bit. If you're tired you won't be able to run to get away." Annabeth scratched her ear and slowed down slightly. Sweat began to make the vial of dummy serum slippery in her hand.

She fell into a trance, feet moving underneath her and forest swimming past as she came closer and closer to her destination. Agent O'Hara started talking to her. "Alright, you're getting close. Go ahead and walk this last little bit, you should see the split off up ahead as you go around that corner. Cough if he's there." Annabeth walked around the corner, taking deep breaths. A small game trail appeared in the trees to the left.

She turned onto the trail and walked a few dozen paces into the woods before reaching a clearing in the aspen trees. Only dry grass grew in the middle. Empty. She scratched her ear. "Not there?" Annabeth scratched again.

A rustling noise came from behind Annabeth in the woods. A large man wearing all black and a face mask stepped out of the woods holding up a gun. "Do you have the serum?"

Annabeth turned white and coughed. "Alright," O'Hara said, starting her ATV, "Annabeth, stall, we're on our way."

"Yeah," Annabeth answered the man. She wiped the vial off on her shirt and held it out to him. He stepped forward and took the vial from her.

"Did you tell anyone about this?"

"No."

He shook the gun at her. "Don't lie to me! Did you tell anyone?"

"Annabeth," Agent O'Hara asked, "are you alright?"

"No." She scratched her ear.

"Annabeth, will you please confirm you're okay?"

"What's wrong with your ear?" The gunman stepped closer, putting the gun to her head. "Are you talking to someone?"

"No." She scratched at her ear again. "I have an ear infection."

Agent O'Hara cursed on the other end. "Alright Annabeth, we're hurrying. One minute. Just hold on." Agent O'Hara revved her ATV and sped ahead of the other officers following her.

"O'Hara," one of them called out, "slow down, this trail is too rough for high speeds!"

"Annabeth is in trouble! We need to get to her!" Agent O'Hara sped around a corner, shouting into the comms, "Annabeth, are you alright?" There was no response. O'Hara muttered a curse. She took one hand off the steering and grabbed her gun. Nearly falling off after going over a rock, she overcorrected and almost hit a tree. Seeing the path up ahead she slammed the brakes and ran, following it into the woods.

As she approached the clearing, she slowed and took soft steps. She saw Annabeth standing in the middle and the masked man behind her. One hand clamped over her mouth, the other holding a gun to the side of her head. Agent

O'Hara stepped out of the trees. "Put the gun down!"

"I don't think so. Little Miss Pretty here is my ticket out of here. So, here's what we're going to do, you're going to put the gun on the ground and kick it over to me. You and whoever else is here is going to get out of my way, and I'm going to leave with the girl. I'll get rid of her once I'm sure you aren't following me. But don't worry, I won't kill her, there's no sense in that. Besides, she already brought me what I needed." He smiled wickedly.

Agent O'Hara dropped her gun on the ground. She kicked it through the dirt toward the gunman. "Annabeth," she groaned, "I told you to bring a gun."

Annabeth was breathing heavily, eyes wide. She tried to say something, but her mouth was covered. The gunman tightened his hand over her mouth. There were sounds in the forest. "Shut it. Tell whoever else is coming to back off!"

Agent O'Hara hesitated but then raised her hand to her ear. "Annabeth has been taken hostage. Our gunman's demands are that we let him go." Several officers burst through the trees.

"Get them out of here!" He gestured with the gun.

O'Hara nodded and the officers retreated from the clearing. She tried to take slow, even breaths. "So, now what?"

"I'm going to leave. And you're going to stay right there. And to make sure you stay there, I'm going to do this." The gunman took the gun away from Annabeth's head and shot O'Hara in the chest. She fell to the ground.

Annabeth stomped on the gunman's foot and punched him in the face. She spun away from him and shot him twice in the leg. He went down with a shout of pain, dropping his gun. Annabeth kicked it away from him. She rushed over to O'Hara. "Are you alright?"

O'Hara nodded. "Bulletproof vest." She saw the Glock in Annabeth's hand. "Where the heck did you hide that?" Annabeth smirked and shrugged, she held out her hand to O'Hara and helped her up off the ground. O'Hara walked over to the gunman and yanked off his mask. "What's your name?"

He grimaced. "Dave Phillips." He reached into his shirt. O'Hara shook her gun at him and he paused, speaking slowly, "It's not a gun. It's a letter from my boss." He handed O'Hara an envelope.

"What's in it?" O'Hara turned it over in her hands, examining it, only touching the corners with her fingertips.

"I don't know," He grimaced, clutching his bleeding leg, "I never read it. He told me to turn it over if I was captured."

"Officers!" The police walked into the clearing. "I need you to secure this man. Take him down to the station. We're going to question him." O'Hara tucked the envelope into her pocket. She glanced down at his wrist and saw two rings of scars, one old and neat, the other fresh and crude. "So, you're an anthrope too?"

Phillips nodded. "All of us are. Everyone that works for my boss. We're all alike. People who know the machine is broken."

"What are you talking about?"

"Everyone keeps calling us terrorists. This isn't terrorism. This is an awakening. There have been movements for decades, all trying to gain equality in the eyes of others. They all worked to some degree or another. Now there's one big group of people that still isn't being treated fair. Us. The anthropes. But now we're doing something. And it's working. Things are getting worse for now, but soon no one will be able to ignore the problem. Then they'll fix it."

"You're crazy." Three police officers picked Phillips up and began to carry him out of the clearing.

Phillips fought against them as he was taken away, "Anthropes have to stand up for themselves now! Just think, how hard was it to get that badge of yours? How hard was it?" Phillips was carried out of the clearing. O'Hara clenched her fists. She took a deep breath and shook it off. Annabeth sat down on a rock at the edge of the clearing. She started crying. O'Hara walked over and sat next to her.

"You okay?"

"I just shot a person."

"A bad person. You had to do that. To keep people safe. Plus, he's still alive."

Annabeth looked at her. "If the ends justify the means, then was he right?"

O'Hara looked down. "You go to a haven school. It's a good place to grow up. But the rest of the world isn't like that. It's a lot worse than you would think out there for people like us. It took me twice as long as everyone else to earn my badge. I was more than qualified, but there was a lot of BS about me being an anthrope. Frankly, no terrorist can ever create change for the better because their actions are evil. Their end is usually a little murky but theoretically justified, in this case equality. Their means are not justified. Terrorism. How could that create positive change? Now what you did, shooting him, was justified because it was out of self-defense, and he was attacking you. The means were necessary. Their actions destroy, yours help protect. You were brave out there. I know you're pretty talented with that chemistry stuff, but if you ever think about going into law enforcement…" O'Hara handed her a card.

"The FBI?"

"Flip it over."

Annabeth turned it over and found O'Hara's handwritten phone number.

"Just give me a call and we can talk about it. No promises but I could give you some pointers. Or just talk if you want. If you ever need a friend."

"Thank you. But I don't think law enforcement is my path."

"What is your path then? Chemistry?"

"I'm not sure. Still trying to find it," Annabeth wiped away her tears, giving a weak smile, "The future is kinda scary, but the good thing is if I keep my options open, I can do anything I want to."

O'Hara nodded, "You can."

CHAPTER 17

David Mitson kicked off his shoes and tore off his socks. He slipped his feet into his dark green crocs as he placed his shoes into a bag. Undoing the top button of his Hawaiian shirt, he slung the duffel bag over his shoulder. He slid the latch of the bathroom stall and walked out into the hall of the elementary school. Squeaking shoes and bouncing basketballs could be heard in the gym only a few paces to his right. A pimply teenage boy wore a cheap black and white shirt with a whistle around his neck. He blew the whistle to signify the end of the quarter.

Mitson stepped into the gym and pulled a chain and a lock from his bag. The door he'd used was positioned near the corner, and on the opposite side of the bleachers was an emergency exit that went outside. He wrapped the chain through and around the door handles and clicked the lock into place, sealing off the hallway exit. Keeping his eyes down he walked past the parents in the bleachers to the emergency exit, lab coat fluttering. He slung another chain over his shoulder and had just reached the door to outside when he felt a tap on his shoulder. A mother holding her three-year-old stood behind him, a band under the child's wrist blinked. The mother had no band. "Excuse me, what are you doing sir?"

Mitson smiled and patted the little boy on the head. He set the bag down on the floor. "Don't you recognize me?" He removed a modified propane tank from the bag and set it on the floor. "You must have seen me on the news." He secured a gas mask over his face. "I'm the Anthrope."

The woman stepped back and pulled her child closer. "Why are you doing this?"

"I'm doing this for your son. I'm doing this so your son will have a better life." He pulled a gun out of his white lab coat and fired it twice in the air. People screamed and panicked. He tossed the gun aside. Mitson opened the valve on the propane tank and blue gas seeped into the air. Everyone yelled and ran away to the other side of the room. Mitson picked up his bag and opened the door. Across the room a half dozen people began to spasm and fall to the floor. He closed the door behind him and used the chain to lock it shut.

He spray painted on the wall, 'HOW LONG CAN YOU IGNORE THE PROBLEM?' Standing in front of a camera he read off a piece of paper. "Anthropes, everyone's talking about you. It's obvious I'm using you as pawns. I too am a pawn to my conscience. I know that things are broken. People think they're victims of the anthropes, but you are the real victims. You've done nothing wrong. Are you going to ignore the problem or are you going to stand up for yourselves? What are you willing to do for change? Think about your children and their future. You decide now what kind of future they're going to have. I'm just a man. An anthrope. The Anthrope. I'm not a terrorist, I'm here to wake you up. Prejudice is universal against anthropes, but it ends now. Throughout history there were awakenings that changed things. I call upon all anthropes to bring the last great awakening. Discrimination is nearing its end on this planet, and it is our responsibility to end it once and for all. These demonstrations will continue until action is taken. Demonstrations of what happens when you discriminate against people with a disease. I am the Anthrope. Act now." He walked away from the camera and climbed into a car.

Agent O'Hara took the letter from the forensics specialist. "Thanks. Nothing?"

"Only prints were Mitson's."

"Thanks anyway." O'Hara closed the door and returned to her desk in the bare room. Annabeth and her dad sat in two chairs in front of her. "Alright, forensics cleared it, Mitson seems to have been the only person to have ever touched this. Also, we figured out who Dave Phillips is. He just recently quit his job as the head computer scientist for a VPN provider based in the same city as Mitson's biochemical company. They must have known each other, and there might be more of them, but we can't just go looking for people who quit their jobs in that area. There could be thousands. He found a way to disable the alarm when they removed their trackers, so we won't be able to find them on the ACC system either. Anyway, I thought you might be interested in hearing what Mitson had to say." She unfolded the paper and began to read to them. "I expected you would take down my man. I've planned ahead and at the very time you find this letter, another attack will be underway, and you will be helpless to stop it. I'm starting an awakening and am myself only a pawn of my conscience here to start the awakening. After that, my purpose is accomplished and my destination irrelevant, only what I have achieved matters. I will make a personal visit to Miss Watson in the coming weeks. Like today's attack, you will not be able to stop it. David Mitson, the Anthrope." O'Hara set the letter down. "As pseudonyms go, I'll give it to him, that's a pretty good one. He was right though. I got a call a few minutes ago. He locked a ten-year-old basketball team and their parents in a school gym and gassed them. Right at the same time we caught Phillips."

Annabeth ran her hands through her hair. "And he's coming here?"

"Sounds like it. Now let's think. This man is a brilliant planner, he won't be leaving anything to chance. He said he's coming after you. We need to be ready for him anywhere in the next few weeks. But whenever he comes you won't be alone. There'll be lots of people there, a gathering of some sort. What gatherings are you going to be at?"

"None," Mr. Watson said, "if he's coming after my daughter, she isn't going anywhere."

"Dad, that's not fair, prom is coming up! I have to go!"

Agent O'Hara snapped her fingers. "Prom! Has it been announced?"

"We announced the details just this morning, but everyone already knew which day." Annabeth opened her phone to check the announcement. "It's a joint prom with our rival school. There's no way he could have planned it already, right?"

"Why would you have a joint prom with your rival school?"

"Because of Lucas," Annabeth sighed, "he got in a fight with some kids there because he was an anthrope. He thought maybe if we had prom together then they might not hate us so much."

O'Hara rocked her head back and forth. "That might be true, but a prom with a haven school involved sounds like the kind of place this Anthrope," she made quotations with her hands, "would want to hang out. So, our plan for catching this guy is to take his challenge. He says we can't stop him. We'll just have to beat him at his game. Plan ahead. Cover all the entrances. Figure out escape routes for everyone and make sure people can get out. Once he shows up, we nab him. Step one of our plan, you're going to announce that you're going to go to prom on whatever social media you use."

"But-" Annabeth paused, "I don't have a date."

O'Hara raised her hands. "So get one."

"I can't just get a date to prom. A boy has to ask me."

"What about Lucas?" Her dad asked. "He seems like a nice boy, and you already had a date with him."

Annabeth threw her hands in the air. "He has to ask me."

"Tell him to ask you."

Annabeth looked at O'Hara in disbelief. "Did you ever go to prom? You don't seem to understand how this works. He asks me. I have to wait until Lucas or someone else asks me."

O'Hara shifted in her chair and rubbed her chin. "How quickly can you get him to ask you?"

Annabeth rolled her eyes and unlocked her phone. She called Lucas. "Hey Lucas, they announced prom this morning."

"I know. It's exciting. It's actually happening."

Annabeth nodded. "Yeah. Super exciting. I'm excited to go."

"I didn't know you already had a date. That was fast."

She facepalmed. "No, I don't have a date, but everyone is already asking each other. I'm sure someone will ask me soon."

"Yeah probably." An awkward silence ensued.

"Well, I've got to go. Talk to you later." She hung up and groaned. "He is so clueless."

"So, is he going to ask you now?"

"Probably," she said, "he's probably going to talk to his friend Vincent about it. Vincent is smart, he'll understand. Sometimes I swear Lucas can be so… anyway, I'm sure he'll ask me sooner or later.

Across town in his basement, Lucas put his phone down. "I just had the weirdest conversation."

Vincent flailed his arms, a VR headset covering his face. "Sounded like it. Was it Annabeth?"

"Yeah. The whole thing was confusing. I'm not sure why she called."

"You guys talked about prom." Vincent pulled off the headset. "She probably wants you to ask her out."

"Then why didn't she just say so?"

"Because women are like quantum physics." Vincent plopped on the couch and handed the headset to Lucas. "They're beautiful but you never really know what the heck is going on on the inside. And every once in a while, something weird happens and they start crying for no reason and you start wondering if it's just that time again but then you remember they have the same breakdown every week and-"

"Vincent," Lucas strapped on the VR headset, "are you still talking about quantum physics?"

"No, admittedly at a certain point the analogy breaks down. But the point remains. Women aren't straightforward. Annabeth was talking to you about her and prom and getting asked out. She was priming you."

"You mean like a mower?" Lucas held up his hand, holding an invisible shotgun.

"No, she was making you think about all those things and hoping you would connect them together and decide to ask her out." Vincent sent a message to Annabeth. *Don't worry. One of us isn't an idiot.* "So, do you have any ideas of how to ask her out?"

"I didn't say I was going to ask her out."

"But I inferred you were going to so I just skipped asking you that question and moved on to the more important question."

"Fine. I was thinking maybe I could make a poster and give her some candy with a pun like, 'I'd be an airhead to not ask you to prom'."

"Lucas," Vincent said, "you are an airhead and if I hadn't suggested it you might not have decided to ask her to prom. And please, don't insult your minimal intelligence with a stupid pun. If it was up to me, people would just ask people to their faces and save money on all those stupid signs and candy. But a dumb tradition is still a tradition."

"If I don't do a poster with a pun, what am I supposed to do?"

Vincent shrugged. "Something extravagant, cheap, and really cool."

"Like?"

"Like…" Vincent grinned. "Do you have any alcohol?"

"Bro, why would I have alcohol?"

"Rubbing alcohol."

"Oh," Lucas said sheepishly, "yes. We have a lot of that."

"Good. Grab as many bottles as you can find and meet me in my car."

"Okay." Lucas took off the headset. "Are you sure this isn't going to be illegal?"

Vincent snapped his fingers and made finger guns. "I'm almost positive it's illegal. But it's one of those laws that was made just to keep people from having fun, you know? It would have been totally okay in the eighties."

"If you say so." Lucas ran off to grab the alcohol. He ran out to Vincent's car and climbed in the passenger seat. Vincent hit the gas and they sped off to Annabeth's house.

"I texted Annabeth and she told me she was on her way home and she's going to be back in about five minutes. Check in the back and make sure I have some chalk laying around."

Lucas dug around the backseat. "What's up with all this?" He held up a multi color pack of Crayola chalk. "Have you been getting in touch with your inner four-year-old?"

"I took my little sister to the park the other day. She always forgets her things." Vincent reached over and fumbled around in the glove box and grabbed a lighter.

"You keep a lighter in the glove box?"

"I keep a lot of things in the glove box. Keep judging, why don't you?" Vincent steered his car over to the curb. He climbed out without turning off the ignition. They were parked around the corner from Annabeth's house.

"Are you going to turn that off?"

"No. Here's another thing I keep in the car." Vincent tossed Lucas a ninja mask. "Put this on. We are ninja." He hurried around the corner to Annabeth's driveway and began writing in chalk. "Grab that alcohol and start pouring it on the ground where I make chalk lines. Make sure you get a lot on the ground. We want this to last a while. And hurry. She'll be here soon."

Lucas began to follow along behind Vincent pouring alcohol all over the driveway. Vincent moved quickly and joined Lucas pouring the pungent liquid everywhere. They finished covering the lines and stepped back to admire their handy work. "So, what now?"

"Well," Vincent said, "we wait for Annabeth to get here and then we run away." A car pulled into the neighborhood. "That was a little faster than expected."

"You know they're going to think we're terrorists. Everyone is freaked out about that kind of stuff."

"Bah, it's just a little neighborhood driveway arson. You can't get arrested for having a good time." Vincent flicked his lighter open and started the flame. He tossed it into the alcohol and the whole driveway was consumed in fire. "Time to go!" They sprinted back to the car.

Mr. Watson yelled. "They're setting our house on fire! It's the terrorists!"

"Relax dad." Annabeth said, laughing at the two boys bent halfway over jumping into their car with ninja masks. "It's not that." She hopped out of the car and climbed onto the hood. The fire spelled out 'PROM? -LUCAS'. "Dad! It's a promposal!"

Mr. Watson got out of the car, eyes wide and fixed on the fire. "From Lucas?"

Annabeth laughed and nodded. "Relax dad. They didn't set the house on fire."

He turned to her, panic in his eyes. "They might have!"

CHAPTER 18

Benny eyed the pins in front of him. All around he could hear them scattering across the greasy wooden lanes and the smell of rubber pizza hung in the air. He picked up a ball and walked smoothly under its weight. Picking up speed, he dropped to one knee and launched the ball forward. It rolled straight, slamming into the pins and sending them flying. One pin in the back rocked slightly back and forth. He stuck his arm out and wiggled his fingers as though he could use the force. The pin fell.

Behind him, his three companions for the evening cheered. He turned and raised his hands. "I'm the best." He walked back to the table and picked up his drink. Taking a few sips, he sniffed, trying to fight back the stuffiness in his nose. "Hey, Claire, I'm going to go to the bathroom really quick. Spring allergies. Be right back." He set down the soda and walked across the bowling alley to the bathrooms. "Well, that's a sketchy looking bathroom if I've ever seen one."

He put his finger through the hole where the handle should have been and pulled the door open. The bathroom smelled like wet paper, sweaty shoes, and dirt. Benny raised an eyebrow at the sinks. What could have been paint but was more likely blood spattered the countertop. Instead of a paper towel dispenser, the wet end of a rotating hand towel hung down the wall and draped several feet across the floor. "No way am I wiping my nose on that thing." He walked over to the sink and used the elbow of his jacket to flip on the water. Praying no one would walk into the bathroom, he blew as much snot as he could onto his hands and washed them off as fast as possible. He dabbed his nose off on his other elbow just as the door creaked open.

Three familiar faces walked into the bathroom and two immediately placed their bodies in front of the door. Benny turned around to face them. "Hello boys." He grinned. "Do I know you? I think we might go to school together. You know what, that's it. We go to school together. What classes do we have, I'm sure there must be one. Is it… AP chemistry? No, there's no way you're in that class."

The foremost boy stepped forward, his enormous belt buckle flashing in the garish fluorescent light. "I think you know exactly where we were acquainted."

"Acquainted? Wow." Benny mocked surprise. "That's a big word for you. Good job. Where'd you learn that one?" Belt Buckle slugged him in the chest. Benny doubled over. "I'd rather you don't do that again. If I fall on the floor, it might start a pandemic."

"You were there at the basketball game. You're one of those Weber freaks."

Benny clutched his stomach. "Actually, I go to Fremont. You and I are on the same team. Really we're all on the same team, you know? All of us on this planet. Fremont kids, Weber kids, we're all just kids. They're trying to make it through high school, we're trying to make it through high school. You know how to throw a punch-" Benny delivered a right cross to Belt Buckle's jaw. "I know how to throw a better one."

Belt Buckle stumbled backwards, hand to his face. "There's no one to bail you out. It's three against one."

Benny raised his hands in protest. "Why are you doing this?"

"You're with those freaks."

"So what? You hate them so much you hate me for not hating them? That doesn't make any sense." Belt Buckle threw another punch at Benny. Benny ducked and put him in a headlock. One of the boys guarding the door stepped forward to help. "Ahh! I wouldn't do that. He's getting a little claustrophobic." The boy stepped back, returning to the door. Benny relaxed a bit and continued, "Listen up. You hate these people, but I don't think you even know why. You were told to hate them, and you listened just because it was your mom or your teacher or some person you saw on TV. Think about it. And while you're doing that, I'm going to leave so your buddy here can get a breather."

The two boys moved to the sides and Benny edged toward the door, dragging Belt Buckle along with him. Benny reached the door and kicked it open with his back foot. He shoved Belt Buckle away and walked back out into the bowling alley. The three boys rushed out after him, but he was already in plain view. He tipped an imaginary hat to them and laughed, walking jauntily back to his double date.

"Benny, hurry up, it's your turn, what took so long?" Claire handed him his ball.

"Well," he took the ball with ease and slipped his fingers into the holes, "I ran into some guys I recognized from school."

Claire noticed his red knuckles as he turned to roll the ball. "Benny!" She stopped him, "Did you get in a fight?"

"What?" He looked down at his hand and hid it behind his back, still holding the bowling ball. "Cuss. Okay fine, do you remember how I told you about that guy at the basketball game? Well, it was the same three guys that attacked him. And they were still a little cranky."

"And you fought them!"

"Just a second, I don't want to keep holding this." Benny rolled a strike. "I wouldn't say I fought them. I threw a punch. Just one." He held up his finger. "But it's fair because they hit me first."

"How did you get out of there?"

"Put one of them in a headlock," Benny shrugged, "then I just walked out."

"Come sit down." Claire dragged him to the table and examined his hand, the other guy getting up to bowl and the girl was off ordering some food. She made a face, "Admittedly I don't really know what to do. That redness will probably just go away, right?"

Benny nodded, "There isn't anything to do. It just has to heal."

"You know," Claire said, "if you count hanging out during and after the game, this is technically our second date and the second time you've gotten in a fight during that date. That's a pretty high percentage."

"That is pretty high," Benny mumbled to himself. "Tell you what, I'll take you out again and we can lower that percentage."

She smiled. "Umm… when were you thinking?"

He rocked his head. "Prom is coming up."

"You're going to ask me to prom like that?"

"Well at first I wasn't going to." He unzipped his jacket. "I actually had this poster with a corny pun with me," he pulled a mini poster out of his jacket and set it on the table in front of her, "but then I thought it was too corny."

She read the poster. "I don't want to sound corny, but will you go to prom with me?" She paused for a second and then looked at him, "That isn't corny. It isn't even a pun."

Benny reached into his pocket and set an ear of corn on the table. "That's fresh by the way."

"You just had that in your jacket this whole time?"

Benny shrugged, "This jacket has really big pockets."

Claire smirked, "One second." She got up and took her turn. The first roll went straight into the gutter but the second scored a spare. She sat back down. "This is an acceptable promposal."

"So…"

"Yes, but not officially. I have to do something back. It's a tradition."

"Ah," Benny said. "In that case I will eagerly await your *official* response."

Lucas walked into the kitchen and sighed. His mom was making a smoothie in the very loud blender. He waited for her to finish and then sighed again. She looked over at him. "Something wrong?"

"No."

"Okay." She started to pour some of the smoothie into a glass. Opening the cupboard, she pulled out another glass and filled it up, setting it on the island's quartz countertop. "Do you want some smoothie?"

"Okay," Lucas said, "you always know how to get me to talk. It's about Annabeth."

Mrs. Harrison pushed the glass over to Lucas. "What about her?"

"I asked her to prom. Now I'm getting stressed about it. What am I going to do?"

"Go with her, I think." She drank her smoothie.

"Yeah, but she thinks I'm an idiot. I feel like an idiot when I'm with her. It took me forever to realize she wanted me to ask her out. She's so smart and I'm… not. Even Vincent keeps telling me I'm totally clueless."

She pulled out her phone. "Why does Vincent think you're clueless?"

"Beats me, I have no clue. He keeps telling me I don't understand Annabeth at all."

His mom nodded, eyes still on the screen. "So, why does Vincent think you're clueless?"

Lucas blinked. "I don't know?"

"That's so interesting." She sent a message. "Sorry, our carpool got canceled, I have to go pick the kids up from soccer practice. Can you come with me?" Bringing her drink with her, she walked out to the garage. Lucas stood and followed her. He pulled his phone out and started sending a message to Vincent. His mom put the car into reverse and started backing out. "So, what's worrying you?"

Lucas mumbled to himself as he typed, "Why do you keep saying I'm clueless?" Lucas hit send. "What?"

She put her hand on Lucas's chair and looked backwards to pull out of the garage. "Did I say you were clueless? I'm sorry, that's not what I meant."

"What did you mean?" Lucas hit send again. "What?"

"I don't remember, what was I saying?" Putting the car into drive she looked over at Lucas. "I'm sorry, where are we going?"

"We were talking about Annabeth."

"No, piano lessons?"

"Soccer?"

His mom nodded. "Right. Let me just make sure I know where we're going and then I will be focused…" She opened up the map on her phone.

Lucas sent another message to Vincent. "Yes you did, you totally called me clueless."

"No," Mrs. Harrison mumbled, face illuminated by the phone screen, "honey, I think you're getting confused."

"What?" Lucas looked up from his phone. "What? Sorry, I was sending a message to Vincent. He says he can't remember what we were talking about earlier today because it was 'too long ago' and he wasn't paying attention."

His mom didn't say anything for a second. "Sorry, I got distracted, what were we talking about?"

Lucas paused, squinting at his phone again. "I don't remember."

"Ok. Do you want to listen to some music?"

"Yeah, that sounds great."

"Ok." She turned on the music and left the driveway. Both of them set their phones down and started listening to the music.

Lucas sat there for a moment before saying anything else. "So, what I was wanting to talk to you about was the fact that I'm kinda second guessing myself with Annabeth. I don't even know why she likes me. We just seem really different. I mean, I know she likes me-"

"Did you guys kiss?"

"She told me that she likes me." Lucas hesitated. "And yes, we kissed, but we're keeping it secret from Vincent."

His mom grinned. "That's fine. As far as why she likes you, she seems like a smart girl, she's very sweet, and she's going to be a student officer. You've got a few things in common."

"I guess in terms of people skills yeah, but in all other aspects we're really different. She's got a really analytical brain, she's really clever," Lucas tapped his head, "like Vincent."

"You think she's more like Vincent?"

Lucas thought about it. "No, it's fifty fifty. Half and half. I don't know, I guess I just feel a little overshadowed by both of them."

"Why? You're a talented kid too. Just because they're both talented doesn't mean you need to feel less so. Vincent's prideful and it can make people feel not so awesome, but when he grows up a little he's going to realize that everyone is awesome. Yes, we have our brain hiccups and fuzzy spots, but you can hold your own bantering with him. You're a great leader and you have lots of great ideas. Like this joint prom. Who would have thought of doing that? And with things the way they are right now, it's going to take a lot of work to hold people together. There was another attack today, did you see the news?"

Lucas nodded. "Yeah."

"Well, people are freaking out about it. Everyone is upset about it for one reason or another. But you're trying to hold people together. Even though everyone else is getting scared, you're being brave."

Lucas smiled for a moment, then he frowned. "People are trying to cancel it. No one wants there to be a brawl."

"What do you think about that?"

"I think we need to be brave and do it anyway." He folded his arms. "I think if we want to help people, we should help them be brave."

"And that's why you're awesome." His mom smiled to herself. "I have awesome kids. And that is why Annabeth likes you. Because you are awesome."

Lucas grinned. "Thanks mom."

CHAPTER 19

Agent O'Hara sat in the Watson's living room, looking at some papers on the coffee table. Annabeth walked in, holding a crumpled ball of paper. She used her foot to fling some discarded packing paper and into an empty box. "Here it is." She handed the paper to O'Hara, then sat on the gray couch.

O'Hara smoothed out the paper on the table, revealing a map. "This is your school? It just looks like a bunch of squished hexagons, or a beehive."

"Yeah, it's kinda confusing at first. So these two sections right here," Annabeth pointed, "those are split levels or extra floors, they're stacked on top of each other."

O'Hara stared blankly. "Who designed this school?"

"Everyone says it was designed as a bunker back in the cold war."

"Was it really?"

"I don't know," Annabeth said, "I'm still kinda new."

"Okay," O'Hara said, drawing on the map in red ink, "it looks like these are all the exits. This one and this one probably aren't going to be used. This one will be the easiest to find right here, right?"

"Yeah," Annabeth nodded, "that's the cafeteria and the dance will be in the commons and there's a big opening between them. This wall right here is one of the only places we actually have windows so everyone should see that it's a way out in an emergency. The front door is over there, that's where everyone will come in."

Mr. Watson walked into the room carrying two glasses of lemonade. He set them down on coasters and peeked at the map. "Do you two need anything else?"

"I'm alright Mr. Watson."

"Thanks dad."

Mr. Watson nodded and left.

"I'll be at the door, letting people in. We'll post men at all the exits, even the weird ones, just in case. You said you're going to be there tomorrow after school to decorate, right?" Annabeth nodded. O'Hara continued. "Ok, I've got to stop by the police station first but then I'll come find you and we'll go over the doors. I'll call your principal and have them email out the emergency plan to everyone. They won't suspect anything, it's standard procedure for school gatherings right now. Sound good?"

"Yeah. One last thing." Annabeth turned on her phone. "I posted that I was going to prom with Lucas, and I got a message back from 'Mitt Davidson' and he said, 'so excited, will be there too'."

O'Hara looked up at her. "We know for sure he's coming."

Annabeth nodded. "He'll be there."

Vincent picked up a purple balloon. He put it to his lips and blew hard three times. Eyes wandering around the huge room lazily, he tied the balloon and tossed it to the side in a massive pile of purple balloons. "Who was the moron that decided we needed a thousand balloons? And who chose the color purple? That's a stupid color. Our school colors are red and black."

"Well," Lucas said, a false grin plastered across his face, "I definitely like the color scheme." He waved his hand frantically in front of his neck, balloon slapping against his hand. "It was a good choice, looks great." He pointed over his shoulder at Annabeth who was in the process of taping all the balloons into a big spiral from atop a ladder.

"Whatever." Vincent blew up another balloon. He set it on the floor and jumped on it. It erupted in an explosion of sound and Annabeth nearly tumbled from the ladder. All around the hexagonal commons of Weber, various students stopped their decorating to look at Vincent. "Sorry! Blew it up too much. My bad. As you were."

Lucas blew up a balloon. "Have you asked anyone to prom yet?"

Vincent stuck a balloon in his mouth and muttered through gritted teeth. "What do you think?"

"Okay, you could always ask Kenzie. You two seemed to hit it off."

"You know," Vincent yawned, "for a student officer, you don't really pay very much attention to people. Kenzie has a boyfriend."

Lucas stopped mid blow. "She does? Who?"

Vincent shrugged. "I don't know. It's a different one every week. But she's always got one. Last week it was Jason."

"Jason…" Lucas trailed off.

"How many Jasons do you know?"

"Apparently none."

"Jason Jones," Vincent ripped open another package of balloons.

"Wait, is he that really tall guy we play Where's Waldo with and we see who can spot him first at school in the crowd?"

"Yes," Vincent nodded, "the guy I always beat you at playing Where's Waldo with."

Lucas folded his arms. "That's not true."

"It is too true. I've beaten you the last three weeks in a row. I sent you a picture of him in the commons this morning."

"Oh, I guess that's right," Lucas paused, "He's like two feet taller than her."

Vincent nodded, "Very sad. They could probably make out while she's standing and he's sitting."

"They could make out with her standing on a chair."

Vincent turned his head and pointed at Lucas. "They could make out on a box."

Lucas pointed back. "They could make out on a fox. Hmm… admittedly that doesn't make much sense."

Vincent shook his head. "Dr. Seuss never really did. He mostly just put a bunch of rhyming words together."

"Maybe he was the one who invented rap. Have you read Fox in Socks? I'm white, but I'm pretty sure even I could make it into a sick rap. Well, that is if I could say it without tripping."

Vincent smirked. "Saying it is supposed to be the hard part about rap. Besides, Scatman invented rap."

"Scatman?"

"Yeah," Vincent said, "Scatman John. He had that one super famous song. Ski ba bop ba dop bop?"

"Oh! That guy! Did he really?"

"No, maybe, probably not." Vincent shrugged. "I feel like the actual story would be less interesting though, so I just pretend."

"Huh."

They picked up a balloon each and blew them up. An awkward silence fell.

Lucas looked over. "But Kenzie. Couldn't you just… next week… for prom?"

"Eh. Not my type." Vincent tied another balloon.

"What is your type?"

"I don't know," He shrugged, "Super hot, super smart, super dumb about people. Preferably they still have their natural hair color. I find it attractive that they're confident enough with themselves that they would leave it the way it is."

"Why would you want them to be super dumb about people?"

Vincent gestured to his face. "Because all the smart pretty ones usually go after you."

"What?" Lucas waved him off, "totally not true."

Vincent pointed at Annabeth.

"Okay, so that's one. Hardly counts at all."

"Jessica Simpson, Katie Wallace, Katie Hansen. A lot of Katies. I'm naming one of my kids Katie. Fingers crossed they inherit my wife's genes. Have you ever noticed girls named Katie are more likely to be really hot?"

"I-"

Vincent raised an eyebrow as he blew up a balloon.

"Actually, I think you're right. That's definitely a thing." Lucas nodded in agreement. "Katie's are hot."

Annabeth rolled her eyes and popped a balloon with the sharp part of her tape dispenser. Lucas jumped and she smirked. She spotted Agent O'Hara walking into the commons. Annabeth climbed down the ladder and waved to her. O'Hara walked over. "Hi Annabeth."

"Hi Age… Aunt O'Hara." Annabeth winked and turned around. "Hey Lucas, Vincent, this is my Aunt O'Hara."

O'Hara waved to them. "Hi boys." Vincent noticed a gun in her suit. O'Hara adjusted her black suit and locked eyes with him. "So, Annabeth, should we go?"

Annabeth nodded. "Yeah."

"Wait," Lucas said, "where are you going?"

"Well," O'Hara lied, "Annabeth was telling me earlier about how different your school was, and I thought it would be fun to check it out."

"Bye guys," Annabeth waved, "I'll be back in a little bit." Annabeth and O'Hara walked off down a hall.

As soon as they were out of earshot Vincent grabbed Lucas. "Dude, that is not her aunt."

"Why wouldn't it be her aunt?"

"This is a school, right?"

"Yeah?" Lucas hesitated. "Is it not?"

"If you tried to bring a gun into school, you would get arrested, right?"

"Yeah. So what?"

"Auntie O'Hara," Vincent made quotations with his hands, "had a gun. It was inside her suit. Side holster. If she was trying to hide it, she needs to try a lot harder. Also, who calls their aunt by their last name?"

Lucas picked up another purple balloon. "So she's a cool, law defying aunt."

"Haven't you noticed Annabeth acting a little weird lately?"

"She has been a little jumpy. But so what?"

"Dude," Vincent grabbed Lucas by the shoulders, "she's an undercover cop. She's got to be. Why else would she wear those clothes and carry a gun?"

"Why would there be an undercover cop at Weber of all places?"

"They still haven't caught the Anthrope."

Lucas let all the air out of a balloon. "Excuse me. You think that lady and Annabeth are trying to catch the Anthrope?"

Vincent nodded. "Yeah. I know that doesn't make very much sense but who else brings a gun to a school? We need to ask them. They need us. If we can hunt down regular anthropes, we can hunt down the Anthrope."

"Mmm, dang, that was pretty cool."

"Thanks. It felt cool." Vincent walked over toward the hall O'Hara and Annabeth had gone down. Lucas followed him. "They went this way. Let's go find them." Vincent hurried down a small set of stairs and jogged down the hall.

Lucas stopped him at a split in the hall, one hall going off at sixty-five degrees, the other at two hundred. "Vincent, which way?"

"Well, if they're trying to take down the Anthrope, and they're checking out the school, they're probably covering all the exits. These stairs go straight to an exit. This way." Vincent took the sixty-five degrees and ran up a set of stairs, then turned the corner. He followed the hall a few dozen paces and found Annabeth and O'Hara examining a door.

Annabeth noticed them coming. "Hey guys, do you need something?"

"Well," Lucas started, "we had a question for you guys, kinda random, mostly theoretical I guess. Basically, what we're trying to say-"

Vincent butted in. "Are you guys trying to take down the Anthrope?"

"No."

"No."

"Okay," Vincent pinched the bridge of his nose, "you guys suck at lying. You're definitely trying to take down the Anthrope." He pointed at O'Hara. "You're a cop. I saw your gun."

O'Hara straightened her suit. "No you didn't."

"Yes, I did. Look, we can help. Lucas and I both know how to use guns. We have experience in high-risk situations. We help track down rogue anthropes." He glanced at Annabeth. "Or ones that just lost track of time. Plus, we know the school a lot better than Annabeth does and you're clearly trying to figure some stuff out."

Annabeth looked at O'Hara and nodded. Then she went white. "Wait, no. I don't want them involved in this."

"Too late," Vincent didn't break eye contact with O'Hara, "Tell us everything. There's no going back now. We can help."

"Alright, in that case, my name is Agent O'Hara," she flashed a badge, "I work for the FBI. Fellow anthrope as I noticed you two are." She pointed to their wrists. "And yes. We are expecting an attack on the joint prom from the Anthrope."

"So just cancel prom." Lucas said. "Problem solved."

O'Hara shook her head. "We need to lure him in to catch him. A joint prom with a haven school is an opportunity too good to pass up. We couldn't get him to come any other way. He sent us a message letting us know he's coming."

Vincent said something under his breath.

"Wait," Lucas said, "We have to let people know."

"No," O'Hara said, "we can't do that. If they know the Anthrope is coming, it'll be all over the news in a few hours. Students won't come, the government will shut prom down. Bye bye goes our window. If we don't stop him here, who knows how many more attacks will happen."

Vincent frowned. "Don't you work for the government?"

"I've been authorized to color out of the lines a little bit. Unofficially, the order is to shoot David Mitson on sight. The same goes to you all by the way. If you kill him, the law won't touch you."

"I'm not killing him," Annabeth said.

"I doubt I'd hesitate." Vincent said. "Thanks for permission. I've never gotten along with terrorists."

Lucas folded his arms. "You've never even met a terrorist."

"We don't know that. But either way, irrelevant," Vincent waved him off, "I would kill a terrorist. No problem. Before Lucas and I officially consult on this terror trap, which is what we're calling this now, I have one question, prom is in the commons, right?"

O'Hara nodded.

Vincent smiled. "I've always dreamed of doing this."

CHAPTER 20

Vincent nearly skipped down the hall. He followed the corridor around a curve and then took a right and then a left. A big space opened in front of them, lined on each side with rusting lockers. "This is senior hall. Lucas, can you run down to the other end and make sure no one comes down this way?" Lucas nodded and ran to the opposite side. "I'm going to need someone to hold a flashlight for me. Annabeth, will you come with me? And Agent O'Hara, can you make sure no one comes in this way?" O'Hara nodded.

Vincent led Annabeth halfway down the hall, stopping just before reaching the bathrooms. He turned to a break in the lockers and moved a garbage can. A metal panel covered a large section of the wall. Annabeth eyed the cover. "I've always wondered what this was for."

"Tunnels."

"These are the tunnels?"

"Well, kinda. The Weber tunnels do exist but they're not what everyone thinks. Everyone talks about the flooded tunnels under the school. That's a bunch of BS. But there are dead spaces in the walls and a few pretty weird rooms with no doors." Vincent pulled his wallet out of his back pocket. He withdrew a peculiar metal frame. A bottle opener, a seat belt cutter, and a few other appendages were evident. He inserted a thinner edge of the metal into one of the screws and began turning. Moving to the other screws, he quickly loosened them and pulled them out by hand. He pulled the panel open and stepped aside. "After you."

Annabeth stepped through the opening and began walking in the darkness, putting a hand onto the wall to her right. Behind her, she heard the panel shut,

117

plunging her into darkness. "Vincent?" There was no sound. "Vincent!" She heard a scuffing noise from the panel. "Vincent!" She edged closer to the panel. The scuffing noise got closer. "Vincent! This isn't funny!" She extended her arms in front of her, creating a buffer space.

Suddenly, it stopped. Edging further still, she tried to turn on her phone. The screen turned on, illuminating her face.

A hand grabbed her ankle. She screamed and kicked. Vincent yelped, grabbing his head. Annabeth turned on her phone's flashlight. "What the heck Vincent!"

"Sorry," he groaned, clutching his head, "seemed like a good idea in my head. If it makes you feel better, it was fun for me up until now."

Annabeth shone her light around. She stood in a narrow corridor, sandwiched between cinder block walls only two or three feet apart. Mortar had dripped down the blocks and the floor was unfinished concrete. She walked a few paces down to the opposite end and touched the wall. "This passage doesn't go very far. How is this going to help anything?"

"These walls are close enough together that they're really easy to climb." He dragged himself to his feet. "Shine your light on me. I need to be able to see." Annabeth shone her light and Vincent jumped, bracing his arms and feet on the walls. He quickly climbed up and over the top of the wall, only ten feet or so. "From up here we can get anywhere. The walls only go up to the ceiling in most places so there's a lot of spots you can access from up here. To my left here we've got the bathrooms." He pointed to something Annabeth couldn't see. "Boy's is right here, and here's the girl's bathroom."

"Wait, do you…"

"Goodness no, I'm not a pervert. Plus, you'd have to take out the entire light fixture, and there's no individual ceiling panels in there. Far too much work." He pulled his phone out of his pocket and turned on the flashlight. "Go ahead and put your phone in your pocket. You'll need both hands to climb up here."

"You want me to climb up there?"

"Yeah. Don't worry, you won't fall. It's not hard. And it's a thousand times more fun than using stairs." Annabeth nodded and stuffed her phone in her back pocket. She braced herself against both walls and climbed up quickly. Vincent gave her his hand and helped her on top of the wall. "Alright," he said, "try not to fall back that way because you'll break your head on the wall. And also try not to fall that way because you'll fall right through the drywall and break your face on the bathroom floor."

"Noted." The two of them crawled across the top of the cinderblock wall toward where they had entered.

Vincent stood up, in front of a rectangular metal duct. "I need you to get your light out again. I'm going to crawl over this air duct, and I've got to get my feet on something solid on this side or else I'll break the duct, fall through the ceiling, and break my face on the ground. If you haven't noticed, face breaking is a bit of a hazard up here. Try to shine it through the gap underneath the duct." Annabeth did what he asked, and Vincent slid his upper body over the air duct and moved his leg over to the other side. After searching for footing for a second, he placed his foot and slid off the air duct. He turned on his light and shone it at Annabeth. "Alright. Come over."

Annabeth crawled up to the air duct. "How do I do this?"

"You're going to want to spread out your body weight on top of the air duct so it doesn't buckle under you. I'm not saying you're fat, but I don't super trust these things to hold anyone's weight."

Annabeth climbed on top of the duct and laid flat on her stomach. "Is this good?"

"Yeah. Now start to turn and try to get a foot down. There's a cinder block right there you can stand on. Do you see it?" Vincent pointed the light down by her feet.

"Yeah. I see it." Annabeth stood up. "That wasn't hard. It was actually kinda fun. Do you and Lucas go up here a lot?"

"We like to explore various ceilings," Vincent said as he stepped onto a board, "Don't step anywhere except the boards or you'll fall and break your face. We found a closet once that took us up above the hall by the library. I found one of those housings for a fire extinguisher and a spray can of cleaner that looks like it was from the eighties. It's proudly presented in my bedroom to this day."

Annabeth followed behind him, always keeping one hand holding tight to the various pipes and metal braces all around. "One question, how exactly is this helping us?"

"Did you see those wood double doors just past the bathroom?"

"Yeah."

"We need to get through that door, but we don't have a key. So instead, we're taking the back road into that room. I always like the road less traveled better anyway." Vincent stepped over a small pipe and onto concrete. "The ground is safe here. These are accesses to these big HVAC systems." He rested his arm on a huge piece of machinery.

Annabeth stepped onto the concrete, noticing writing on the wall. "What's that on the wall over there?"

"Names. Graduation years. When people come up here, they leave their names." Vincent pointed to his name and Annabeth saw that Lucas had written his name beside it. "You'll have to come back up here another time when you have something to write with so you can leave your mark. Let's go. This next part is easy." A path of metal grids led them to another concrete pad with another big machine on top of it. Another metal grid led to another pad, but Vincent turned left just before reaching it. A staircase took them three steps up, across a panel, then three steps down, bridging over an air duct. A ladder appeared on the wall next to them. Vincent reached out to an electrical box and flipped a switch. Lights turned on all around them revealing a door to the left. "Would have been nice to have that before, right?"

Annabeth nodded and looked around. With the extra light, she could see even better the chaos of ducts, wires, plumbing and more, all shoved into a few feet of space. Annabeth put a hand on one of the rungs of a short ladder that led to a hatch just above them. "Are we going up this ladder?"

"Yes, but not yet." Vincent reached out to the door and opened it. "We still need to get the others." He turned around and dropped. His hands and shoes screeched on the sides of the metal ladder. "Come down if you want. You're also free to stay, we'll be going back up in a minute."

"I'll come down." She hurried down the ladder and began to examine the room as Vincent felt the wall for a light switch. The lights flickered on, revealing more machinery and a dingy couch sitting in the middle of the open room. The floor was unpolished concrete with several stains on it. "What is this room?"

"To be honest," Vincent answered, "I've never figured out exactly what all these machines do. A ton of these pipes are connected to a boiler underneath us. Around that corner there's a hole in the floor and another ladder that goes to the boiler room." Vincent walked over to a pair of wooden doors. He opened one and stepped out into the hall. Before he let go, he wedged a rubber stopper into the jam. "And here we have the hall." He walked around the corner and started putting the screws back into the metal panel they had entered through. "You can go get Agent O'Hara and Lucas now. Also, you're covered in dust."

Annabeth looked down at her shirt and saw a layer of gray dust coating nearly every inch. "So are you," she said.

Vincent shrugged. "I like the dust. I'm going to leave it."

Annabeth rolled her eyes and dusted herself off and ran to get Agent O'Hara and Lucas. When the three of them returned, they found Vincent sprawled out on the couch inside the machine room. "Howdeedo everyone? Welcome to the Weber Underground." He sprung up and began climbing the ladder. "Follow me and watch your step."

Annabeth and O'Hara climbed up after him. Lucas pulled the door stop out and took to the ladder. Vincent climbed the second ladder and pushed open the hatch at the top. Bright sunlight poured in. He climbed over the lip and helped Annabeth and O'Hara onto the roof. "Welcome to the Weber Aboveground!"

"Vincent," Annabeth said, squinting, "weren't we already above ground?"

"Mmm, yeah, but there weren't any windows so you couldn't prove it. Anyway, this is the roof."

Lucas climbed out of the hatch and walked over to them, shoes scuffing against the rubbery white material. Annabeth jumped up and down on the roof. "What is this? It feels bouncy."

"That's for the snow. Because it snows so much, the roof is designed to sag a little."

Agent O'Hara spoke up. "I know I said it was okay to color outside of the lines a little bit, and sneaking onto the roof is probably a bit out of the lines, but I don't really see why this is helpful."

Vincent lifted a finger in the air, "That will all make sense in a moment. Allow me to explain. Follow." Vincent led them to the edge of the hexagonal section of the roof. He swung his leg over the edge and climbed down a ladder. "We're setting a trap." He raised his voice as he crossed another section of the roof. "We want to be able to swoop in on this crazy dude and catch him before he has a chance to hurt anyone. Well, you know how in movies, the SWAT Team always busts in through the windows and catches the bad guy just at the last moment?" He started climbing up another ladder.

"We do that sometimes," Agent O'Hara said, following up the ladder, "but not very often. That's mostly just a movie thing."

"But you *do* do it," Vincent countered, "And that is the important thing. Our school is built perfectly for this. You see, our school has very few windows, so in most places it would be impossible to do this. In most of the places we do have windows, it's in a door on the ground, so the SWAT guys would probably just go through the door. Is it effective to bust through doors? Yes. Is it as cool? No." He led them down another ladder.

"Vincent," Annabeth yelled, "what is your point?"

"I'm getting there! There is one single spot in the whole school where the busting through the window stunt would actually work." He hurried across another section and went up another ladder. "This is the last ladder, I swear." Everyone followed him up and they stopped around a hexagonal window pointing up out of the roof. "We are currently standing directly above the commons. The location of the joint prom. The Anthrope shows up, reveals himself, we have all the students run away and we come in from all the exits and the roof and nab him. We can only hide so many police in plain sight. But up here on the roof, we could hide a small army and he would never see it coming," Vincent accepted a fist bump from Lucas, "And we can sneak them up here, so we wouldn't even have to tell the admin about this. Completely under the radar."

Agent O'Hara was silent, looking at the ground, thinking.

"Well," Vincent said, "what do you think?"

O'Hara looked up at him. "Let's go catch ourselves a terrorist."

Belt Buckle took a sip of his milkshake and relaxed into the chair at the burger joint. His buddies sat at the bar with him, facing out the large windows. They were looking at something on their phones, laughing at videos Not A. Cowboy had saved. Belt Buckle dipped a few fries in fry sauce and munched on them as he pulled out his phone as well. A notification for the news app appeared and he tapped it. It pulled up an article with the headline 'Reactions Across America After Anthrope Attacks'. He scrolled down and saw a few pictures of protests, marches, and vandalism.

One photo displayed a burned down house with a family of seven staring at the ashes. Another showed a man in a hospital gurney, his jaw wired shut and his legs in casts. "Hey guys, look at this."

Not A. Cowboy looked over at him. "What's that?"

Belt Buckle frowned. "I guess this is what people have been doing after those terrorist attacks."

Not A. Cowboy took the phone and scrolled through the photos, showing them to their other buddy. "This is pretty serious stuff." He took another bite of his burger.

Belt Buckle nodded. "Yeah, it's pretty bad."

Their other buddy spoke up. "I mean, things definitely got out of hand there, but people are just trying to express that the anthropes are causing some serious problems, which is true. They're having a negative impact on society. They're dangerous, they make taxes go up-"

"I don't think that's actually true-"

"-and now a bunch of people are getting killed because of them."

Not A. Cowboy nodded and handed the phone back to Belt Buckle. "There's also a history of high crime rates and poverty in anthrope neighborhoods."

Belt Buckle finished off his fries. "That's true." He took another sip of his milkshake. "But regardless, things are getting out of hand."

Not A. Cowboy stood up and went to throw his garbage in the trash bin. "Yeah, but do you want them moving in next door? Have to lock your doors every night and make your kids come home early on curfew? Always be scared of some accident where they don't get to the anthrope prison on time? They should just stay away from everyone else, it's better that way." The three of them walked to the door and went out to their truck.

Belt Buckle hopped into the driver's seat and put the key in the ignition. The engine turned over for a second before starting, spitting out a cloud of smog. "I definitely don't want to deal with them personally, there's enough places they can go that they don't have to be anywhere near me." They pulled out of the parking lot and started down the main street.

Their other buddy pulled his phone out and started looking at memes again, occasionally showing them to Not. A Cowboy. Belt Buckle kept his eyes focused on the road. They took several turns and went through a pleasant looking neighborhood with a park in it. A woman was pushing a stroller along the walkway and had stopped to talk to a man in a hoodie. He raised his hands in exasperation and then struck her, knocking her to the ground. Belt Buckle slammed the brakes and pulled over.

He left the key in the ignition and ran over to them. The man was kicking the woman and screaming. "Run away! Run away! Run away!" Belt Buckle tackled the man to the ground and wrestled with him.

Belt Buckle tried to pin the thrashing man. "What are you doing?"

"Get off of me!" The man rolled away from him, but Not A. Cowboy and their other buddy pinned him to the ground, still thrashing and yelling.

Belt Buckle stood and went over to the woman sprawled on the ground. "Are you okay, miss?"

She started crying, shoulders heaving.

The man yelled, "Run away! Get out of here!"

The woman tried to sit up, hair covering most of her face. Belt Buckle offered his hand to help her up. She reached out and he saw a band of raised skin around her wrist. He recoiled, pulling his hand from the woman. She sniffed and looked at him. "Why do you hate us so much? What did we ever do to you?"

Belt Buckle looked over at her stroller where a one-year-old and a three-year-old were wailing, each had a ring scar around their wrist. "I-" He gave her his hand. "I'm sorry. I didn't..."

She brushed his hand away and stood up alone. Clutching her ribs she took hold of her stroller and started to walk away with her children. "Thank you."

The man yelled out from where he was pinned. "Find somewhere else to live! There's kids here!"

She limped slightly as she left, "That was brave of you. I hope everyone else can be a little braver too. Too many people are scared."

"That's right! Get out of here! Find somewhere else to live!" Not A. Cowboy clamped his hand over the man's mouth and looked at Belt Buckle. Belt Buckle looked back at him, unable to say anything as tears filled his eyes.

CHAPTER 21

Lucas picked up his chicken sandwich and glanced over at Annabeth. He slowly set the sandwich down and kept his eyes on her. "Hey Annabeth?"

"Yeah?" She munched a carrot, shoulders and arms pulled in. As usual her miniature tupperwares were spread out across the table. No one else had joined them.

"You need to unwind."

"Why do you say that?"

Lucas let go of his sandwich and wiped his hands off. "Because you look like you're in shock." Lucas scooted over and sat right next to her. "Your shoulders are pinned against your neck." He pushed her shoulders down. "Your hands are shaking." He grabbed her hands. "And you're shivering in a sweatshirt inside of a building." He pulled a jacket out of his backpack and handed it to her.

She frowned, "Do you just keep that in your backpack?"

"Yeah," Lucas shrugged, "Might as well. People get cold and it's not like I keep a hundred textbooks in there. I've got space." He shook the jacket, and she accepted it.

"Okay," she said, pulling the jacket over her sweatshirt, "what do you propose I do to unwind?"

"Mmm… come to a party at my house tonight?"

"You're having a party tonight?"

"If you say yes."

Annabeth rubbed her forehead. "I've got to study for my chemistry test."

"You know all that already."

"I know how to do real chemistry, that doesn't mean I know all the nonsense they're putting on the test. This is an American public school. And a haven school at that."

"Fair. What's your grade in that class?"

"One hundred percent." Annabeth looked at the floor.

Lucas raised an eyebrow, "And you can't miss a few points?"

"My dad wants me to have all A's."

"Your dad knows we're dealing with a terrorist," Lucas paused, "Wait, does your dad know?"

She nodded.

"Oh," Lucas said, settling back into his seat, "Well, then he should understand that you need to relax a bit. So is that a yes?"

"Lucas, I- fine. Yes. I will be at your house. But let me tell you something. It better be wild, like super wild, wild enough that someone is going to break something. Because if I'm not getting a perfect score on that test, it's going to be worth it. Just, no alcohol or anything like that. That's too wild."

Lucas laughed. "Don't even worry about it. My uncle has been through rehab more times than I can count. I decided I wasn't going to drink when I was six."

Annabeth nodded and closed her eyes. "I decided that three years ago after a drunk driver hit our car. And…" She shook her head.

Lucas turned pale, looking around as if trying to escape the conversation. He eventually stopped gaping to say, "I'm sorry."

"It's alright," She leaned her head on his shoulder, letting out a shaky breath, "Not your fault."

Lucas put his arm around her and pulled her closer.

Vincent emerged from the churning masses of the student body with a lunch tray in his hand and a grin on his face. He took one look at Lucas and Annabeth and turned around, vanishing just as fast as his smile had.

Lucas rubbed her shoulder, "I'm still sorry."

Vincent took a bite of his pizza off at the other end of the cafeteria. Kenzie twirled her hair. "So those dudes were just sitting there cuddling?"

"I don't know," he grumbled, "I only saw them from behind. But seriously, those two are together all the time. Holding hands, kissing, whatever it is they do. I don't know, I think they usually try to hide it from me. Regardless, I don't want to watch that."

"I think that because you're used to spending so much time with Lucas, you're getting a little jealous of how much time he's giving Annabeth. Jonathan's homies keep complaining that he's spending too much time around me. That's just the kind of thing that happens when you're in a relationship."

"Who's Jonathan?"

"Jonathan Davis. My boyfriend."

"Oh. Where's he?"

Kenzie shrugged. "Bro, I don't know. I haven't seen him yet today."

A tall lanky boy walked up to the table. "Hey Kenzie, I'm skipping lunch today. I'm going to go workout." He gave her a kiss and walked off.

"Okay. See ya."

Vincent rubbed his forehead. "This is why we have a mono problem at our school," he grumbled, "it's because of you."

"What?" Kenzie said, staring at Jonathan as he walked away, "Did you say something?"

"Nope."

"Oh," she said, "well, like I was saying, you just need to get used to Lucas being busy with girls. Maybe you should get a girlfriend. It might help. Which reminds me, do you need a date for prom? I know a girl."

Vincent shook his head. "No thanks. Waiting for the right one. No point in forcing something to happen when it's not right."

"Eh, I don't agree with that mentality," Kenzie said, "Jonathan and I are together for two reasons. He has a super-hot friend, and I need someone to go to prom with."

"That seems a little…"

"Shallow? Yeah, it totally is. But both of us are okay with it. I guess it just depends on what you're looking for in a relationship. Both of us understand it's a short-term thing and we're helping each other out."

Vincent squirmed in his seat. "Not that I'm really an expert but I feel like that's not the right way to go about it either. I might be a little too reserved, but you just kissed that guy like it was nothing."

"It's fun."

Vincent frowned. "That's not what kissing is for."

Kenzie shrugged. "Maybe. Lots of people do it that way though."

"Just because everyone does it doesn't mean it won't affect more serious relationships later."

Kenzie thought about it for a second. "You could be right. Anyway, back to the topic at hand. I think most kids in high school know when they start a relationship that it's only going to be temporary, but they want to learn how to be in a relationship and they like the other person enough that they just don't care. What I don't understand is how Lucas and Annabeth ended up together. Lucas is totally crazy for her, but I'm not sure what she sees in him. And I'm not trying to dig on Lucas. It's just that he and Annabeth don't seem like a good match to me. She's insanely smart and he's just a little above average. Maybe it's his personality. But if I was Annabeth, I would be with someone that's also super smart and attractive, someone like you."

Vincent took a bite of pizza, blinking once.

Kenzie apologized. "That was a little awkward."

"Yes it was," Vincent said, "It was very awkward. Besides, I don't think Annabeth is my type anyway."

"I'm going to venture back into awkward territory and say I don't believe you." She pointed at him, a mischievous smile on her face, "I think you're jealous of Lucas."

Vincent choked on his pizza. "What? Jealous? Because of him and Annabeth? That's ridiculous." He coughed and took a drink of his chocolate milk, eyes watering.

"Are you crying?"

"I choked." He took another drink and muttered an insult directed at Kenzie.

"You totally are."

"No I'm not!"

"Dude, you are, you aren't even looking at me."

Vincent looked her in the eye, "Yes I am."

"Can you look me in the eye and tell me you aren't the slightest bit jealous?"

His face was granite. "I'm not jealous of Lucas."

"I don't believe you."

"Okay," Vincent tossed his hands in the air, "fine, don't believe me. Whatever." Vincent stood up and picked up his lunch tray. "But you're making something out of nothing." He turned and headed for a trash can. "She's crazy." He let out a shaky breath. After dumping his trash, he walked out into the commons and looked up at the windows. His phone rang and he answered Lucas's call. "What's up?"

"Can you come with me to the store after school? I'm going to throw a party and I want to get some snacks."

"Sure," Vincent said, "what's the occasion?"

"With this whole Anthrope thing going on, and prom in two days, we need to chill."

"Okay, I'm down. Oh, wait, can we have Benny come with us?"

"Sure, why?"

"Well," Vincent said, "he's in our prom group and we haven't really talked to him since he bailed you out at Fremont. And on top of that, I'd like to have a guy like Benny around when the Anthrope comes. I get the feeling he's been in more than his fair share of fist fights."

The back wheel of the shopping cart squeaked as it rolled down the drink aisle at Walmart. Lucas tossed a case of Orange Fanta into the cart. Vincent fiddled with a Rubik's Cube. Benny watched Vincent. "You know you can look up the instructions for that on the internet."

"That takes away the fun of it." Vincent turned the cube. "It took the guy that invented this a month to solve it. I bet I can do it faster. If I look it up, then there's nothing special about solving it."

"Okay, whatever. You said on the phone there was something you wanted to talk about. Something about Annabeth."

"Yeah," Lucas said, "about that. Umm, this is hard to explain. So you know how sometimes in life, confusing and unexplainable things happen totally out of the blue?"

"Yeah?"

"Well, it's kinda like that. Umm-"

Vincent cut him off. "The Anthrope is going to attack us at prom."

Benny froze. "He what?"

"The Anthrope is coming to prom and he's going to attack us. We've only known about this for a little while. Annabeth found out first. We can't stop it, but we're going to catch him."

"Vincent, is this a joke?"

"No, I don't make jokes."

Benny looked at Lucas. Lucas nodded. "That's why we're throwing a party. We're all mad stressed. Kind of a last hurrah before willingly throwing ourselves into a traumatizing event."

"If you guys are really being serious, why don't we stop it? Why doesn't everyone already know about this?"

Lucas shook his head. "We can't. We have to catch him. We're working with the FBI-"

"Dang that sounds cool-"

"-and one of their agents is coordinating this whole thing. The Anthrope said we couldn't stop him from attacking. And so far, the police haven't been able to do anything. He's clever. No one knows where his money is coming from. He's already got cars and supplies all over the place. He turned into a ghost a few months back and since then the only times he's ever popped up are these attacks. But we know he's coming. And we know when. And we need to stop him here or else more people are going to get hurt."

Benny lowered his voice. "People will get hurt here. A lot of them. Prom is going to be at least two thousand kids, probably more. There are hundreds of anthropes at your school. If he gasses people, game over. No one is ready for this. None of the students are going to know what to do."

"Relax," Vincent said, "we're going to stop him before he can do anything and we're bringing a bunch of hidden cops, so he has no chance. I have a good feeling about it. Spiritually. And if something goes wrong, we sent out emails to people with escape routes."

"I saw that email. You know what I did with it? I deleted it without even looking at it."

Lucas scratched his cheek. "Benny, look, this is already in motion. We're not changing our minds. But we wanted to tell you because if something does go wrong, we want you to be ready."

"And you're right by the way," Vincent said, "If this goes wrong, then we're never going to be fully prepared. We're dead men. If you'd like though, Lucas and I are both hiding tranq guns in our suits. I think Annabeth is going to try to keep a rifle in her dress. We can get you one. Your dad is going to be there too. We're bringing as many guns as we can."

"My dad's onboard with this?" Benny folded his arms. "I hate this. But okay. Also, related to prom, is it too late to switch restaurants? I only work in the summer and I'm a little tight on spending money."

Vincent laughed. "I feel you. I thought you guys should go to McDonalds, but Lucas said it had to be nice."

"Well," Lucas said, "there was another restaurant I had in mind that's a little cheaper." He winked at Vincent.

Vincent winked back.

"What's the catch?" Benny asked.

"We'd have to trust Vincent far more than any sane person should."

Annabeth knocked on the front door of Lucas's house. The red door swung open and she was greeted by the smell of hot pizza. "Hey Vincent."

"Hey Annabeth. And- Agent O'Hara? Is something wrong? You're dressed like... Annabeth."

O'Hara shrugged. "Annabeth let me know that you were having a party, and I thought I would come undercover just in case. Any gatherings still hold a risk. And yeah, these clothes are Annabeth's. I didn't exactly pack for a party."

Vincent nodded and stepped aside to let them in. "Then in that case, what am I going to call you? I feel like Agent O'Hara isn't a good cover name."

"My first name is Katie."

Vincent coughed. "Katie? Really? Huh. Interesting. Well, everyone is downstairs right now, if you're hungry there's pizza and snacks in the kitchen. Sodas in the fridge."

"I didn't eat before this," Annabeth said, "I need some pizza."

"Me too," Katie said, "I don't think I even had lunch." The two walked past the living room to the kitchen.

Vincent closed the door and hurried down the stairs. Lucas stood against one wall, watching the final round of around the world at the ping pong table. "Lucas! You'll never believe who just walked through the front door. I'll give you a hint. Their first name is Katie."

"Wait, one of my exes is here?"

"Aside from the one cuddling up on the couch over there, and the one snooping around your bedroom, no. I'll give you a hint. Their last name is O'Hara."

"Katie O'Hara?" Lucas shook his head. "Doesn't ring a bell."

"Agent O'Hara."

"Wait, Agent O'Hara's first name is Katie? Katie as in the name we decided was abnormally hot?" Lucas put his hand to his mouth. Vincent nodded and the two burst into laughter. "Wait, why is she here?"

"Annabeth invited her just in case. It's so trippy though, she's wearing some of Annabeth's clothes and I think she's wearing makeup too. She looks like a regular teenager. And not to be weird or anything, but I think the Katie rule holds true for her too."

"Woah. I'm totally with you on that though." Lucas grabbed his cup from the windowsill and took a drink. "How old is she?"

"She's got to be in her twenties."

"That's weird. How much you want to bet someone is going to start flirting with her?"

"Guaranteed. Anyway, just a heads up. Call her Katie. I'm gonna go upstairs and kick Katie Hansen out of your bedroom. There's still some of that Diet Dr. Pepper I left in your fridge, right?"

"Yeah. At least five more cans."

"Hmm. Well, I guess I'll have to make do with what I've got." Vincent turned and headed back upstairs.

CHAPTER 22

Vincent popped open a can of soda and took a long drink. He sat in the living room near the front door, looking at a chessboard. After setting his drink down, he moved the king's pawn two spaces and flipped the chessboard around so the red pieces were in front of him. Annabeth set down a folding chair on the other side of the table. She flipped the board back around and sat down in front of the red pieces. "Mind if I join you?"

"Free country."

"Hmm. Deja vu." Annabeth moved her king's pawn forward, blocking Vincent's pawn. "Do you remember the last time we had a conversation that started like that?" Vincent shook his head and moved his queen's pawn one space. Annabeth gave him a skeptical look. "In the ACC, up on the catwalk." She brought out her kingside knight, attacking Vincent's pawn.

"Empty threat. You don't have the set up to make that worthwhile. These moves are textbook." He countered by bringing out his queenside knight, leaving his bishop open. "And I have the set up to make it hurt."

Annabeth moved her queen's pawn up two spaces, attacking. "True, but you're in a tough spot to stop that. Are you sure you don't remember that conversation?"

"I can take the exchange. In the end, we come out even. Your queen is exposed in the center with only a single pawn and then it's my move."

Annabeth propped up her head with her hands. "A pawn is enough to support a queen. I feel like you're avoiding the subject which to me implies you do remember that conversation. And it's your move."

Vincent took the exchange after some thinking. He swapped his pawn for hers and set it to the side. Annabeth took his pawn with her knight. Vincent countered by taking her knight with his. Annabeth ended the exchange by taking his knight with her queen. Vincent set his queen's bishop in front of the queen, doubling it behind a pawn. "I don't have any weak points."

"You don't have any attacking capabilities." Annabeth moved her center pawn forward, bringing it diagonally ahead of the queen. "And therefore, I can do as I please while you are reduced to countering me. We're both employing a similar tactic though. We're each using a pawn to strengthen another piece. Pawns are useful for a time, but eventually you have to step out and make the moves with the powerful pieces. And because you're playing a defensive game, you have to wait for me to give you an opportunity. Except now it's your move and you have nowhere to go."

Vincent grumbled and took a sip of his Diet Dr. Pepper, examining the board methodically, tracing interactions between various pieces with his eyes. "If I take your pawn your queen will be exposed."

"Like I said, once the pawn is out of the way you still have a queen to deal with." After hovering over the piece for a while, Vincent took her pawn. Annabeth accepted the trade and took his pawn with her queen. "Check."

Vincent muttered something under his breath. "I've got three options. My bishop, my knight, or my queen. I don't like any of them." He moved his queen diagonally, protecting the king. "This is the most offensive move I have."

Annabeth immediately moved her queenside bishop out, placing it diagonally behind the queen. "Take the trade and we're back in the same spot as before."

Vincent smiled. "You can't use your queen. That's the only thing stopping me from killing your king."

"And you can't take my queen either. If you do, you'll have to pay a steep price."

"A trade." Vincent took her queen, and she took his, leaving her lone bishop in the center.

"But you don't have a plan anymore. That gives me the advantage."

Vincent stared at the board. "Element of surprise. I like to surprise myself."

Lucas's head appeared out of the stairwell to the basement next to them. "Hey guys, can I have you stay a bit after to talk about... prom?"

Annabeth nodded. "Yep. I'll be there."

"You're going to need help with the rest of the pizza." Vincent castled while Annabeth was looking away.

"Alright, thanks. Have fun. And Vincent..."

"Yeah?"

"Stop thinking so hard," Lucas winked at Annabeth, "It's coming out your ears."

Annabeth laughed at Vincent and Lucas went downstairs. "I saw that castle by the way." Vincent shrugged and took a drink. She moved out her remaining knight. "Lucas is right. You think too much. Your moves are too slow."

"It might be a little slower, but I win more chess games by thinking longer."

"How long are you willing to wait to win?" Annabeth asked. When Vincent didn't answer she continued with the topic at hand. "So anyway, you do remember that night."

"So what if I do?" Vincent moved his rook, attacking the bishop.

Annabeth moved a pawn forward two spaces, protecting the bishop. "Just wondering. What do you remember?"

"Enough." Vincent doubled his bishops, threatening her bishop again.

Annabeth nodded. "Do you have a date for prom?" She brought her knight out.

"Who's changing the subject now?" Vincent brought his remaining knight out, up against the edge of the board.

"I'm just wondering. Do you?" Annabeth advanced her dark bishop, blocking Vincent's knight.

Vincent grumbled and moved his knight further, placing it alongside Annabeth's foremost pawn. "No. I do not. Nor do I intend to find one. Happy?"

"Oh, come on. There's got to be someone you'd want to go with." Annabeth ignored the attack on her bishop and castled.

Vincent took her bishop with his knight. Annabeth took the trade, killing his horse with her pawn. Vincent countered by killing her pawn with his rook. "No. There's no one. I'd rather be watching for the Anthrope with a gun than dancing anyway. I don't dance. Your move."

Annabeth moved her kingside castle out, challenging Vincent's rook. Vincent brought his second rook onto the same file, doubling. Annabeth moved her knight forward, threatening two pawns and a light bishop. "You do you I guess."

"That was a weird move. It's very low risk for me. I'm guaranteed to win any exchange." He moved his king behind the center of a row of three pawns. "And now there aren't any loose ends."

"Calculated risk." Annabeth took Vincent's bishop. Vincent killed her knight with a pawn. Annabeth moved her dark bishop, pinning Vincent's king in the corner.

"Oh come on, what are you going to do with that?" Vincent took her rook, and she took his. Vincent used his second rook to kill hers, checking the king.

Annabeth moved her king diagonally out of check, attacking the rook. "I have a feeling I'm better with pawns than you are."

"But now I'm up a pawn and a rook. Simplifying the game just makes my advantage more drastic and harder for you to deal with." Vincent moved his rook away from the king.

"Okay," Annabeth said, pausing, "so admittedly, I didn't actually think that move through. Maybe you're right about thinking for so long. But maybe I'm just letting you win. Maybe I don't like the red team, and I'm just sending them after you so you can kill them."

"Right, because that makes sense. Care to explain why you're killing so many of my guys in the process?"

"I can't let them know I'm playing them." Annabeth picked up a pawn but then set it back. She picked up another but put it back as well. Selecting a third pawn, she moved it forward two spaces.

"Hesitation?" Vincent moved a pawn forward, opening a path between his rook and her bishop, attacking.

"No. I saw that move coming. The other two would have ruined my escape route." She picked up her bishop and retreated to safety while also attacking his rook.

Vincent moved his rook out of danger and attacked her king. "Check."

Annabeth moved her king behind the bishop. Vincent advanced a pawn. Annabeth countered by advancing her own pawn, inviting an attack from Vincent. They traded pawns, leaving Annabeth's king directly across from Vincent's.

Vincent moved his rook to attack the king. Annabeth stared at the board for a while. She moved her bishop, acting as a meat shield for the king.

Vincent smiled and took her bishop. She took his bishop with her pawn. Her king hid behind a pawn in front of Vincent's king, a rook, and two pawns. Vincent tapped the table with his finger. "I'm still up a rook and a pawn."

"Doesn't matter. This is nearly a pawn game."

Vincent shrugged. "If you say so." He moved his king forward into the center of an arrow shape made of two pawns and headed by a rook.

Annabeth moved one of her pawns up two spaces, backing up the pawn in front of the king.

Vincent hummed. "You know what? I can kill both of your pawns right now if I want."

"So do it."

"I'd rather not. I felt like you were playing with me at the beginning, so I'm going to make this last a little longer." Vincent picked up his castle and moved it to the other side of the board, where two of Annabeth's pawns watched three of Vincent's from across the board, blocking one of his pawns. "Have at it. Show me your pawn game."

"I'm going to get my queen back."

"No you aren't."

"You'll see." Annabeth picked up her second pawn and moved it forward.

Vincent moved the pawn across from her advancing pawn up. "I dare you."

"With pleasure." Annabeth took the trade. Vincent took her pawn with his king, leaving it directly in front of her pawn backed up by her king. His pawn was a knight's jump away. Annabeth moved one of her pawns across the board.

Vincent shrugged and maneuvered his king around the side of Annabeth's pawn. He set the king down and immediately smacked himself in the forehead. "That was the most wrong move I could have made." He groaned while Annabeth seized the opportunity. She moved her king forward, bringing it closer to Vincent's pawn while protecting her own.

"That was a very wrong move." She smiled. "I'm glad you made it though."

Vincent grumbled and moved the pawn forward, attacking her king. He let go of the piece and looked up at Annabeth. She frowned and moved her king backwards. Vincent brought his king back in front of the pawn. "I'm glad I was able to fix it." Annabeth moved her king behind the pawn. Vincent moved his rook forward, blocking one of Annabeth's pawns. "Oh look at that, check."

Annabeth moved her king out of check, toward her two pawns, abandoning her other pawn to be killed. Vincent pounced and ended the pawn. Annabeth moved her king closer to her other two pawns. Vincent advanced the pawn closest to his king. Annabeth groaned. "Pawn box."

"Choices choices."

Annabeth moved her king back, trying to cut off the pawn before it could reach the other side. Vincent advanced the pawn. Annabeth moved her king.

"See if I didn't have my king, I would be guaranteed to lose. Because I have my king, I can promote my pawn every time, it just might take a while. But because I have my rook, I can win this every time, very quickly." Vincent set his castle in front of Annabeth's king.

"Alright, fine then. I resign, my position is hopeless. Well played."

Vincent nodded. "You as well. Why did you bring that night up?"

Annabeth shrugged. "I don't know. I guess I was just wondering if… anything has changed or if it's still the same."

"Why should I tell you?"

She sighed. "I guess there's no other reason than I asked."

"Hmm..." Vincent stared off into space. "Lame reason." He stood up and walked downstairs.

CHAPTER 23

Benny stretched his arms. He adjusted the couch cushion behind him and let out a deep breath, then took a big bite of his pizza. Two other couches were situated in the room, forming a U with his couch on one end. In the center was a table with a chess board on it, most of the pieces removed. Near where Benny sat, between the couch and the table, was a folding chair. A girl with short blond hair sat on the couch opposite him, and a boy sat next to her, inching closer and closer.

"Hey, your name is Katie, right?"

"Yup." She looked at the floor.

"My name is Mark. I've never seen you around school before. Are you from Fremont?"

The girl nodded, not looking at him.

"Is something wrong?"

"I… have a boyfriend."

The boy made a face. "Are you sure?"

"I think I would know if I have a boyfriend or not."

"It just seemed like maybe you were saying that because you didn't want to talk to me." The boy rested his arm on the back of the couch, right behind her.

She turned and pressed her elbow down hard into the inside of his. He grimaced and she gave him an angry smile. "You got me. I don't have a boyfriend. But I'm not looking either. And I'm definitely not looking for someone to try to suck my face off tonight, so get lost."

The boy fidgeted and got up after unpinning himself from her elbow. "Nice meeting you too."

Benny snorted and dusted the cornmeal off his hands. He picked up his plate and walked around the coffee table and sat next to her. "That was pretty cool. Way intense, but cool I guess."

"Thanks." She rubbed her hands together awkwardly.

"I heard you say your name is Katie. Is your last name O'Hara?"

She nodded slowly, visibly tense.

"As in Agent O'Hara?"

O'Hara glanced over into the kitchen and saw three girls talking about Lucas. She lowered her voice, "Who told you that?"

"Lucas and Vincent," Benny said, almost whispering, "My dad works at the ACC, he's coming to prom as a backup. They thought I would be able to help. I know how to use a gun and I'm a student officer. People will listen to me in an emergency."

O'Hara nodded. "Did those two tell anyone else?"

"No."

"Good. They better not." She folded her arms. "This operation is getting out of hand. Too many minors involved."

Benny nodded. "My lips are sealed, even though I'm still not sure about this. Also, just out of curiosity, how old are you? You look like a teenager."

"Twenty-five."

"You can be an FBI agent that young?"

She nodded. "Twenty-three is the minimum age." She wiped her palms off on her jeans.

"I'm sorry, am I making you uncomfortable?" Benny asked, giving her a bit of space, "You seem kinda nervous."

"This is my first party in a while," she laughed, "Kinda silly. I've been in five shootouts in the last year. I've had guns to my head. I've got three guns on me right now and yet I'm afraid of a bunch of teenagers."

"An FBI agent that's afraid of a party. And here I thought all government employees were boring."

"Your dad works for the government."

Benny rubbed his chin, and the corner of his mouth raised. "Maybe that's where I got that idea from. Anyway, I was just curious, how exactly are we justifying inviting a terrorist to prom without warning anyone?"

"The government has always been a little unorthodox when it comes to anthropes. A lot of paranoid fat old men that are afraid they're going to get eaten by a werewolf. Their policies don't make sense, aren't effective, and are mostly ignored. In cases with anthropes, it's up to the individual law enforcement officers to decide what to do, which in this instance is me. To answer your question, it's mostly a question of bad and worse. Sure, letting a terrorist attack your prom with a bunch of unsuspecting kids is bad, but isn't letting this guy run around worse?"

Benny rocked his head, "Depends on how much goes wrong."

"Fair enough. We're doing our best to make sure as little goes wrong as possible."

"This guy planned his last two attacks perfectly. The bank had eleven anthropes. The four customers were just random chance, but seven employees were anthropes. That bank had several dozen workers and just by random chance all of the anthropes that worked there were working at that time? And that basketball game. One of the teams was half anthrope along with a bunch of parents and the referee. None of the other teams in that whole state had that many anthropes. You've seen the news. Some people think it's a conspiracy theory, but this guy had to have gotten inside their computer systems and figured out the best place to strike. He's smart and he might know what we're planning."

O'Hara snorted. "Yeah right. The ACC system is the most protected isolated mainframe in the world. There's more sensitive information on there than any other mainframe in existence. The federal government has a perpetual fund of ten million dollars for anyone who can figure out a way in. No one's done it for twelve years. Not even the Russians have gotten in. It'd be easier to steal nuclear launch codes. But either way, there's no way he can take down the entire SWAT team without us seeing him coming."

Benny nodded. "One question. Do you have a cover for prom, or are you just going to be waiting outside?"

"I need to be close on the inside, so I can be keeping an eye out for the Anthrope. I tried to be in charge of tickets at the door, but there was this crazy mom who nearly fought me over it. So, I'm still trying to figure it out. Maybe I could just go and stand around, but I'd also like to be able to stick close with Annabeth during her day date."

"Oh, I'm in her group."

"Oh fun." An awkward silence fell.

"Wait, you're hiding three guns?" Benny noticed a slight bulge under her arm. "There's one right there, right?"

"Just to be clear, you're guessing where I have my concealed carries?"

"Hmm, on second thought, maybe not the best idea."

"I've got one under each arm, and then there's one other spot Annabeth told me about, but I'm not going to go into that one."

Benny nodded, "Ah. Well, I'm going to head downstairs and rejoin the party.

If you're feeling up to it, you should come join us. It's pretty fun down there." He stuffed the rest of his pizza crust into his mouth.

Katie nodded but didn't move. Benny went into the kitchen and threw away his paper plate. He hurried downstairs and joined Lucas in karaoke. After a few minutes he saw O'Hara come down the stairs and join Annabeth on the couch talking to Vincent.

"Bye, see you tomorrow!" Lucas shut the front door and let out a sigh. "That's the last one. Hey everyone, meet downstairs!"

Benny and Vincent walked out of the kitchen and followed Lucas down to the basement. Annabeth and Agent O'Hara were already waiting on the couches. Lucas overheard Benny talking to Vincent. "What about this one?" He showed Vincent his phone. "She's pretty cute, right? You could go with her. No one asked her yet and she's feeling really bad about it."

Vincent rolled his eyes. "No."

"Oh, I have a friend who just moved from England. She has a super cool accent and she's really smart."

"No."

"C'mon man, you've got to go."

Annabeth sat down next to Lucas. "What are they talking about?"

"Benny is trying to set Vincent up for prom. It isn't really working."

Agent O'Hara sat down next to Annabeth. "Okay everyone, I thought we should just review all of our plans. Are you guys ready?" Everyone nodded and gave the affirmative. "Alright. So, at prom, we've got armed SWAT with both lethal and tranq weapons at every exit ready to disable or evacuate. We've got the other half of the SWAT team on the roof who will be ready to break through the skylights. Benny's dad, Mr. Anderson, will have the ACC truck parked nearby with the majority of the ACC's arsenal ready and the holding space prepared. We've also rented box trucks for the same reason. I will be there undercover, as close to you all as possible, I just need to figure out what my cover is going to be. We will also have communication devices in case we're separated."

Benny showed Vincent his phone. "What about this one," he whispered, "I went double with her to a shooting range once. She's good. We could use that. Plus she's cute."

"I'm sorry," Agent O'Hara said passive aggressively, "is there something I should know about?"

Vincent shook his head. "Not important."

"I vote we kick them out," Annabeth said, "they're just going to get themselves hurt."

Vincent raised a hand in objection. "I find that comment to be both hurtful and false. Other than the actual FBI agent I am verifiably the most qualified person here to deal with terrorism."

Lucas folded his arms. "I've been trained as an emergency guardian too."

"I score higher in marksmanship, endurance, strength, crisis management, and overall field record," Vincent said, "I am the highest ranked emergency guardian at the ACC."

Lucas rolled his eyes. "I didn't get turned into a rabbit."

"And I am still easily the highest ranked."

Annabeth leaned over to O'Hara, "Can we please ditch the boys? Leave them in protective custody or something?"

O'Hara shook her head. "You're safer with them around. All of us are."

"They won't be." Annabeth replied, "They'll be safer if they never go. This is my fault, let's leave them out of it."

O'Hara cleared her throat, silencing Lucas and Vincent. "I'm going to continue. Only relevant commentaries from this point on." She eyed the boys. "All of us will have gas masks. They'll be just big enough to cover your mouth and nose, so we can fit them in our pockets and then we won't have to worry about the gas. I will be armed. Benny, Vincent, and Lucas will be armed as well. Annabeth, you'll need to show me your dress so we can figure out what kind of weapons we can hide. Depending on where I am, I might be able to carry extra weapons for you. If I can find the right cov-"

"Hey Annabeth," Lucas cut in, "Where did you say you got your dress?"

"A little shop down on 24th street. You're acting weird, why are you changing the subject?"

"I'm not," he said through gritted teeth, "Hi mom!"

"Hey Lucas, hey everyone, how are you all doing?"

Everyone turned and saw Lucas's mom walking into the basement. "We're good mom! How was your date?"

"Your dad nearly spilled his drink all over me twice, so nothing out of the ordinary. It was pretty good though."

"That's good," Lucas said, "there's some pizza left upstairs if you or dad are still hungry."

"I'm pretty sure he found it already. You guys have fun." She walked upstairs.

Benny whispered to Vincent, showing him his phone again. "What about her? Dude, I swear, she's perfect, super smart, super cute-"

"If she's so perfect, why doesn't she have a date yet?"

"She and her boyfriend just barely broke up. No one wants to ask her."

Agent O'Hara cleared her throat.

"Sorry." Vincent looked away. "Benny was trying to set me up."

"For prom?"

"Yeah. I'm not going."

Agent O'Hara froze. "Is there any particular reason?"

"Umm… not interested?"

"Terrible reason. Perfect." O'Hara turned to Annabeth. "Annabeth, where did you say you got your dress?"

"A shop on 24th street, why?"

"I need a dress. Vincent, find something nice to wear. We're going to prom together."

"Woah," Vincent sat up, "first off, against the rules, I have to ask you. Second, that sounds ridiculously illegal. I'm a minor. And third, why?"

"I need a cover for prom. I want to stay close to Annabeth the whole time. If you go with me, we can join their group and that solves both of those problems."

"Awesome." Vincent tossed his hands in the air. "I look forward to the day when my kids see our pictures and they ask me who you are and I have to explain how I ended up going to prom with some twenty something year old lady who I met when she was pretending to be their godfather's girlfriend's aunt while hunting down terrorists for the government."

"Look on the bright side," Lucas said, "now you don't have to make food and drive us around anymore."

"I'd be more comfortable making food."

O'Hara rolled her eyes. "Vincent, we don't have to dance or anything. I just need you to be there so I can blend in with the crowd and not stand out."

Vincent grumbled and mumbled under his breath. "Alright, fine."

"Wait," Benny said, "does this mean we have to pay for the food again?"

O'Hara shook her head. "I have funding for any mission related spending. I can pay for the food."

Annabeth spoke up, "I feel like that's against the rules."

"The government won't even notice."

"I think she meant the rules of the date," Lucas said, "guys ask, guys pay."

"I don't know if you guys noticed this, but we're already breaking a few of those silly rules." O'Hara shrugged. "Who even cares?"

Vincent snorted. "I sure as heck don't."

CHAPTER 24

Lucas straightened his bowtie. "Alright boys, is everything looking good?"

Two sophomore boys wearing black jackets and headsets sat at two control panels in a booth. One of them adjusted sliders on his board while the other opened files on a monitor. The boy moving sliders stood up and grabbed two remotes. He turned on projectors and then twisted two keys and screens on the opposite side of the auditorium began to roll out on the wall. "Yeah, we've just got to get this music pulled up real quick and do a fast sound check and we'll be all set. We'll just follow you on the slides. Feel free to use either of the mics. And just give us the thumbs up when you're ready for the music." He pulled a paper out of his jacket. "And you want us to play the first three songs until you're ready to start, right?"

"Yup. Thanks, you guys. Tell the guys up in the catwalk I said hi." Lucas began going down the stairs past rows of flip down seats.

The boy flipped the mic on his headset down. "Hey guys, the bossman says hi." He paused. "They said good luck."

Lucas gave a thumbs up. "Thanks boys. You too." He put his hand on the railing in the middle of the stairs. The auditorium was shaped like a big octagon, and the stage down below thrust out into the audience, also a big octagon. As he descended, he turned one more time and made a heart with his hands to the boys. "Love you techies! We'd fall apart without you!"

The boy on the computer laughed softly to himself. "We know."

The bell rang and students slowly began to trickle into the auditorium. The techies turned on the first song, slowly cranking up the music as the auditorium filled. One of the boys pulled a bag out of his pocket. "I grabbed these from the classroom." He shook the bag, jangling two orange tablets inside.

"Mmm, Vitamin C, or should I say Vitamin Yes!" They each took their tablets.

The other boy bit into his, turning it into powder. "Is it just me or do these taste like Froot Loops?"

"They definitely do. I love it. And whether or not these actually do anything, it's a tradition. Healthy cast."

"Healthy cast."

Down by the stage, Lucas rubbed his palms together, fidgeting in his chair. Someone tapped him on the shoulder. "Mind if I join you?"

Lucas turned and saw Benny all dressed up. "Hey man, come sit down."

Benny took a seat in one of the chairs next to Lucas. "How'd you get stuck doing this thing by yourself?"

Lucas shrugged. "My idea. No one else wants to get blamed for it. Bad street cred."

"As it stands, I'm still not happy we're going through with this, so I'm blaming you too."

"Well, sorry." Lucas glanced at the time, then the nearly full auditorium. "Are you ready? Usually we're not the biggest fans of Fremont, but I'll try to give you the best intro I can. Wish me luck." He stood up and walked up to a mic stand.

"Break a leg."

Lucas grabbed the mic, and the music lowered. "Hey guys." Everyone began to cheer.

"Oh, stop, you're making me blush."

Someone near the back jumped up and shouted. "Do the howl!"

"What was that?" Lucas put his hand to his ear.

"Howl!"

"Oh, the howl, I don't know, my throat is feeling a little rusty today. Only if you really want me to." His buddies on the front row flipped out, chanting. The hype spread and soon the whole auditorium was screaming for him to do the howl. "Well, if that's what you really want..." He threw his head back and howled into the microphone. The students all joined in, howling with him. Eventually it died out. "You guys are fun. Hey, so we've got a little PowerPoint we put together for y'all, because tomorrow just so happens to be a big day. Tomorrow is… my birthday!" He laughed. "Just kidding. Kidding. It's prom." He grinned.

Benny rolled his eyes. Lucas went on. "Yeah, so this year, as you know, we're doing something pretty special, we're having a joint prom with Fremont."

Everyone booed. "Yeah, I know," Lucas scratched the back of his neck, "I used to feel the same way. This joint prom thing, it was actually my idea, and I know a lot of people don't like it so that's why I'm here explaining why we're doing it. Anyway, please hold your tomatoes." The crowd had gone cold, no one laughed. "So here's the story, not too long ago I was at the big basketball game, shoutout to my boys on the basketball team, and I went to the bathroom-" He paused, "I guess I didn't need to say that. Oh well, anyway, I won't go into the whole story, but some guys came into the bathroom and tried to beat me up for being an anthrope. I kept thinking about why and I decided it's probably because these guys are just afraid of us because they don't know us. They just know what it says on the news about how scary and dangerous anthropes are. So anyway, they're trying to beat me up and believe it or not, as ripped as I am," he waved his hand across his neck, "I actually couldn't hold my own against three other guys.

"But," he continued, "my buddy Vincent and a new friend of mine came and bailed me out. His name is Benny, he's a student body officer at Fremont, he's not an anthrope, but he's got a lot of connections to anthropes. He stepped into the middle of that fight and helped me out. We've become good friends already and I think the world needs more people like Benny. People who aren't scared because they know. So I got thinking, if everyone knew us like Benny does, maybe it'd fix things. That's basically the idea behind the whole prom, a big 'get to know you' so we can stop fighting.

"So, to go over a few more things about the dance, we invited Benny to come and talk for a second with you guys. Let's give a round of applause for Benny!"

The crowd gave a halfhearted cheer. Lucas shrugged as he handed off the microphone to Benny. "Hey guys! I'm sorry, I know you don't want to hear from me, you'd rather hear the 'wolfman', so I'll keep this short. First, thanks for inviting us to your turf, in case you're wondering, we are going to have police here to arrest anyone who tries to vandalize or disrespect your wonderful school, so don't worry about that. We had an assembly yesterday to talk about respecting you guys and your school. Second, I think you're all aware of the terrorist attacks from the guy who's calling himself the Anthrope. Obviously, we have nothing to worry about, but just in case, the federal government is requiring every school event to have information available about emergency escape routes, so the administration sent out emails to everyone about that. And like I said before, we will have police officers here, so if you see any of them, don't worry, they're just trying to make sure we're all as safe as possible. Like I said, probably nothing to worry about, but just make sure you review that email.

And third, I don't know about you guys, but I am super stoked for prom!" The students cheered. Benny laughed. "Thanks guys for having me. Lucas is going to come back out here now and he's going to announce your nominees for prom royalty. Bye guys!"

"Benny, are you sure it's okay if you stay for lunch?" Annabeth set her tray down.

"Yeah," Benny picked up one of his tacos, "it's totally fine, it's the day before prom and I haven't skipped a day of school all year. Plus, it's just lunch. They won't even miss me. Thanks Vincent for the food by the way." He took a big bite and the shell cracked along the bottom and everything spilled out. "Awesome. Cafeteria food!"

"You owe me a buck fifty." Vincent took a bite of his taco and frowned. "I actually don't mind the food. Just every once in a while, it needs a little extra salt." Vincent reached into his backpack. "Which is why I always bring this." He pulled out a plastic bag with a saltshaker inside. "Anyone need some salt for their taco?" Vincent used the salt and then offered it to the others. Lucas stretched out his hand and took the shaker.

"Well," Annabeth said, "it's definitely a nice surprise for you to stay."

"Ooh! Ooh!" Vincent swallowed a bite of taco. "Guys, I'm brilliant and I need to tell you about it. I had this thought the other day. Everything you didn't know about was meant to be a surprise. Like when you find out about something that you didn't know, it was supposed to be a surprise when you found out."

"Umm," Annabeth said, "I don't agree."

Vincent waved his hand as he took a drink of chocolate milk. "No really, imagine you have a surprise birthday party. You didn't know about it because it was meant to be a surprise. Even if you find out early it was supposed to be a surprise."

"Yeah," Lucas said, "but that doesn't apply to everything. Like what about an assignment you didn't know about?"

"That's almost always because you have an evil teacher. They don't want you to know because they hate you and want to surprise you with a bad grade."

"I don't think that's true, but I guess I can pretend," Benny said, "but what about if someone in your family gets in a car crash but you don't know about it until later? That's horrible, you need to know about that right away."

Vincent didn't miss a beat. "Sometimes if you find out about stuff like that too soon, you overreact and freak out but then they get discharged from the hospital later that night because they're totally fine and the car crash wasn't even that bad."

"How about this," Lucas folded his arms, "I forgot to pay off my credit card last month."

"That's definitely meant to be a surprise. There's a reason they don't remind you the first time around about money you owe them."

Benny nodded solemnly. "Fair."

"Look," Annabeth said, "Vincent, not everything you don't know is meant to be a surprise."

"Then why don't I know about it?" Vincent raised his eyebrows conspiratorially.

"Nope," Annabeth threw her hands in the air and stood, "I'm done, you handle this Lucas."

Lucas leaned over to Vincent as Annabeth walked off. "I'm actually totally on your side here. Just don't tell Annabeth."

Annabeth walked back and picked up her tray. "I want my lunch. I'm going to sit with Kenzie."

"Oh my goodness," Vincent called out, "that's a wonderful idea! I'll come with you."

Annabeth called back. "I'd rather you didn't!"

Vincent got up and followed Annabeth. Kenzie sat at a table alone except for her boyfriend Jonathan, both looking down at their phones. Annabeth sat down next to Kenzie. Vincent sat down across the table from the others and immediately began sharing his theory. "Hey, Kenzie, you can't prove me wrong. Everything you don't already know was meant to be a surprise."

"Vincent, I'm busy."

Jonathan looked up from his phone. "Wait, what do you mean?"

"So imagine, it's your birthday and someone is throwing you a surprise party. Whether or not you find out when you're supposed to, it was supposed to be a surprise, right?"

Jonathan nodded slowly. "I think so. Yeah. Sure. Makes sense."

"So in that instance, it doesn't matter how you find out, but it was supposed to be a surprise. Even if it wasn't. But even then, it would be."

"Alright, I think I'm still with you man."

"Now imagine the same thing applies to everything. You didn't know there was another assignment in English, but that was because your teacher is evil and you weren't supposed to find out until your grade tanked. Or you forgot to pay off your credit card and they didn't tell you because they wanted you to have to pay a bunch of interest."

"Woah, Kenzie, this dude is smart. Everything is supposed to be a surprise."

Kenzie rolled her eyes but didn't look at Vincent. "Vincent, if that was true, then what about cancer? Maybe you test positive and you don't get your results right away because it takes a while to do the test. That's not supposed to be a surprise, it was just slow."

"Or maybe the lab actually could test faster but they're in cahoots with the cancer people at the hospital and the longer you have cancer, the worse it gets and the more money they make off of you."

"Dude," Jonathan's jaw dropped, "have you taken the ACT? I bet you could get a perfect score."

"I dry tested and got a thirty-three."

Annabeth snorted.

"Oh please," Vincent folded his arms, "like you got a better score."

"Thirty-five." She shrugged. Jonathan lost his mind. "Only taken it once." Jonathan's jaw dropped off.

Vincent grumbled. "Whatever."

"I can print out the transcript if you'd like."

Kenzie spoke up, still watching her phone, scrolling through her social media feed. "Oh, I've got one! When Columbus found out the world was round! No one knew it was round before then, so no one could have meant for it to be a secret! Your theory just got scooby dooed!"

Vincent shook his head. "Kenzie, you have caused me tremendous physical and emotional pain. Literally everything you just said was wrong. First, the world is totally flat. This is very easy to prove. Have you ever seen a 3D picture of the earth? No. You haven't. Because you can't take a 3D picture of a flat object." He kept a straight face, but his eyes twinkled. "Second, Columbus didn't create the hoax of a round planet." He grabbed a napkin and pulled a case out of his backpack. Opening it he withdrew a feather quill and a small ink bottle.

Kenzie looked at him as if he was crazy, "You just had that?"

Vincent dipped the quill in the ink. "I was going to make a replica of the Declaration of Independence with a treasure map on the back. Not the point." He drew a circle. "This is the Earth." He wrote Europe, Asia, and America spaced out 120 degrees from each other. "Columbus started here in Europe, everyone always went around Africa down here, but he went the other way and ran into America." He drew a line from Europe and went around the circle to America. "Now, Columbus never actually proved anything in this venture. At this point in time, it was a commonly held belief that the whole world was shaped like a rectangular map. Columbus had only discovered that the map was bigger than they thought. It was Magellan who made the most important discovery. He was the first person to sail all the way around the world, well, actually he died in Oceana, but that's not important, he gets credit. When he made it all the way around the world, people began to realize that it wasn't a rectangular map, it was a round one and it was possible to sail all the way around it." Vincent extended the line from America around Asia and back to Europe. "And thus we see, Magellan is the man responsible for this round Earth hoax."

"Woah," Jonathan said, "is that really true?"

"I'm hurt. I would never lie."

Annabeth rolled her eyes, "Of course he's lying. If the Earth was a disk-"

"-Space Frisbee-"

"Whatever, if it was a Space Frisbee, then explain gravity."

"Simple. Frisbees obey the law of gravity. They fall. The Earth is falling endlessly through space toward a supermassive black hole and there's a drag zone that cancels out the wind from us falling, so we don't notice anything except for a little bit of wind here and there. Viola! Gravity!"

"And this black hole has been pulling us for thousands of years and we haven't been obliterated?"

"It's really big." Vincent waved his hand. "It grabbed us when we were in a galaxy far, far away. When Sir Isaac Newton, an admired Space Frisbist, calculated gravity, his numbers were accurate. Now that we're finding them to be slightly off, people are blaming 'dark matter' when really the distortion is caused by the spacetime warping of the super massive black hole."

"That's crazy. When is the black hole going to destroy us?"

Vincent shook his head. "Never, time slows down the closer we get. Good news is that when we get really close, we'll be able to jump super high like we're on a trampoline."

"Jonathan," Kenzie still didn't look up from her phone, "he's just messing with you."

"But he looks so serious."

"I am serious." Vincent stared into Jonathan's soul. "Do not insult me by thinking me a liar. I detest such untrue thoughts." He raised his hand, shaking spastically, and slowly reached for Jonathan's throat. "It fills me with a murderous rage. Even now I tremble at the very idea of it."

"Woah, woah! Don't worry man. I believe you."

"Good man." Vincent continued. "Kenzie, back to your incredibly wrong statement. The whole issue with Columbus. Sailors had been aware of a very very slight curvature of the Earth, which is why we can't see very far. They knew the Earth was still mostly flat except for the edges of the frisbee but considered creating a hoax nonetheless because sailors are an unruly lot. And the last bit. When the sailors figured out the Earth was flat, there was no one keeping the information from them, right? Wrong! At least, no mortal man. Whether you believe in a higher power, fate, or just pure dumb luck, there is some powerful force out there that had intended for it to be a surprise. So, like I said, literally everything you said was wrong."

Annabeth sighed. "I swear Vincent, you only have energy when we don't have the energy to put up with it." She stabbed her fork into the side of her taco. "Are you done?"

"Have I made my point?"

"Vincent," she gave him a dry glare, "we're bleeding."

Vincent stood and nodded cordially. "Good day."

CHAPTER 25

Agent O'Hara walked out of the dressing room at the dress boutique. She wore a blue satin dress that hung perfectly to the floor. "How about this one?"

"Oh my goodness," Annabeth said, "that's perfect! Spin!" O'Hara spun and the bottom of the dress spun out like a church bell. "That's so perfect."

"I know, right! Only problem is the price tag, but then again, that's not my problem!"

Back at home Vincent dug through his drawers. "Come on, I know I've got a bowtie somewhere!"

Lucas went through the closet, sliding clothes and hangers along, one by one. "Hey, I found a white shirt!"

"Sweet! I might not need it though." Vincent jerked his thumb over his shoulder to his bed. A t-shirt with a picture of a tuxedo was slightly wrinkled but spread out on the sheets.

Lucas looked at the shirt. "I applaud the resourcefulness, but Agent O'Hara is getting something nice, you should too."

"Dude, I don't even want to do this." Vincent shut his drawer. "It's so weird. She's an adult and I'm only seventeen. It's an eight-year gap. So many things are wrong about that." He opened a new drawer and began pawing through it.

"It's only weird if you make it weird."

"I know," O'Hara said, "but he's a teenage boy, and unless they've gotten a lot smarter since I was in high school, a lot of things could go wrong. What if he tries to kiss me or something?"

"Ew," Annabeth wrinkled her nose, "that would be super weird. Okay, it's only weird if one of you makes it weird. But Vincent is a good guy and he's a lot smarter than that too, he wouldn't do that. My guess is you'll have a hard time getting him to talk to you in the first place."

"Dude," Vincent tied the bowtie around his neck, "I'm not even going to want to talk to her. Because if I start talking to her, she's going to think I'm flirting with her."

"Yeah," Lucas said, "but if you don't talk to her, she's going to try to talk to you, and then she's going to think that you think that she's flirting with you."

Agent O'Hara frowned. "But if he doesn't talk to me, then I'm in an awkward position."

"How so?" Annabeth asked.

"If I'm trying to talk to him, but he isn't talking back, he might think I'm trying to flirt with him. And then it will get ridiculously awkward."

"C'mon Vincent," Lucas said, "she's an adult woman. She isn't going to think that."

"No, c'mon you, Lucas! She's an adult woman. That's why it's such a problem." Vincent sat down on his bed and ran his hands through his hair. "I'm telling you, tomorrow is going to be the most awkward day of my life."

"Vincent, it's only awkward if you make it awkward."

"I'm not going to make it awkward, but what if he makes it awkward?" Agent O'Hara grimaced.

"He's not going to make it awkward. He isn't an idiot."

Vincent folded his arms across his chest. "Look, I get that she isn't an idiot, but just because she's an adult doesn't mean she won't make it weird. Adults are just us with more wrinkles and a little more practice winging it."

"Well then in that case, she's just a teenager with more wrinkles and a little more practice winging it."

"Dude, don't be weird. She looks exactly like one of us. And she's a government super cop! Which would be super-hot if she wasn't eight years older than me. Actually, kinda still is."

"It doesn't help that Vincent is the kind of guy I would go out with if he was a lot older and I wasn't so busy all the time. Ugh, that sounded so weird coming out of my mouth."

Lucas nudged Vincent. "If it helps anything dude, Annabeth is nine months older than me."

Annabeth nudged O'Hara. "If it helps anything, I'm like nine months older than Lucas."

"Yeah, except pretend or real this is both wrong and illegal."

Annabeth and Lucas nodded. "You're right. This is super weird."

Annabeth laid her head on her arms, trying to get comfortable in the ACC rec room. She heard a clang from the other side of the table. "Mind if I sit here?" She lifted her head and turned to see Vincent pulling out a chair, a gauntlet on his arm. "Actually, I don't care, I'm going to sit down." He had set two Diet Dr. Peppers on the table. "You look pretty tired. Have one, you need it."

Annabeth yawned and grabbed the can. She popped the top open and took a drink. "Thanks Vincent."

He waved it off. "Don't mention it. But also, don't expect me to share again. These are precious." He opened his and took a drink. "How's Kenzie doing?"

Annabeth lifted her arm and took a look at her gauntlet. "Everything is normal. She's asleep, so better than me." She rested her head on her hand and began to drift off.

Vincent nodded. "Do you need to say something to me?"

Annabeth's eyes shot open. "What?"

"Do you need to say something?"

"I don't think I follow." She took a drink of soda and fought to keep her eyes open.

"Last night at the party. When we were playing chess. You were talking about the first time we were here together. There's something you want to say. You wouldn't have brought it up otherwise."

"Vincent," she yawned, "do we really need to do this now?"

"Yes, we're doing this right now. I'll go first. Yes, I'm still into you. Now you get to tell me what you wanted to say." He took a drink without breaking eye contact.

"Vincent-"

"Annabeth." He set his drink on the table and a few drops splashed out. He grumbled. "You opened this can of worms, not me, you started this last night, and now we're going to finish it. What do you need to say? Straight to my face. Woman up and say it."

"Vincent, you are so difficult!"

He folded his arms and tipped his chair back. "I could say the same to you!"

"Hey!" Annabeth and Vincent turned to see a short man sitting on a couch near the door, holding his hands to his head. "Will you two keep it quiet! I have a headache!" An awkward silence fell. "Thank you!"

Annabeth huffed. "Look, Vincent, you're great. You're smart and funny and I won't deny you're good looking, but you push people away and you do it on purpose. In spite of that, I could maybe see something working out between us, but not now. Lucas has been trying to figure out how to tell you. That's why I brought it up last night, he and I are-”

“Go figure.” Vincent rolled his eyes.

“Vincent, I get that you're jealous of Lucas and all but you're acting like something unfair is happening here.”

Vincent threw his hands in the air. “Why Lucas? Of all the guys, you picked the 'nice' one. Was he just your rebound from Benny? Is that what it is? They're pretty much the same person.”

Annabeth glared at him. “Shut your mouth. Lucas is your best friend. You don't mean any of that. Yeah, sure, it was a rebound, but it's more than that now. And I like nice guys more than I like condescending jerks like you.” She stood up and left.

Benny laid on his bed strumming his guitar. There were two other guitars hanging on the wall, a black acoustic and a red electric. Rock albums filled the rest of the wall space. There came a knock at his door. “Come in,” he said.

His dad, Mr. Anderson came in and sat rigidly on the bed. “Hey Benny. How's it going?”

“Good.” Benny sat up. “I'm doing really well.”

“That's great.” Mr. Anderson sat there for a second. “So, you're going to prom, right?”

“Yup.”

Mr. Anderson nodded slowly. “How are you feeling about that?”

“Good.”

“That's good.” There was an awkward pause. “Have you thought about not going?”

Benny blinked. “No.”

“Oh.”

Benny waited for his dad to say something else. After a moment he opened his mouth again. “Should I not go?”

Mr. Anderson shrugged. “Maybe not. Maybe it would be better not to.”

“Is there a reason?”

Mr. Anderson shook his head. “No.”

“Are you worried about something?”

“Well, there's a terrorist.”

Benny nodded. “Yeah, there is.”

"Well, I'm going to go to work." Mr. Anderson stood. He grabbed the door handle, then froze. "You're going with Claire?"

"I am."

"Oh," Mr. Anderson said, "Do you like her that much?"

Benny nodded again. "She's alright."

"Do you really want to go with her?"

"Yeah." Benny shrugged.

"Okay." Mr. Anderson opened the door but didn't walk through it. "The neighbors have a date night on the same day as prom. I bet they'll need someone to babysit."

Benny pursed his lips. "I hope they can find someone."

"Yeah, me too."

Benny pulled a string on his guitar. It twanged. "Do you want me to not go for some reason?"

"No."

"Okay."

His dad stepped into the hallway. "Be safe."

"Like with my seatbelt?"

"Yeah…"

Benny gave a thumbs up. "Ok. I will."

"And generally. Avoid dangerous things."

"Ok."

"There could be dangerous things. Like moshing," he hesitated, "Or a terrorist."

"Do you think the terrorist is going to be there?"

"No."

Benny smiled without teeth or eyes. "Alright."

"Love you, Benny."

"Love you, Dad."

The door closed.

Then it opened. "Have you heard anything about prom? Or what's going to happen?"

Benny shook his head. "I think there's going to be fruit punch. And music."

"Be careful."

"Ok."

The door closed again. Benny's dad called out through the door. "Are you sure you want to go?"

"What?"

"Nothing! Good night!"

CHAPTER 26

"Alright boys, are you ready for the day date to begin?"

Vincent and Benny cheered. Lucas pulled the car into Annabeth's driveway. He and Vincent climbed out of the car and went up to the front door. He knocked and the door swung open, revealing Mr. Watson standing in front of a pile of boxes that had somehow grown, not shrunk. Tension was visible in his face, his posture, the way he'd done the buttons wrong, everything. "Hey Lucas. And you must be Vincent. Here for Annabeth and Agent O'Hara?"

"Yup."

Annabeth appeared behind her dad, wearing an oversized sweater and old jeans with paint. "Hi Lucas." Her voice turned cold. "Hi Vincent." She squeezed past her dad, Agent O'Hara followed, having dressed similarly with a plastic grocery bag in her hand.

"Annabeth, honey, what time are you going to get back?"

"Umm…" Annabeth looked at the boys.

Lucas answered. "Our last thing ends at three and then we'll come back to change."

"Alright, have fun." Mr. Watson tried to smile. "Stay safe."

Annabeth nodded. "We will dad. Don't worry." Mr. Watson closed the door.

Annabeth and Agent O'Hara followed the boys back to the car. Vincent climbed into the back next to Benny and let the girls take the seats in the middle. They closed the door and Lucas pulled away from the curb. "Alrighty, welcome to the magic carriage. We're going to go pick up Claire and then we'll get started." Lucas turned the radio on and lowered the volume. "Hey Benny, how

158

do we get to her house?"

"You need to head toward the interstate. It's just on the other side."

"Alright cool." Lucas turned the volume up a little and turned a corner.

"So, where are we going?" Annabeth asked.

"We can't tell you that. It's a super secret." Vincent grinned. "In fact, once we pick up Claire, we're going to make you wear blindfolds until we get there."

Agent O'Hara frowned. "I can't tell if you're joking or not."

Vincent held up three blindfolds. "Nope. It was my idea. What's in the bag?"

Agent O'Hara opened the bag. She began passing out small electronic devices. "These are our communication devices. Stick them in your ears. They're small and they blend in with your skin so they shouldn't be noticeable, powered by Bluetooth, and they're all automatically linked together. Just touch them and they'll start transmitting. Mine is connected to the SWAT team's control center, so I'll be able to give you all constant updates."

Vincent stuck his in his ear and pressed the button, "Dope. This is like a spy movie."

Lucas's eyes exploded as he heard Vincent, "Vincent, we're never texting again. The sound quality on these things is amazing!"

"Hey geniuses," Annabeth said, "they're Bluetooth, you didn't even turn them on. You have to hook them up to your phones. You're just hearing each other talking." She pulled out her phone and began connecting her earpiece.

"Just remember," Agent O'Hara put her earpiece in, "Claire doesn't know about any of this, and we want to keep it that way. Don't use these unless we're separated or something is going very wrong."

Everyone started connecting their earpieces. Vincent grumbled as he connected his phone's Bluetooth to all the wrong earpieces. Benny gave Lucas a few more directions and they eventually pulled up to Claire's house. "Benny, is this it?"

"Yup. I'll go get her." Benny squished past Annabeth and climbed out of the car. He walked up to the front door and knocked. After a few moments, a short girl with long brown hair opened the door. They hugged and walked back to the car. Benny opened the door and let her in first. "Hey everyone, this is Claire. Claire, this is Katie, Vincent, Annabeth who I think you already know, and Lucas is driving."

Claire waved and climbed into the back, pausing to glare at Annabeth. Benny sat down between her and Vincent. Vincent grinned and held up the blindfolds. "It's time." He handed out the blindfolds and the girls began to secure them in place.

"Why are we putting these on?" Claire asked.

Vincent chuckled to himself. "We want our first stop to be a surprise. And like I always say, everything you didn't know was meant to be a surprise." Lucas hit the gas and they sped off, heading downtown.

Annabeth groaned. "Someone else take this one."

"Uhh..." Lucas said, "what about cancer?" He winked in the rearview mirror.

"It's funny you should say that, Kenzie said the exact same thing. Whatever higher power you believe in, be it deity, luck, a space crab, or even a spaghetti monster, they wanted you to not find out about your cancer."

"Why?" Claire asked.

"I don't know. I don't understand the space crab."

Claire muttered to herself. "I meant why a space crab or a spaghetti monster?"

Agent O'Hara rolled her eyes under her blindfold. "You believe in a space crab?"

"Who's to say I don't?"

"Me," Lucas said, "because I see you at church every week."

"Silence Lucas. Space crab is a dual religion. I can believe in God and a space crab. The space crab is of less importance and doesn't have divine power, but it exists nonetheless. Many believe our Space Frisbee, also known as Earth, is one of the previous shells of the space crab."

Agent O'Hara frowned. "But if you believe God made the universe-"

"He also made the space crab."

"Why would he make a space crab?"

Vincent shrugged. "How should I know? Maybe he wanted a pet. He didn't need to make us, but he did because he wanted to. Besides, have you ever heard of a hot DOG?"

Annabeth sighed. "Vincent, we all know what a hot dog is."

"I'm not talking about that kind of hot dog. I mean a hot Dust-Obscured Galaxy. It's a space thing and an acronym. But it's a silly acronym. God made that. Why not a space crab?"

"I actually have heard of that kind of hot DOG," Annabeth said, "but it's not usually the first kind to pop into my head. And space crab isn't an acronym, so your point is moot."

"I could make it an acronym." Vincent hummed to himself. "Ooh, I've got it. Spacecrab Parts A Crustacean's Exoskeleton Cuz Rage Abounds Baby!" He mused to himself. "Really you could just have CRAB be a motto. Cuz rage abounds baby."

"I've got one!"

"Lucas," Annabeth said, "just pay attention to the road."

"No no," he insisted, "this one is good. Small Pants Are Chafing Elephants Cuz Rage Abounds Baby!"

"Oh look at that," Vincent said, "you stole my catch phrase."

"My turn," Benny said, "how about this, Some People Always C Exorcisms Cuz Rage Abounds Baby!"

Vincent tossed his hands in the air. "Are we all just going to use my CRAB now?"

Claire bounced in her seat. "I've got one! Superb Plant Acne Creates Evil Cuz Rage Abounds Baby!"

"Cool, everyone is stealing my idea now."

Annabeth huffed, "First off, this is stupid. Second, Shiny Prussian Alien Currency with Exceptional Crowns, Rings, And Bling."

"Of course Annabeth is the first one to not steal my ideas."

After quite a while, the car slowed to a halt. "Are we there?" Annabeth asked.

"Yeah," Lucas said, "but you have to leave your blindfolds on. I'm going to get out and get something. Be back in a minute." Lucas climbed out of the car and walked into a small building. He walked back out a minute later clutching four pieces of paper and a handful of pens. "Alright, girls - and Benny- here's the deal, we need you to sign something."

"What about the fine print?" Annabeth asked, "If we can't see it, then how do we know we aren't selling our souls to someone?"

"Vincent, check the fine print for soul selling." Lucas handed Vincent one of the papers.

Vincent held the paper directly to his forehead and blinked. "Nope, no soul selling."

Lucas put a paper and a pen in the hands of each of the girls. "Relax, it's just a safety waiver in case any of us are disemboweled to make sure we can't sue anyone. That doesn't mean this is dangerous though. They have the exact same thing at trampoline parks."

Claire smirked. "So what you're saying is we aren't at a trampoline park."

Benny laughed. "Yeah, this is a little different. If you need to you can peek for a second to sign it. But don't look anywhere but the waiver." The three girls lifted their blindfolds and began signing the waivers. Benny filled his out too. "Are you guys going to do one?"

Vincent smiled. "We've already been here. Many times. Many many times."

Lucas grinned. "So many times. Everyone done? Cool." He collected the papers and walked inside. He came back out a minute later. "Girls, make sure your blindfolds are on. We're going to get out of the car now. Careful climbing out." Annabeth got up and he helped her out of the car. "Once you get out of the car just step off to the side." He got O'Hara and Claire out. Benny and Vincent climbed out and the boys all led their dates inside. They walked through the front door and into the lobby.

The building wasn't large, but it had the feeling of a warehouse to it from the low budget materials and unfinished look. A heavyset man with a nametag that read Drake stood at a cash register. "Did they sign the safety waivers with blindfolds on?"

"No," Lucas let the door close behind him, "they took them off, but they don't know where we are."

"So they signed the waiver but don't know what they signed?"

"Yeah," Lucas frowned, "can we just let that slide?"

"If they all give consent." The girls nodded. "Well cool. Here's a basket, go ahead and fill it with as much stuff as you want. You know the drill. Two dollars per pound of material. We've got a two for one on printers right now."

Vincent walked over to some crude two by four shelves full of old printers. He stacked two on top of each other and picked them up. "Sick."

Lucas walked over to a shelf full of glass. Cups, plates, vases, all kinds of household ornaments. Lucas took the basket and began filling it with china tea sets. "Hey Benny, while we're doing this, can you go with the girls into the next room to get suited up?"

"I'll take you guys." Drake came out from behind the counter and walked through a door. "Follow me."

Benny herded the girls through the door. "You can take your blindfolds off." The girls took off their blindfolds. "But you aren't going to be able to figure out where we are from this room." They groaned.

Drake handed them all plastic suits. "Put these on." He walked into a small closet and brought out padded vests. "These go over your chest. Make sure they're tight." He tossed them on the floor at their feet while they struggled to put on the suits. Going into the closet one last time, he brought out helmets with face covers.

Vincent stuck his head in the door. "Hey, we've got all our stuff. Can you come weigh it for us?"

"Yup." Drake set down the helmets and walked out of the room. He walked back in a minute later. Lucas followed carrying an enormous basket filled with glass. Vincent closed the door behind him with his foot, balancing four printers on top of each other.

Benny laughed. "I thought we were only going to get two printers."

"We were but then they had the two for one thing and so we had enough money for four." Vincent set the printers down and he and Lucas grabbed two of the suits off hooks and put them on. Once everyone was dressed Vincent and Lucas picked up their things and Drake took them through another door.

The room was concrete all around except for the light in the ceiling and a camera on the wall. In the center of the room was a concrete pillar about two feet high covered in leather scraps. Several metal pipes and baseball bats leaned against one wall. Annabeth squinted. "Will someone please explain what exactly we're doing here?"

Drake smiled. "Basically, you're about to do whatever you want. Those bats and pipes are yours to use as you please. Just try to only maim the things you've bought to maim. Don't hit each other with anything. You can throw things at the walls if you want, but don't hit the ceiling because of the lights, or that camera on the wall. Fifty dollar fine if you break either. Be safe but have fun." He walked out of the room and closed the door.

"Wait, we're about to do what?" Claire asked.

"Allow me to demonstrate." Vincent picked up a bat and a teacup. He tossed the teacup into the air and smashed it into smithereens with the bat. "Does that answer your question?" The girls exchanged looks and rushed to grab bats. "We're going to do the printers last, those are the most fun. But anything in the basket you can break."

Agent O'Hara picked up a china teapot. "My grandmother used to have some like this. Shame to destroy it. Oh well." She set the teapot on the ground and smashed it with a huge crowbar. Annabeth hurled a wine glass at the wall.

Lucas picked up an armful of glass. "Benny, Vincent, batting practice? I'll pitch." He tossed a coffee mug and Vincent whacked it out of the air, showering the room in glass. Lucas lobbed a cracked vase to Benny and he swung down, breaking the vase between his bat and the floor.

Claire choked up on her bat. "Throw me one!" Lucas launched a drinking glass at her and she swung, exploding the glass in every direction.

"Hey, check this out." Vincent picked up a glass chihuahua statue. "My neighbor has one of these. It's so annoying." He set it on the floor and did a few practice swings. "My spirit animal is a dog, but I don't think these yippy things should even count as dogs." He obliterated the chihuahua like it was a golf ball.

Agent O'Hara picked up a ceramic Buddha statue that was missing half its head. "Really Lucas? I feel like this is disrespectful."

"That was Vincent! Not me!"

Vincent raised his hands defensively. "He was giving me a weird look with that one eye.”

“Would you smash a Christus?”

“I don’t know,” Vincent grinned, “Maybe not, but statues are just statues. Besides, we paid two dollars for that Buddha. I’m pretty sure Buddha wouldn’t want us to waste two dollars. He sounds like a pretty chill guy. But if you really don’t want to smash it, I can do it.”

“Eh, what the heck, no hard feelings Buddha.” O’Hara underhanded the statue into the air and smashed it into smithereens. An hour and a couple dozen pounds of glass later, the basket was empty.

“Well, only one thing left to do now.” Lucas picked up a printer. He set it on the short column in the middle of the room. “Beat the crap out of these.” He lifted his bat overhead and with one mighty swing-

The lights shut off, plunging them into complete darkness.

O’Hara pressed her earpiece. “Weapons. I think… I think he’s here.” She pulled her gun out and flipped off the safety. “Everyone,” she said out loud, “hold still, don’t move. I don’t want you to trip. There’s glass everywhere.” Lucas and Annabeth pulled out Glocks. There was a scraping sound of broken glass and metal as Vincent picked up the crowbar O’Hara had discarded. O’Hara used her earpiece again. “Vincent, quiet! We’re trying to stay quiet so we don’t get shot or gassed.”

“I can’t see anything,” Claire said, sliding her feet through the wreckage, “Don’t pick up your feet or you might get impaled.”

“Hush,” O’Hara whispered, “I’m trying to listen. No one turn on any lights.”

Claire frowned. “But don’t we need to-”

“Hush!” Footsteps quietly approached the door. The handle squeaked slightly as it turned. O’Hara crawled toward the door in the darkness. The door slowly creaked open. Faint light cast the shadow of a large man across the floor. The man took a step into the room. Agent O’Hara jumped and knocked the man to the floor. She jammed her forearm into his neck against the ground and put her gun to his head. “David Mitson, you’re under arrest! You have the right to remain silent. Everything you say can and will be used against you in a court of law.”

Claire stood up. “Katie! What the heck are you doing? That’s Drake!”

Drake groaned. “What’s wrong with you? I was coming to make sure you guys were alright. The power went out.”

O’Hara climbed off and extended him a hand, giving him a sheepish look that almost could have been apologetic. “How often does the power go out here?”

"Never," Drake answered, backing away from O'Hara and looking at her gun nervously. He turned a flashlight on, revealing that nearly everyone had a gun drawn except himself and Claire.

"Go stand in the corner over there, it's the last spot anyone will see from the door," Katie demanded, "Our lives may be in danger. Hurry."

Drake picked himself up and staggered into the back corner. "Why do you all have guns?"

Benny motioned for Claire to go stand in the corner with Drake. "You heard of the Anthrope?"

Drake nodded.

"Yeah, that's why." Benny gave Claire a look that said, I'll explain later.

Vincent ducked out of the room and peered around the corner. O'Hara, Benny, Lucas, and Annabeth followed him out into the hall. They walked into the lobby and looked out the window. The neon sign in the shop across the street was flashing.

O'Hara shook her head. "He's got to be here. We lost power but they're untouched? No way."

Drake stuck his head out the door, Claire behind him. "Who exactly are you?"

O'Hara flashed her badge. "Agent Katie O'Hara. FBI. Please go back in there. Benny, go with him. Wait with the girl. We're going to check this out. We have reason to believe the Anthrope is on the premises. Do not call anyone, especially the police." O'Hara walked slowly toward the front door, back to the wall. Vincent did the same across the room and they reached the front window, checking the street for anyone. They nodded to each other and O'Hara walked out the door. "Try to keep your weapons out of sight. We don't want to draw attention. Annabeth and Lucas, guard the door. Vincent, come with me."

O'Hara walked around a corner and into an alleyway. She pointed her gun down the alley and waved over her shoulder for Vincent to follow. They walked down the side of the alley. "O'Hara, there's no one here."

"Yeah, but look at this." The powerline was ripped apart and sparks shot out in all directions. "There was someone here."

"Why?"

O'Hara stuffed her gun back into her clothes. "He's taunting us." She walked out of the alley and returned to the door.

"Did you find anything?" Annabeth asked.

"Someone destroyed the power supply."

"That's kinda weird," Lucas said, "there's a power van across the street. They left their window open and the engine is idling."

O'Hara squinted and spotted a jagged line where the window should have been. "No they didn't. Someone broke that window. That van was stolen." She drew her gun and sprinted toward the van. A man jumped into the driver's seat and pulled out into the street. Agent O'Hara ran after the van. "Get the car! Get it now!"

Vincent sprinted to the car and Lucas threw him the keys. Lucas and Annabeth sprinted toward the van with O'Hara. Vincent jammed the key into the ignition and started the car. He raced down the street after them. As he passed O'Hara she shouted to him. "Don't slow down! Follow him! If you shoot, aim for the tires!"

Vincent hit the gas and tore down the road. He drew his gun and opened the window. Barely keeping on the road, he stuck half his body out the window and fired three shots at the van's tires. The man in the van fired back, shattering the windshield. Vincent ducked but didn't slow. His right tires hopped the curb. Vincent fired again through the windshield and what was left of it shattered into pieces. He was gaining on the van. "Come 'ere you little-"

The man fired back at him, popping both of his front tires. The car jerked and Vincent smacked his forehead on the dashboard. He swerved and crashed into a fire hydrant. Spots swam in his eyes and he put the car in reverse, but the tires wouldn't move. He pounded the steering wheel and the airbags deployed.

Vincent gasped for breath and tried to open the door. When it didn't budge, he stuck his head out the window and saw the door was crumpled. With a groan, he climbed out the broken windshield, shattered glass biting into his skin. Water showered down around him from the broken hydrant. Blood seeped into his eyes. Dazed, he touched his forehead, hand coming away covered in blood. He wheezed. "Uh oh..." He passed out on the hood.

<h1 style="text-align:center">CHAPTER 27</h1>

Lucas watched the crash. He put his finger to his ear. "Vincent?" No response. "Vincent? Buddy, are you there? Vincent! Can you hear me?" Lucas took off down the road.

"Lucas!" Annabeth ran after him.

O'Hara put a hand to her head. "Oh no." She opened her phone. Her finger hovered over the nine. She shook her head and stuffed the phone in her pocket. She followed.

Lucas gasped for breath and his muscles burned, not slowing. "Vincent! Vincent!" The name ripped itself from his throat. "Vincent!" He saw the car up ahead, smashed into a fire hydrant. Water went everywhere. "Vincent!" He reached the car and found Vincent unconscious on the hood. "Hey! Buddy, come on, wake up!" A massive bloodstain covered Vincent's shirt. Lucas put his ear to Vincent's bloody chest. His heart pattered weakly.

Annabeth skidded to a stop. "Lucas, is he-"

"No." Lucas shook his head, tears blurring his eyes. "He's going to be fine."

O'Hara arrived, shoes crunching on the broken glass. "I need to call an ambulance. He's going to die."

Vincent shot up, gasping for breath. "Am I dead? I think I'm dead, man."

Lucas laughed in shock and hugged his best friend. "No. You're alive."

Annabeth pulled them apart. "Lay down Vincent. You were shot."

He resisted but eventually laid down. "You really can't feel it that much. What do you know? Hey Lucas, the movies were telling the truth." He laughed again but his smile quickly faded, and he was able to swallow with some exertion. "How long until I'm gone? Wait, wait, O'Hara, put that phone down!"

"I'm calling an ambulance."

"Don't," he wheezed, "If you do, then everyone will know what's going on and they'll try to stop us and then we won't catch him."

O'Hara shook her head. "Vincent, you're going to die if I don't."

"Then I can die knowing I was the most heroic of everyone. It's like it says in John fifteen thirteen. I'm willing to sacrifice to catch him. If you call that ambulance, this will all be wasted."

O'Hara spoke into the phone. "Hello, yes, someone was shot."

"No!" Vincent coughed blood. "End the call! Lucas, make her end the call! Stop her! Stop her. Listen, you need to let me die so no one else has to." He let out a ragged breath and stared into the sky. "Let me die. Let me be the dead man." He shook his head and closed his eyes.

O'Hara handed the phone off to Annabeth. She ripped off her jacket and pressed it into Vincent's chest. "Vincent, I'm not letting you die. We're going to catch him and you're going to live to see it. For goodness sakes you're my date to prom, don't you dare die right now!"

Vincent coughed but didn't open his eyes. "Quite frankly, I don't think this could ever work out. Too much between us. Age mostly." He wiped his bloody hand on his pants.

"They'll be here in three minutes." Annabeth said. "Vincent, just hold on. They're going to get here."

Vincent's breathing grew weaker and weaker as the minutes passed. The lights of an ambulance flew down the street toward them. Two EMTs immediately climbed out. "What happened?"

O'Hara flashed her badge. "Agent O'Hara. This is official business. Top secret. Do not discuss any of this without permission from me. He was shot in the chest. As far as I can tell, he also has a minor head wound and a concussion."

The EMTs quickly loaded Vincent onto a stretcher and rolled him into the back. Lucas and Annabeth climbed in with him.

O'Hara looked at Lucas. "I'm going to get Benny and Claire. I'll bring them to the hospital as soon as I can. I'm going to have to call the agency for a favor."

Lucas nodded. "Hurry." The EMT shut the doors, and the ambulance drove to the hospital. Vincent's breathing stabilized a little as an oxygen mask was secured over his face. Annabeth hid her face in her hands and began to sob. Lucas put an arm around her. "Hey. It's going to be alright. Vincent's going to be okay."

Annabeth looked up at him with red eyes. "This feels like my fault."

"What do you mean?"

"I'm the one who got us all into this. I started this and now," she gestured to Vincent, "Vincent is paying for it. This is the last thing I wanted to happen."

Lucas lowered his voice. "Hey, this is not your fault. If you want to know whose fault this is, I'll give you a name. The Anthrope. It's not your fault. Okay?"

Annabeth nodded and wiped away a tear.

O'Hara waved down a big, blacked out hummer. "Benny, Claire, come on. We've got to hurry. Drake!"

The hefty employee stuck his head out the door. "Yeah?"

"A police patrol car will be here in two minutes, we're putting you into protective custody. Don't talk about any of this."

He gave a thumbs up and went back inside. O'Hara climbed into the driver's seat as a man dressed in street clothes with a mask shifted over into the passenger seat. "Benny, Claire, the man in the passenger seat is currently undercover. That's why he's wearing a mask. Don't look at him if you can help it."

Claire leaned over to Benny. "Benny, I don't want to be part of this. Vincent got shot and… he might die. I'm scared."

Benny nodded. "Me too. We can put you into protective custody with Drake." He took off his jacket and handed it to her. "Here, you're shaking."

She smiled. "Thanks. So, you're like a secret agent now?"

"No." Benny chuckled. "I don't think so. I think this is a one-time thing. I kinda got involved on accident. Lucas and Vincent got me involved and they found out from Annabeth."

"How did Annabeth get involved?"

Benny scratched his head. "I don't really know. Really, I don't think I can tell you what I do know. O'Hara, Claire wants to go into protective custody too!"

"Who?" O'Hara turned around and saw Claire. "Oh, right. Get out of the car, the police cruiser is just around the corner, they'll take you and Drake down to the police station."

"How old are you?"

"Twenty-five." O'Hara reached back and opened the door for her.

"Dang. Fooled me. I thought you were a senior." Claire got out of the car, and they sped away.

When they arrived at the hospital, they hurried in and found Vincent unconscious in the ER. Annabeth sat in a chair in the corner and Lucas stood next to Vincent, watching over him. "Hey guys."

"Is he okay?"

Lucas nodded. "Sedated. He lost a lot of blood. But they're giving him a transfusion." He pointed to a sack of blood hooked up to Vincent's arm. "He won't be able to go anywhere for a couple days. They got him patched up, but if he exerts himself too much, the wound could reopen. We're down a man for prom."

Benny spoke up. "Claire's gone too."

O'Hara nodded. "Benny and I can go together then. I need to get in. We have to continue with the plan."

"Can we just leave them?" Annabeth asked. "Vincent already got hurt, I don't want anyone else to be in danger."

"I'm coming," Benny said.

Lucas nodded and looked Annabeth in the eyes. "Don't you trust us? We want to help."

Annabeth grabbed O'Hara by the arm. "Please?" Her eyes reflected fear.

O'Hara glanced at the boys, then Annabeth, and shook her head. "We need everyone." She checked the time on her phone. "We also need to go soon. We've got to get back home, change into our clothes, and then go get dinner and pictures. I know it's going to be hard, but we need to pretend like everything is perfectly normal." She turned and walked out of the room. Everyone but Lucas followed.

O'Hara stuck her head back into the room. "Hey. Lucas, are you coming?"

Lucas looked down at Vincent. "He's my best friend. I nearly lost him." He faced O'Hara. "The Anthrope did this. I'm going to make sure he pays, and that no one has to lose anyone."

CHAPTER 28

Vincent opened his eyes. A cold sensation covered his skin. He sat up to grab a blanket at the end of his bed when a stabbing pain erupted in his chest. "Ah, that wasn't a good feeling." He looked down at his chest and found himself wearing a thin hospital gown. An IV needle connected to his veins, supplying him with blood. Gently, he felt out his chest and discovered thick bandages. "What happened to me?" He carefully took the blanket and laid back down. His eyes fell on a whiteboard that listed his information. "Chest wound? Oh. Right." He began to sweat and kicked off the blanket. The chills quickly returned, and he wrapped himself in the blanket again. "Time, time, time, time… six thirty." He tapped his palm to his forehead. "Prom starts in thirty minutes. I missed dinner. Food."

He noticed a blueberry muffin and a cup of fruit sitting next to a bottle of water on a nearby table. Taking the muffin, he began to stuff his face. He sat up in his bed. "Fruit?" He snorted and ignored the rest of his food.

A nurse walked into the room. "Oh good. You're awake. Vincent, do you know where you are?"

Vincent downed the water, clearing his throat. "Yeah. I'm in a hospital that serves blueberry muffins and fruit cups. Both have fruit. Which makes me wonder, does anyone ever make muffins with vegetables like carrots or celery? I've also got a hole in my chest and the blood of someone else, who I'm hoping doesn't have AIDS, in my veins."

"That's very good." She made a note on a clipboard. "And no, you're not going to get AIDS, we screen the donors. If you'd like another muffin, I suppose I could check with the cafeteria."

"That's alright. I can't stay long." His vision spun. "Prom starts in thirty minutes. Granted, I always like to be fashionably late, but I still need to get dressed and then get to the school within an hour. Unless you have muffins to go. If you have those, then I would like another."

"Vincent. I know you may be disappointed to hear this, but you aren't going to prom. You are in no condition to go anywhere. In fact, you're probably going to be staying here for several days."

Vincent shook his head and laughed, ignoring nausea. "No, I have to go. I'm supposed to go with Katie. She's going to be disappointed. I'm pretty sure she never went to prom. I think she was really shy when she was younger. And of course I'm not even supposed to talk about our secret mission." He swung his leg over the side of the gurney and felt pain. "Ouch."

The nurse grabbed him and pushed him back into the bed. "Vincent, look. I'm not allowed to let you leave. If you keep trying, I'm going to have to call security. Please lay down."

Vincent nodded and laid down. "Did anyone tell my mom that I got shot?"

"No. We were asked not to contact anyone about your injuries. Only three staff even know you're here."

"Good. If my mom knew I got shot, she would kill me. Thank you. If they have any, can you bring me a chocolate chip muffin?"

"I'll look into that." The nurse turned and walked out of the room.

Vincent waved and smiled. He waited for several moments before swinging his legs around and getting down, still feeling chills. "Nice lady." Vincent unplugged all the machines from the wall and ripped sensors and needles from his body, only leaving the blood bag attached. He dragged the IV pole with him over to the window and grabbed his pants where they lay in a heap with his other things. A few blood stains were spattered across the front. "Those were my favorite pants." He put his pants on, tucking in the gown. His shirt had a big blood stain and a hole in the front.

Vincent put it on and folded his arms over the blood stain. "That hides it well enough." He checked his phone and discovered his earpiece was still connected. With a grimace, he unhooked the blood bag from its stand and dropped it down his shirt. "Let's roll." As he walked out of the room, he picked up the fruit cup and tossed it in the trash. He passed through the door and sniffed. "Ammonia." The nurse from earlier was on the phone at a big desk in the middle of the hall. Vincent ducked into a nearby room. An elderly man slept soundly in a bed.

Vincent plucked the sleeping man's muffin off the table. "You can have mine when it comes." He peeked out into the hall. The nurse got up and walked over to an elevator. Vincent folded his arms over his chest and walked out the room. He took the stairs and hurried down to the ground floor, nearly falling down multiple flights.

Ignoring signs to find the lobby, he went the other way. After turning a corner, he spotted a large metal door. "This looks like an exterior door." He stumbled toward it and changed direction at the last second to throw up both of the muffins into a drinking fountain. With a grimace, he wiped his mouth and went through the door. He found himself in a back parking lot. A row of ambulances caught his eye. Vincent staggered up to the first ambulance. He opened the door and hoisted himself up, grunting in pain.

The keys were in the ignition. Vincent started the ambulance and pulled out of its parking spot. He drove around the corner and into the street. "Where am I?" He scanned street signs. "Twelfth street. Thirty minutes. That's not that much time… Forget fashionably late, I never liked fashion anyway. I need to be there as fast as I can." He fumbled around on the dash and turned on the sirens. "That should work. Wait a second, this is Thirteenth Street." Making a sharp U-turn, he headed the other direction, towards Weber. An alarm went off at the hospital as he passed it and a voice came over the radio.

"Ambulance One. Where did you go? A patient with low blood levels has disappeared. Ambulance One. Where are you?"

Vincent grabbed the radio. "Stuff it ammonia man!"

"Is this Vincent?"

He squeezed the button on the handpiece, "Go scrub yourself!"

"Vincent, I need you to stop the vehicle. Stop and tell us where you are. We'll come pick you up. You aren't thinking clearly. You're in no condition to drive. You're still at high risk for reopening your wound."

Vincent took a right turn at thirty miles an hour and began rolling down the passenger window. "You are correct, my main male nurse man! I'm feeling nauseous, I've got chills, my chest really hurts, my vision is spinning a little, and I am definitely not thinking clearly! But what I do know is that I need to go get ice cream right now! So you can come get me if you want, but not before I get ice cream!" Vincent tossed the handpiece out of the opposite window, letting it dangle by the cord. He chuckled. "Ice cream. Dang it, now I want to stop for ice cream." He floored the gas, and the needle rose to eighty-five on a forty-five road, cars ahead frantically pulling aside to let him pass. "No time for ice cream. Gotta pick up my suit." A bead of sweat began to form on his forehead, and he ripped off his shirt without slowing down. He cranked down his own window and the tape on his bandage began to flap in the wind, air cool against his bare abdomen.

Vincent flipped on his left turn signal and switched lanes to the right. "Could I get ice cream?" He grabbed at the collar of his hospital gown and ripped open the front. "Goodness, it's hot." Vincent glanced down at his chest and saw a large bandage that had been mostly soaked through with his blood. He retched in the passenger seat and kept driving.

When he arrived home, he snuck in through the back door. "Where did I leave that stupid suit?" He rummaged around his closet. "There you are." Vincent took off his pants and put the suit on. He tossed his untied bowtie over his shoulder and went back to the door. Sweat dripped from his forehead and landed on his bare foot. "I need to cool off. I'm going to die in this stupid suit." He went up the stairs and found his mother on the couch.

"Hi Vincent. Weren't you supposed to come back earlier? And how did you get in?"

"I like to leave the back door unlocked for when I sneak out at night with Lucas. Anyway, plans changed and I need to grab the ice cream." He walked into the kitchen and opened the freezer. Ice cream in hand, he took a spoon and headed back downstairs.

"Vincent, did you say you sneak out with Lucas?" She looked him over, hair a mess and face pale and sweaty. "You don't look well. Maybe you should stay home."

"Can't. Katie is waiting for me."

"Oh yeah. She seems nice. Have fun. We're going to talk about sneaking out later. Bye!"

Vincent waved and hurried down the stairs. He closed the exterior door behind him and opened the ice cream. One hand holding the ice cream and the spoon, and the other trying to scoop it, he nearly fell over backwards as he climbed back into the stolen ambulance. "Prom, here I come!"

CHAPTER 29

Lucas stood in a throbbing mass of humanity in the Weber commons that smelled like fertilizer and cologne. He wiped his forehead and shouted over the blasting music. "Hey Annabeth! I'm getting a little hot! I'm going to go get some water! You want to come?"

She put a hand to her ear. "What?"

"Water?"

"Yeah! Thanks!"

Lucas turned and took a step into the bouncing mass of high school. He paused after a few steps with her not following "Wait, did she mean... Whatever. I'll just get her some." He wove through the crowd toward the water tables. As he approached, he heard two voices shouting over the music.

"You couldn't really clone your brain into someone else's brain because you'd have to map out your brain's signals consistently and you can't do that!"

"But you technically could because you could detect the negative charge of the electron as it travels between neurons!"

"Technically, you aren't just yeeting an electron between neurons, the charge passes down a chain of ions and stuff!"

Lucas frowned. "That sounds like Vincent."

"Oh, yeah! I forgot about that!"

"No you didn't! You never knew that! You just lied to sound smart!"

Lucas pulled out of the crowd and into empty space to find Vincent talking to another boy. The boy looked awkward. "I'm just going to get my drink and go!" He left.

"Poser!" Vincent downed the entire dixie cup in one go.

Lucas walked up to Vincent. "Vincent! What are you doing here?"

"I came to help!"

"We told the nurses not to let you come! You didn't even have a car!"

Vincent shrugged and took another shot of water. "I took an ambulance!"

Lucas grabbed him and dragged him down a hall where the music was quieter and the lights were off. "You stole an ambulance!"

Vincent blinked several times and sighed. "This is better. My head doesn't hurt so much here. The ambulance, right. No, yes, kinda, I'm probably going to give it back."

"You were shot! You can't be here. You don't have enough blood in your body right now. You aren't thinking straight." Lucas's wrist tracker flashed.

"I am too. I'm thinking straighter than ever. You should try nearly dying, it's good for the soul. I actually said a little prayer and it was really great. But the point here is that you are my best friend. And I tolerate Annabeth. I'm not letting you two be here and risk your lives without me. Benny and O'Hara are pretty cool too. You need everybody you can get to help." Vincent's tracker flashed.

"No, Vincent, we don't. We really don't. Nothing is going to go wrong. He shows his face, SWAT team busts in and takes him out. We're fine."

Vincent rolled his eyes. "Oh, come on, something is going to go wrong. Our job is to make as little as possible go wrong. This guy, how did he know we were in that rage room?"

Lucas froze. "How did he?"

"I don't know. I didn't tell him. You and Benny are the only other two who knew we were going. But he could have put a bug in our car or something."

"How would he do that?" Lucas's tracker flashed.

"I don't know…" Vincent grabbed Lucas's arm, just below the wristband. He tapped the strip of raised skin. "The trackers. That guy, Dave Philips, they said he was a computer programmer, right? Remember how Benny said he might have hacked the ACC system?"

Lucas's eyes grew wide. "There's no way! That thing's unhackable!" He paused. "But that's the only explanation."

"Exactly. He was only tracking Annabeth though, he probably doesn't know about us. But that means Annabeth is in more danger than anyone. He'll go straight to her."

"Oh no. We need to get back to them, right now." Lucas turned and hurried down the hall. Vincent staggered along behind him. They wove through the crowd and found O'Hara and Benny.

Lucas got there first. "O'Hara! Where's Annabeth?"

"Katie. Remember? And I think she went to go to the bathroom." Vincent burst through the crowd. O'Hara did a double take. "Vincent? How did you get here?"

"I borrowed an ambulance, but that's not important. Annabeth is in danger. The Anthrope is in the ACC database, he can track any of us. And he wants her."

O'Hara put her hand to her mouth. "I can go get her."

The power shut off, plunging them into darkness and silence.

They all froze for a second before bursting into action. O'Hara drew her weapon and handed an extra to Vincent after a moment of hesitation. Lucas and Benny followed suit. O'Hara lowered her voice. "Hide your weapons until we see him. No false alarms this time." All around them, the lights from phones turned on, lighting the commons. Voices mumbled, trying to figure out what was going on.

Lucas looked around. "Oh no, Annabeth!" He ran off into the crowd.

"Lucas!" Vincent tried to go after him but O'Hara grabbed his arm.

"You do not get to run. You walk unless someone is chasing you. And you're staying right here." O'Hara put her finger to her ear. "All units, be ready. Power has been cut. Wait for my signal. Do you copy?"

Nothing.

"Do you copy?"

Nothing.

"Does anyone copy?" She looked at Vincent and Benny. "Radio silence. I think we're alone."

Vincent shook his head. "We're dead men."

A half dozen bodies crashed through the skylights, gunshots ringing. They hit the ground with a thud. The students yelled and moved back but the gunfire stopped. The SWAT team lay still on the ground. O'Hara pushed through the crowd, Benny and Vincent behind her. She felt the pulse of one of the men. "He's dead." She looked at the boys. "So, who was shooting?"

Another SWAT fell from above, landing on his feet, slowed by a tether. He unstrapped a massive gas tank from his back and opened the valve. Blue gas spewed out, filling the room rapidly. O'Hara fired several times at the figure. The bullets thudded into him, but he strode forward regardless. He lifted his gun and shot O'Hara in the shoulder, and she fell to the ground.

The figure walked up to the DJ's table and picked up a megaphone, looking at the terrified students all huddling on the floor in front of him. "I am the Anthrope."

CHAPTER 30

The students ran for their lives, phone lights bobbing up and down, voices in a full-blown cacophony of yelling and screaming. They went every direction, down halls, into classrooms, toward closets. Most ran for the cafeteria, where massive glass panes covered one wall. Two sets of double doors were on the far ends. The first students reached the doors and pulled. They only gave slightly before the chains holding them caught. "Move! Out of the way!" Lucas shoved his way to the front and shot the windows, sending glass everywhere. "Get out! Hurry!" He looked behind him and saw a girl fall to the ground, shaking. Blue gas spewed from the air vents, quickly filling the air. He fumbled in his suit and put on his mask. "Don't breathe the gas! It's coming from the vents!" Students ran out the window and he moved on to shoot out more of the huge panes. Then he pulled out his tranquilizer gun and began firing at those who fell on the ground.

Benny and Vincent dragged O'Hara away from where the Anthrope stood watching the chaos, taking it in like a man standing in the sun on a cool day. O'Hara reached under the hem of her dress with her good arm and unstrapped a pair of gas masks. She handed one to Vincent. "This was supposed to be Annabeth's." She put the other one on. Benny kept breathing normally. Vincent ripped off his bowtie and began wrapping it around O'Hara's shoulder.

A pair of boys spasmed on the ground next to the gas canister. Benny stepped forward and shot the boys on the floor with his tranquilizer gun. "We need to move them!" He grabbed one of them by the leg and tried to drag him, but the boy transformed into a bear. The bear roused slightly, and Benny shot it again.

The other boy turned into a big lizard. O'Hara looked at them, clutching her shoulder. "The bear stays, the lizard we'll just bring with us until we can set him loose outside. He shouldn't be any trouble." Benny picked up the lizard and put him over his shoulder. Blue gas hung in the air, making the commons hazy and blurred. "I can't see the Anthrope. We'll deal with him later. For now, we need to get everyone out of the building."

Lucas heard a growl behind him by the windows in the cafeteria. He turned in time to see a wolf jump on him. The wolf knocked him to the ground and snapped at his face. Lucas wrestled the wolf back with one arm, rolling in the shattered glass and tranqed it in the neck with the other. The wolf slackened a little and then slumped to the ground beside him. He stood and saw several more animals rise, blocking students from their escape. "Everyone, run!" He shouted, "Find other exits! Take cover in the classrooms if you have to! Run!"

Lucas loaded a new magazine into his tranq gun and fired at several large animals. A cat purred against his leg. "Not the time kitty!" He picked it up and tossed it outside. "Run away!" Across the cafeteria, he saw Kenzie through the haze, limping with her hand over her mouth. He ran over to her. "What happened?"

She mumbled through her hand. "I tripped and hurt my leg. Lucas, that's a tranquilizer gun, right?"

He nodded.

"Shoot me."

He nodded and shot her in the arm four times. "That should knock you out for a few hours. Hopefully this will be over by then."

She nodded and took her hand off her mouth and drew in a deep breath. "Thanks Lucas." She collapsed, shaking. Lucas ran away, heading for the front entrance. O'Hara, Benny, and Vincent materialized out of the gas at the bottom of the steps to the cafeteria.

"Lucas!" Vincent hobbled closer, clutching his chest and holding up his phone light, which was scattered and bounced around by the ever-thickening gas. "Did you find Annabeth?"

"No. I tried her comms but that didn't work. Then I called into the bathroom, but no one responded. I don't know what happened."

"No shot," Vincent whispered. "I called 911. They'll be here soon."

Benny had a lizard draped over his shoulder. He hung up the phone. "My dad didn't answer."

O'Hara kept looking over her shoulder. "We can't stay out in the open like this. Something is going to eat us." No more than a few dozen feet away, a howl erupted. She lowered her voice. "We need to take cover. Lights off. Lucas,

Vincent, where can we hide?" More howls joined together.

Vincent pointed to the opposite side of the commons. "Main office. Follow." Vincent stumbled away. "Wolf pack. We're dead men."

Benny frowned. "How did they have time to form a pack?"

Vincent clutched his chest and went faster. "They all transform on the full moon, like Lucas. They've been a pack for a while. Except Lucas doesn't really play nice with them. And they've probably got his scent. Which means they're following us." The howling followed them and O'Hara broke into a sprint. "See?" Vincent pointed ahead and tried to keep up. Footpads drummed on the floor behind them. "We're dead!"

They rushed into the main office, Vincent falling several paces behind, clutching his chest. Three wolves were gaining on him. "Vincent!" Lucas tossed him the American flag. Vincent swung it like a staff and cracked one of the wolves on the head. The other two dodged and Vincent kept running, still swinging as he practically fell over into the office. Lucas slammed the door behind him. As the door latched in place, they heard a thump and then scratching at the door. Lucas deadbolted it.

The pack howled. O'Hara turned on her light and peered out the tiny window. "Now we're stuck."

Lucas explored the office. "Not necessarily. We need to either get past or take out those wolves. It would be better to take them out though. Only problem is we need a clear line of sight to tranq them, and if we open that door, they'll maul us." The wolves clawed at the door more aggressively.

O'Hara double checked the deadbolt. "Are there other doors?"

"Yeah, but like I said, it would be best to take them out. And I happen to know that the ceilings here are at least ten feet, probably twelve, and a wolf can only jump about six feet vertical." Lucas climbed on top of a desk. "What does this mean you may ask?" He punched one of the ceiling tiles and it fell to the ground. "It means I'm going on an adventure." He reached into the ceiling and shone his light around. His eyes landed on a wooden board. "There we go." Lucas hopped over to another desk and removed the ceiling tile above him. He climbed up into the ceiling and got on the board. "O'Hara, you got any more magazines? I'm almost out."

O'Hara lifted up the hem of her dress and unstrapped a magazine of tranquilizers from her leg. "Here."

"Thanks." Lucas took the magazines and crawled across the boards toward the hallway. He quietly removed a panel and could barely see the hallway beneath him. "Alright," he leveled his gun at the wolf at the door, "sleepy night night." Lucas fired twice, taking the wolf in the neck. He fired darts at all six of the other wolves, dropping them all. "Anyone feel left out?" He turned his phone light on and checked the hall, only to find it empty. Putting his hand to his ear, he grinned. "Y'all can come out now. We're clear." The door slowly opened and O'Hara stepped into the hall, gun in front of her.

She whispered up to him. "Lucas, where all can you get from there?"

He shrugged, letting his arms dangle out of the hole in the ceiling. "Pretty much everywhere except for the commons. The ceiling there is solid concrete. They use the boards up here to access and change lights and stuff."

"So, we could get to one of the exits if we want, right?"

Lucas paused. "Yeah. Actually, we could totally do that."

O'Hara walked back into the office and began to climb up into the ceiling with her one good arm. "Benny, help Vincent up."

Vincent chuckled. "Are you sure you don't want to wait a little longer?"

O'Hara stuck her head out the hole. "Why would we wait here? People need our help."

"Because if we leave, we might be wasting our most valuable asset." Vincent turned and waved over his shoulder for them to follow.

O'Hara dropped from the ceiling. Benny paused. "Vincent, what exactly is this asset?"

"Benny, you're just gonna have to follow me. You're gonna see it in like five seconds. Lucas! Hang on up there!" Vincent walked across the office into a smaller room, the size of a closet. A dozen screens filled one wall, each displaying a different part of the school.

Benny gasped. "How are these on?"

"Security system. It's designed to run on battery for hours. Cameras too. We can see everything in this whole school. Except the bathrooms. That would be illegal."

O'Hara sat down in an office chair in front of the console. "Your school has cameras everywhere?"

"Yup."

"And you and Lucas still sneak into the ceiling?"

"Yup."

Benny fist bumped Vincent. "Balls, man." He ate a chip and wiped the grease onto his suit. "I bet I can operate this thing. It looks like all the cameras are labeled with room numbers. You guys go up there. I'll let you know what's going on around you."

Vincent eyed Benny. "Where'd you find a bag of chips?"

"It was just sitting out. I'd offer you one, but you can't take off the gas mask." He shrugged and ate another chip. O'Hara got up and Benny sat down at the controls. "Sweet." He pressed a few buttons. "Seems straightforward." He put his hand to his earpiece. "Testing testing. Am I coming through?"

O'Hara nodded. "All set then, you navigate from here." She walked back out into the main office area.

Lucas half dangled out of the ceiling. "What happened?"

Vincent walked up to the desk and climbed on top. "The security cameras are still working. Benny is going to stay and be our eyes." He looked up at Lucas. "Oh boy, I've been wanting to sneak around school like this during class, but this is even better. There's wild animals this time." He climbed on top of the desk and tried to lift himself. O'Hara helped him from below and Lucas grabbed his arms from above. "Relax guys, I'm not some invalid."

Lucas rolled his eyes. "Right now, you are. Just accept it. You need help."

"I do not need help, I have never needed help, I will never need help." Vincent folded his arms as O'Hara climbed up. "Katie didn't need help a minute ago and her arm got shot. I could have gotten up on my own."

"Mmhmm," Lucas shone his light around, showing boards sitting on metal straps that held the ceiling panels. "Anyway, Katie, welcome to the boardwalk. I'll be your captain tonight, Lucas Harrison. You'll notice to your right and to your left there are ceiling panels. If you stand on them you will fall through and possibly die, from either injury or animal. Notice the boards have been placed on metal straps that are able to hold our weight. Just try to only have two people on a board at a time. Remember that there may be vicious animals underneath you at any time so stay quiet and don't fall. The exits are all around you, but we don't recommend you take them. Thank you and have a nice flight. The front door is this way." Lucas turned and walked forward.

O'Hara put her hand to her ear. "Annabeth. Annabeth. Come in. Do you copy?" She paused. "Annabeth. Do you copy?"

"Any luck?" Vincent asked.

O'Hara shook her head.

"She's fine," Lucas said, "She probably just dropped her phone while she was escaping."

Benny began to speak to them over the comms, "Quiet. Do you hear that?" Everyone stopped. Lucas knelt down and peered through the hole around a fire sprinkler. Benny continued, "There's someone below you. Two people."

O'Hara flipped the safety off her gun. "Who is it?"

"It looks like... SWAT. But the whole SWAT team is…"

Lucas grimaced. "It's him."

"Yeah," Benny said. "The other guy, I can't tell, but they're wearing one of those ACC suits. See if you can hear what they're saying."

Lucas put his ear to the hole, listening to what they said, relaying the words to the others. "You were wrong. This thing doesn't work. They aren't here. It's not a perfect system." Lucas looked up. "But they're close. I'll deal with them. You take care of the rest."

O'Hara frowned. "There's someone else with them? He's always worked alone."

"Based on their voice it's a young man, maybe college age, could be a little younger." He peered down the hole. "Something on his arm."

"It's hard to see them," Benny said, "But the Anthrope does have some sort of tech on his arm, actually, both of them do. It's got a screen."

Vincent rubbed his forehead and cursed. "Tracking gauntlet. They can use them to keep tabs on us. That means they know exactly where all the anthropes in the building are. They can avoid the anthropes and hunt down everyone else. The trackers can tell them if people are transformed or not."

"When I was helping people get out by the cafeteria," Lucas said, "I saw gas coming out of the vents. It's everywhere. Even if people took shelter in classrooms, they couldn't escape it. Clothes can't filter the gas out of the air. Any anthrope stuck in this building has transformed."

Benny spoke over the comms. "They're gone. Keep moving."

CHAPTER 31

The Anthrope stalked down the dark hall, breathing heavily through his gas mask. He had an assault rifle slung over his back and another in his hand with a light strapped to it. A classroom to his left was closed and he could make out some kind of cloth stuffed under the door. "Idiots. That won't do anything." He tried the handle. Locked.

He fired three shots at the lock. The door swung open. He walked into the room and clicked on a flashlight and immediately a chair was smashed over his head. Two boys jumped on him and pinned him to the ground. Another boy kneed him in the stomach and began to punch him in the face. The Anthrope wrenched his arm away from one of the boys and slugged him in the jaw, knocking him unconscious. With his free hand, he grabbed a syringe from his waist and jabbed it into the boy who was beating him. He depressed the plunger and the boy fell to the floor, spasming. The Anthrope beat the other boy off of him and stood up. Three girls cowered in the corner. "Please don't hurt us!" One of them begged.

"I'm not going to." The sound of ripping cloth came from behind him. "He is." The Anthrope rushed from the room as a disoriented lion climbed to its feet. The girls huddled together and tried to make themselves small.

One of the boys got up and yelled at the lion. "Hey! This way! After me!" He turned and ran from the room. The lion hesitated and then followed. The girls picked themselves up from the floor and walked over to the last boy, knocked out on the floor.

"Tanner, are you alright? Can you hear me?"

One of the girls felt for his pulse. "He's okay." She stood up and went over to the door. Closing it, she jammed the cloth back underneath to seal off the air again. "We need to wait this out and hope Kyle's okay."

Meanwhile, Lucas lifted a ceiling tile and stuck his head down into a hallway. "Those are the front doors. They're chained shut. And… there are bodies."

"Bodies?"

Lucas nodded. "Two boys, three girls, and there's a dolphin on the ground that can't breathe. It's nearly dead. They must have been trying to get out when people started transforming."

"Is there anything we can do about the doors?"

Lucas shot out the glass and it broke in tiny pieces. "That's about it."

Benny spoke up. "Hey, that other guy is coming your way fast!"

Lucas quickly put the tile back in place. Within seconds, they heard footsteps under them. Lucas found another sprinkler hole and looked down below. All he could see was the faint shadow of a person cast by starlight. "What do we do?"

"He's not going anywhere. I think he's waiting, or maybe listening. Stay quiet. He's got a gun."

"I'm going down there." Vincent moved to grab a ceiling tile.

O'Hara shook her head. "No Vincent."

He stopped. "Why not?"

"We can deal with them later. We need to focus on getting people out. That's our main goal."

Vincent frowned. "The whole point of this was to catch this guy."

"No, we didn't come here to catch that guy, we're here for David Mitson. He's just a henchman."

Lucas furrowed his brow. "But they're working together. So we should be going after both of them. We can split up. We can confront this guy and the Anthrope and get people out."

"I know you're here!" The voice below called. "I know you can hear me. I know you're trying to find the girl. Come out and I'll tell you what I did to her."

"What's he saying?" Benny asked.

Lucas closed his eyes. "I need to go down there."

"Lucas," O'Hara grimaced and tightened the bandage around her bleeding shoulder, "you can't. He's going to kill you."

A tear glistened in his eye. "You don't know that. But I need to know. I need to know she's okay."

O'Hara put a hand on his shoulder. "Lucas, I get it, really, I do. I've been in situations like this before on missions. But we need to accept that she probably isn't okay."

"Come out, and I can take you to her!"

Lucas gaped, but only tears came out. He pointed at the ground below them. Vincent stood up and gave him a hug. "Buddy, it's going to be okay."

"She's not." Lucas pulled back.

Vincent looked him in the eyes. "I'll go with you."

O'Hara shook her head. "No. Vincent, you and I are going to go help as many people as we can to get out. You and I are injured. We're in no condition to fight. Benny, keep your eyes on Lucas. Lucas, take that guy out and hold the doors, we're gonna need a safe exit for all these students."

Vincent grumbled. "I'm fine."

"You don't have enough blood in your body."

He opened his suit and showed them the blood bag still hooked up to his veins. It was nearly empty. "I'm almost back to normal."

"You still have a bullet hole in your chest and it could reopen if you exert yourself too much. We might not be able to get an ambulance this time."

Vincent rolled his eyes. "Look, I am invincible. I got in a car crash and got shot and I lived. Not only that, I'm walking around only a few hours later. Add that to my track record of seventeen years without dying once, it's pretty obvious I can't be killed. Plus there's an ambulance parked just outside."

"Vincent," O'Hara growled, "that's the kind of thing that makes me think you're going to get yourself killed. You aren't careful enough. You stole an ambulance for goodness sake. Besides, I need you to help me navigate up here. I don't know the layout of the school very well, and I definitely don't know it from inside the ceiling."

"I'd recommend you hurry and show yourself! She might not be alive next time you see her otherwise!"

Vincent looked Lucas in the eyes. "Don't die." He put his hand to his ear. "Benny, don't let him die."

Lucas laughed. "Keep him safe, please."

Vincent turned and began walking the other way on the boards. He glared at Lucas. "Not an invalid." O'Hara followed him.

Lucas crouched and quietly moved the tile in the ceiling. Faint screams and animal calls filled the air. He lowered himself into the hall behind the dark figure. The man wore a gas mask that covered his whole head and a bodysuit from the ACC. He looked down at a tracking gauntlet. Lucas approached as quietly as he could. He counted in his head. One, two, three.

He jumped, knocking the masked figure to the ground. The man thrashed and punched him in the chest. Lucas punched back and pinned his arms. He slid the man's sleeve up and found a raised band of skin. A light flashed.

"Anthrope." Lucas frowned. "Can't take the mask off in here. He'll transform." He glanced over his shoulder at the doors with the glass shot out. "Benny, can we get them through there?"

"Probably. It'll be hard though."

The man struggled underneath him. "Lucas, let me go!"

"What?" Lucas bent his arm back painfully. "How do you know my name?"

The man grunted in pain. "I know everything about you. I know things you don't understand. I'm trying to make the world a better place. Equality."

"You're a terrorist. It'll never work." Lucas ripped the gauntlet off the man's arm and slipped it on. "This however is helpful. I can see where all the anthropes are. And we're right here…" A tiger jumped out of the mist and roared. "I'm dead!" He jumped and rolled off to the side as the tiger batted at his head. Lucas readied his gun and fired three tranq darts into the tiger. It stepped forward clumsily and raised a paw. Losing balance quickly, it fell to the ground. Lucas picked himself up. The man was gone.

He put his hand to his ear. "Hey guys, I lost him, but I've got his gauntlet. We've got another pair of eyes."

CHAPTER 32

Vincent lifted a tile in the ceiling. He peered down into a classroom. "This is a rescue," he whispered, "anyone in here?"

"Who is that?"

"My name is Vincent. I'm with FBI Agent O'Hara, she's the one who tried to shoot the Anthrope. We're going to help you escape."

A boy crawled out from under a desk, holding a makeshift club. "Where are you?" He walked toward the door.

"I'm in the ceiling. There are paths up here we can take to the front door to get you out." Vincent clicked on a flashlight. "Is there anyone else here?"

The boy nodded. "Girls, come out. It's safe." Three girls came out from under the desks. The boy pushed a desk under the hole in the ceiling. He climbed on top and Vincent helped lift him up into the ceiling. The two worked together to get the three girls up.

O'Hara looked them over. "Are you all okay?"

"We are, but two of our friends aren't."

O'Hara furrowed her brow. "What happened?"

"The Anthrope came. The guys tried to fight him, but he stabbed Jake in the neck and he turned into an Anthrope. He was a lion. But I swear he wasn't before. Our other friend got him to chase him out of the room. Tanner got knocked out."

Tanner stammered. "I- I did the best I could."

Vincent nodded. "That's good enough. You're going to be okay. Follow us, we're going to stop at another classroom before we take you to the exit." He put his hand to his ear. "Alright Benny, that was room 217. That was my English class. You said there's people in 218 too?"

"Yeah. Three people."

"Roger that. Heading that way. Everyone, please be advised, the Anthrope appears to have some kind of bioweapon that can be used to create dangerous anthropes." Vincent waved over his shoulder and everyone followed. "That looks like a wall." Vincent lifted a panel and stuck his head down into the room. "Anyone in here?"

A boy stepped out of a corner holding a gun. "Who's there?"

"My name is Vincent. I'm here to help. Put the gun away. You don't need it anymore."

"How do I know you aren't about to shoot me?" The boy stepped out into the center of the room, shining a flashlight, looking for the source of the voice.

"Because, if I was going to shoot you, I would have done it by now." Vincent cocked his gun.

The boy put his hands up. "Alright. Alright. You want me to drop my gun?"

"You might need it. Put it in your pants and have it ready. Is there anyone else in the room?"

"Yeah, my two buddies. Come out guys."

Vincent turned on his light and let them see him. "Move a desk under me. We're getting people out through the ceiling. It's just the three of you? No girls?"

The boy with the gun moved a desk under Vincent and began to climb up. "They were all anthropes. We don't know where they are."

Vincent helped the boy up and got his first good look at him. "Hey, wait a minute. I know you. You're the guy I beat the crap out of at the basketball game. You had the massive belt buckle." He put his hand to his ear. "Hey Benny, it's those guys who we fought at the basketball game! You remember them?"

"Yeah. They jumped me at the bowling alley too."

The last of the boys climbed up into the ceiling. Vincent frowned. "You guys went to prom with anthropes? You guys hate anthropes."

The boys shifted uncomfortably. "We did. But we were stupid. I'm- sorry."

"Me too."

"Yeah, what he said."

Vincent nodded and smiled. "You have restored my faith in humanity. We're going to take these guys back to the front door and get them out. But if you're willing, we could use your help getting more people out."

The boys exchanged glances. "We're in."

Vincent nodded. "We need to make one stop on the way." He put his hand to his ear. "Benny, we're going to come by the office. We've got a few guys who are going to help out. I wanna pick up a tranq gun for them. Can we grab yours?"

"Sure thing. I'll be waiting."

"Katie, you lead."

O'Hara nodded and turned the other way and led everyone back towards the office. She stuck her head down into the hole. "Benny?"

He walked over from the door. "Here. Just checking outside. It's getting kinda quiet." He handed her his tranq gun. "I'm going to keep the other one just in case."

"Alright. Hey, can you tell how many Anthropes are out there?"

"Hundreds. They're all over. Dangerous ones though, only dozens. Most of them are on the west side of the building, but a decent number are wandering over this way. Most of the students are to the west too."

"Thanks." She continued on toward the front door.

Benny sat back down in front of the security feed. "Lucas, status?"

"I was chasing that guy, but he went into a hotbed of anthropes, so I let him go." Lucas glanced down at the gauntlet. "Also, there's only one other anthrope besides us and that mystery guy in the whole building that hasn't transformed. It must be Mitson. He's on the east side of the school by the science classes. I've got a clear path to a classroom. I wonder if I could get stuff from there to set up some kind of barricade around the front door so we can keep the anthropes out so there's a safe place for when people come out of the ceiling."

Benny paused and checked out the cameras. "What are you going to use?"

"Desks and stuff."

"Okay, I'll watch your back on the cameras. And don't forget to watch out with the gauntlet. Go for it."

Lucas nodded. He held his tranq gun in his right hand and a Glock in the left. Flipping off the safety, he proceeded down the hall, back to one wall. A roar sounded from the distance. He eyed the classroom and ducked inside. Moving quickly, he stacked two pairs of desks and dragged them out, back to the front doors. He pushed the first stack against the west wall and the second stack next to the first, beginning to block off the more dangerous side of the school.

Lucas checked the gauntlet, and saw he was still clear. He went back and collected four more desks and brought them back. When he returned, O'Hara and Vincent were helping students out of the ceiling and out the shattered front doors. Lucas walked up and saw Belt Buckle and his friends. "Oh, hey you guys. What's up?"

Belt Buckle raised his hands. "Relax. We're cool now. Your friend was right. We're all on the same team. You look like you need help. I've got one of those tranquilizer guns and a gun of my own. What do you want us to do?"

"You brought a gun into a school on a date?"

"I'm from Fremont. There's a terrorist on the loose."

"Fair."

Vincent stuck his head down into the hall. "Hey, Katie and I are going to go back for more people."

Lucas gave him a thumbs up and Vincent disappeared into the ceiling. "I'm making a barricade in this main area here. There's a classroom down this way where I'm getting desks." Lucas started walking down the hall. He felt something on his leg. That something hissed. Lucas checked the tracking gauntlet. "Oh crap." He looked down and saw a twenty-five-foot python beginning to wrap around him. "Shoot." He fired a tranquilizer into its neck. "Guys?" He fired three more darts into the snake and then dropped his guns. The cowboys grabbed the python and began to pry at it, but it moved upward, wrapping Lucas's leg completely.

Belt Buckle grunted but the python didn't budge. "It isn't working!"

"Use the tranq gun," Lucas said. Belt Buckle fired his pistol three times into the body of the snake. It slackened and fell to the floor around Lucas. Lucas stepped away from the body. "What did you do?"

"I saved your life."

Lucas pointed at the snake. "That is a person. A human person! With a family that loves them and cares about them. They had a future. And you just killed them."

Belt Buckle shoved his gun back into his pants. "They were going to kill you."

"The tranquilizers would have worked. We just needed more. That's a lot of snake for just a few darts." The snake began to move and slowly slithered away. Lucas let out a sigh of relief. "Oh, thank goodness. Next time, just use the tranquilizers. Okay?"

"Okay."

Lucas checked the gauntlet and picked up his guns. "We're all clear. Don't let me forget to check this thing. It tells me where all the anthropes are." He led them down the hall and into the classroom. They each brought back four desks and pushed them into place, finishing the barricade. A wall two desks high blocked off the hallway in both directions. "Looks good." He turned and looked through the barricade to his left toward the auxiliary gym. "Is that… a baby giraffe?"

A single giraffe's head was visible a few feet above the ground. It began walking closer and the head rose as it went up the bleacher stairs. Lucas simply stared. The adult giraffe turned and walked down a different hall.

Lucas turned back to the others and pointed open mouthed at where the giraffe had been.

"What? Is there something wrong with the barricade?"

"Never mind. The barricade is good. Only problem is we need more guns. And ammo."

"Where would we even get more?"

Lucas paused. He set his tranquilizer gun down and walked over to the front door. "I'll be back with some. Just shoot anything that's big and moves. With the tranquilizers." He ducked through the broken pane and stepped out into the fresh night air. "That's nice." He dashed off to the west parking lot. As he made his way around the building, he shot out all the glass he could see. His legs burned as he sprinted up the hill. When he crested the hill, he found an empty parking lot, with a large ACC van parked right in the middle.

He sprinted over to the van, lungs burning. The back door was open and swung in the gentle breeze. Lucas frowned and looked inside. Benny's dad was slumped on the floor, two tranq darts in his neck. Bullet holes riddled the inside of the van. Mr. Anderson held a gun in his hand and had a pulse, though it was faint. Lucas shut the doors behind him and climbed into the front. He turned the key and pulled out of the parking lot.

Taking a right turn, he headed to the entrance of the school. He drove up into the drop off area and parked the van in front of the front door. With as many tranq guns as he could pile into his arms, he ran back up to the school. "Hey! I've got those guns!" Belt Buckle appeared and Lucas handed him the guns through the door. "These should help. They only have one magazine each. I'm going to go grab as much ammo as I can. You stay here." He turned and ran back to the van.

After finding a box, he piled as much ammo as he could inside. He glanced down at the gauntlet and realized he had moved past the edges of the map. "Let's fix that." He pinched the screen and it shrunk, showing all of the parking lots around Weber. He saw his own dot on the screen, then squinted. Touching the screen, he zoomed in and saw the dot turned into three. Lucas felt a prick in his neck. He turned and saw two men dressed as SWAT, one holding a tranq gun. "Dang it." He passed out.

CHAPTER 33

"Listen up punks," The unfamiliar voice came over their comms, causing Vincent and O'Hara to look at each other wide eyed, "We've got one of your guys, Lucas. We also have the girl, Annabeth. We know the boy's anthrope is a wolf. All of you will be outside and unarmed in twenty minutes or the boy is going to go anthrope and eat her. If you want to save either of them, surrender now."

Vincent and O'Hara froze. O'Hara was the first to break the silence. She turned to the students they were rescuing. "Okay everyone. Change of plans. We've got an area set up by the front doors that is perfectly safe for you all but we're not going to take you outside because it isn't safe yet. Let's hurry."

Benny stood up in a rush, knocking over the chair behind him. He put his hand to his ear. "I'll meet you guys by the front door." He hurried into the main office and climbed up into the ceiling and began crawling.

Lucas groaned and opened his eyes. He was tied up in a small and dark room with one blinding light in the center. His gas mask was missing. A thin man in a full ACC bodysuit set down a syringe of serum on some large metal shelves stocked with sports equipment. There was a SWAT outfit lying on the floor in the back corner. "Oh good. You're awake. I'm sure you're familiar with Annabeth." He gestured behind him and walked away.

"Lucas? Are you awake?"

"Annabeth?" Lucas squinted.

"Lucas. I think we're in one of the maintenance buildings. Maybe it's the storage for football or all the old track stuff or something."

"Annabeth! You're alive!"

"Yeah. I am. I was worried about you guys. Is everyone okay?"

"Yeah, we're alright. Vincent's here. He stole an ambulance. We've been trying to get people out of the building, but they sealed all the exits and took out the SWAT team. I'm so glad you're okay."

"Lucas, you need to know something. They're using us. They used your earpiece to tell everyone if they didn't come out here, they would make you go anthrope with me in here."

Lucas took a second. "That's okay. They're going to come rescue us."

"It's a trap Lucas."

"This whole thing was a trap." He shifted in the ropes, trying to wiggle loose. "They'll take them down."

"The Anthrope has at least five other goons with him. They've got weapons. And they won't take the others to us unless they're unarmed."

"Vincent is smart. He can figure something out."

Annabeth shook her head. "Vincent can't do anything. If it's just him and Benny and O'Hara, they aren't going to be able to do anything."

"It's not just them. There's three boys from Fremont with them. They can surprise them. They can rescue us."

Annabeth started crying. "Lucas, you don't understand."

"What don't I understand?"

"Look at that camera over there." A camera was mounted on a shelf with a red light blinking. She whispered right into his ear. "They don't want to take us prisoners, they just want us to hold still for the video. They're going to kill us and everyone else."

Vincent stood in front of the school, gas mask in one hand, gun in the other. O'Hara and Benny stood behind him. Vincent shouted at the top of his lungs. "Hey you punks! We're here! Now take us to our friends!" He fired several shots into the air. "You hear me you punks? We're here!"

A masked man in a SWAT uniform walked around the corner, leveling an AR-15 at them. "Weapons on the ground!"

Vincent threw the gun aside and it skidded in the broken glass. "We don't have any weapons!"

The man walked closer, and three others also dressed like SWAT came around the corner. "On the ground, arms and legs spread out. We're going to check you." He kept his gun pointed at the three of them while the others checked for weapons, pistols to the back of their heads.

"They're all clear."

The man nodded. "Good. Put them against the wall." One of the others forced them to the wall. "Now the three boys waiting inside with guns. You come out too. Leave your weapons or we'll kill you." He waited a moment. "Now or we shoot them!"

The Fremont boys crawled out the broken doors.

"Check them!" The thugs checked the Fremont boys for weapons. They tossed Belt Buckle's gun aside. "To the boss! Hands on your heads. Single file. Six feet apart." The gunmen lined them up and marched them around the building.

O'Hara whispered. "Where are we going?"

"I think the football field," Vincent said.

"Quiet! No talking!"

They marched in silence up to the football field and headed toward the concession booth. The gunmen led them around and through a set of doors into the equipment room. A stocky man also dressed as SWAT walked up to them. A pistol was clutched in his hand and an AR-15 hung from his neck. He took off his helmet. David Mitson. The Anthrope. "Hi. I've been expecting you. You're here for your friends."

Another fake SWAT walked into the back of the room and pulled sacks off Lucas and Annabeth's heads. They were both gagged and tied to shelving units. Lucas immediately began to thrash and scream.

"Lucas!" Vincent rushed forward to his friend. The Anthrope grabbed him and threw him to the ground.

"I wouldn't recommend that." The Anthrope pointed a Glock in his face. "You won't help them dead." Vincent kicked the gun away and got up. He ran over to Lucas. The Anthrope shot him in the leg and he fell to the floor, just feet short of Lucas. Lucas screamed and struggled to get free with no success. "Of course, you realize I'm going to kill all of you. Otherwise, I wouldn't have stuck around. More than anything I wanted to get a good video of your deaths to show the world that there's no point in fighting the revolution." He paused as one of his goons dragged Vincent back to the others. "I would be remiss if I didn't try to convince you that I'm right however. You all can understand the discrimination against us. It's everywhere and it's the rule, not the exception.

It's been impossible to dissuade the public of their beliefs about us, we've made no progress, and so now to ensure a better future, there must be an awakening."

Vincent grunted from the floor. "An evil tree cannot bring forth good fruit. It'll never work."

The Anthrope walked over to Vincent and kicked him in the side. He looked over at his prisoners. "You three. You aren't anthropes. You've seen it from the other side, haven't you?"

Belt Buckle spat at his feet. "Yeah. Like heck. But you know what? You're wrong. I used to hate them but then I realized how stupid that was. I changed. People listen, but they won't listen to you. Not after everything you've done." He spat again.

The Anthrope shot him in the foot. Belt Buckle howled. The Anthrope gritted his teeth. "People listen to fear." He turned and paced. "What did it take before you listened to them, huh? You are listening to me right now." He turned to look at them. "Look how many guns are pointed at you."

"Eight." Vincent groaned from the floor.

The Anthrope paused. "Eight?"

Vincent nodded. "Count them if you want."

He shook his head. "There aren't eight. There's only six. I'm pointing a gun at you, and I've only got five other people with guns."

"I'm telling you. It's eight."

The Anthrope turned and counted the guns of his men, keeping his pistol trained on Vincent. "One, two, three-"

"Now it's seven," Vincent muttered.

"Four, five." The Anthrope turned back to face them. "Six. You counted wrong."

"Back to eight."

The Anthrope counted the guns again. "One, two-"

"Seven."

"Three, four, five, six!"

"Eight."

"There are six guns pointed at you, you idiot!" The Anthrope crouched and smacked Vincent.

Vincent laughed a little to himself as he propped himself up on his elbow, bleeding a little in the corner of his mouth. He pointed at the gun dangling from the Anthrope's neck. "Then what do you call that big metal pew pew around your neck?"

The Anthrope looked down at his AR-15, pointed directly at Vincent's face.

He growled. "Seven then."

"You were wrong the first time. You might need to accept you're still wrong. Check again."

The Anthrope turned and checked for the eighth gun.

"Well now it's seven."

The Anthrope threw his AR-15 off to the side. "Now it's six!"

"Still seven." Vincent coughed, sending specks of blood into his elbow. "You haven't found the last one."

O'Hara leaned down. "Vincent, I might stop if I were you."

"Listen, boy," The Anthrope grabbed Vincent's face, "If one of you had a gun, my men would have found it. And if you did have one, you would have used it by now. So I know you're wrong."

Vincent spat in his face. "Duh. Why would we point it at ourselves? That would be stupid."

The Anthrope stood and wiped the spit from his face. He glared at Vincent. "Then where, I ask, is the eighth-"

"Seventh."

"Seventh! Gun!"

Vincent pointed. "Officer Scott is holding it. He's hiding in that shelf right there." He pointed at a shelf.

The Anthrope turned and fired several shots into the equipment room. He squinted into the darkness. At last, his eyes caught a glimpse of an old starter pistol, he went over and picked it up. "You idiot, did you really think that would fool me?"

There was a scrape of metal against concrete. "No, but it worked just fine enough." Annabeth picked up Mitson's AR-15 from the floor and trained it on him. "Drop the gun, Mitson. You're not killing my friends." The ropes that had held her bound lay in a pile on the ground next to Lucas. Mitson's gun and the starter pistol clattered to the floor beside him. Annabeth looked at the thugs in the warehouse, each appearing surprised. "Any questions?

The thugs each lowered their weapons.

Benny whispered to O'Hara, shocked, "How'd she get out?"

Agent O'Hara grinned. "That's my girl. David Mitson, you're under arrest."

Annabeth turned around and pointed the gun at Katie. "Not so fast." Her friends' eyes widened. She closed her eyes for a moment and took a deep breath. "Mitson, you're done playing boss. Tie them up."

No one moved at all.

Then Mitson growled and grabbed a coil of rope and knelt down beside Katie, taking her wrist in his hand. "This wasn't the plan."

Annabeth shook her head. "This wasn't your plan. You were never in charge. I was willing to keep going with it until you decided to kill my friends."

Lucas went pale. Vincent coughed more blood. "Who are you?"

Annabeth turned to look at him. "I'm the real Anthrope."

"Mitson was just a pawn," Benny mumbled to himself.

Vincent staggered to his feet. "So then, if the pawn's out of the way, what's the queen going to do?"

Annabeth pointed the gun at him. "Checkmate. Stand down Vincent. We're going to tie you up and then we're taking the chopper on the roof out of here. We've got an appointment."

He took deep heavy breaths and wiped the blood from his mouth. "I always knew you were bad news. I hated you from day one."

"We both know that isn't true." She gestured to the ground with the gun. "I liked you Vincent, I really did. But there was something bigger than either of us. Get on the ground."

Vincent shook his head. "No."

"Vincent, I have a gun you stubborn idiot."

Vincent began to unbutton his shirt and bare his chest, revealing a bloodied bandage. "Shoot me then."

Annabeth hesitated and glanced over to Mitson who was still tying O'Hara up.

"You won't. You're not going to kill us. Give me the gun." Vincent reached his hand out, edging closer and closer.

"No. No one is killing anyone. We're not here to destroy. We're supposed to be here to help." She spoke to the thugs. "Don't shoot them."

Vincent's hand touched the barrel of the AR-15. Annabeth kicked him in the chest and he fell to the ground with a gasp of pain. Blood began to spread. Benny grabbed the loose end of the rope and wrapped it around Mitson's neck. Belt Buckle and his buddies jumped up and tackled the goons. Benny passed the ends of the rope to O'Hara's tied hands and grabbed the legs of the thugs standing next to him.

Lucas managed to get a hand free. Annabeth came over and kneed him in the groin. He tried to double over but she grabbed his arm and pinned it against the shelves. "Lucas, you were never supposed to be here." She took his gag off and he didn't say anything. "I tried to protect you."

His expression was painful. "Was it all a lie?"

"Not everything."

Mitson threw O'Hara off himself and got the rope off his neck. He pulled a knife on her and raised it to strike.

A crack resounded through the room. The knife fell limply underneath Mitson and he fell lifelessly to the ground, a hole through his skull.

Five more gunshots rang out and each of the fake SWAT fell to the ground. Then last of all Vincent's arm fell limply into the growing pool of blood around him, his stitches burst wide open. The Anthrope's gun lay next to his hand.

Annabeth looked around, now alone with her friends. She stepped away from Lucas and leaned against one of the metal shelves and put her hands behind her head. Lucas looked at his best friend. "No." He ripped himself free of the ropes. "No!" He grabbed Annabeth. "You did this!" He threw her to the side and she hit her head against the metal shelf, falling still on the floor. Lucas dropped to his knees and grabbed Vincent. "Vincent!"

O'Hara unwrapped the rope from around her hands. She rushed over to Vincent. "What happened?"

Lucas shook his head over and over, cradling Vincent. "Her fault, her fault, her fault."

O'Hara turned to see Annabeth unconscious on the floor, bleeding from a minor head wound.

Sirens filled the air. O'Hara walked past Benny and the Fremont boys checking the thugs for life and put her head out the door. Ambulances and police cruisers swarmed into the parking lot and toward the school. O'Hara broke into a sprint. She stopped at the first ambulance and grabbed the first EMT she could. "Someone is bleeding to death up there. The men responsible for this are there too. I think some of them are still alive. Take officers with you. Go!" The EMT nodded and rushed to obey. O'Hara ran up to a police officer. "This was an attack by the Anthrope. There are tranquilizer guns by the front door. People are stuck inside." She flashed her badge. "I'm taking control and turning this into a rescue operation. Who's your commanding officer?"

In the equipment room, Lucas cried out for his friend.

CHAPTER 34

Benny walked with a guard up to a metal door. The guard swiped an ID card, and the door opened. "You've got five minutes. We'll be recording your conversation."

Benny nodded. He stepped through the door, and it closed behind him. For a full minute he looked at the ground silently. "I didn't realize you were in maximum security."

Annabeth hesitated. "They moved me here after one of the others was killed by his cellmate."

"Ah."

"I'm sorry."

"Shut up. You don't have the right to say those words."

Annabeth looked down.

Benny stepped closer to the metal bars. "How could you?"

"Do you really want the answer?"

"No."

"How is everyone doing?"

"You want to know how traumatized everyone is? You want to know how much this is destroying us? Your dad won't even open the front door. O'Hara thinks she's a failure because she didn't figure it out sooner, she tried to turn in her badge. Lucas is completely heartbroken. He hasn't said a word since coming out of shock." Benny folded his arms. "I'm the only one who would come, and frankly I'm exercising a lot of self-restraint not to strangle you through these bars."

"When is Vin-"

"Don't say his name." There was a long pause. "It's Thursday."

Annabeth touched the stitches in her forehead. "Can you say something for me?"

"I won't."

Annabeth nodded. "I didn't want any of you involved. I was trying to save you, I sacrificed everything. I was going to stay to be with Lucas, Mitson was supposed to take over, and no one would have ever known about me. Until he tried to kill you. That's what ruined everything, he double crossed me. None of this would have happened."

"None of this would have happened?" Benny laughed with rage. "None of this would have happened?" He clapped his hands together. "Oh, that's so perfect. You're absolutely psychotic!" He pounded the bars.

"It should have worked," Annabeth whispered, "it almost worked. My plan was perfect. I knew how to counter every trap and precaution we set. It was the big one. We brought everyone in for it. We spent millions to get it just right. It should have worked."

Benny lowered his voice. "Thirty-seven."

"Thirty-seven," Annabeth repeated, eyes full of understanding.

"Do you know what thirty-seven is?"

"I have the newspaper come. It's the number of people that died in the attacks."

"It's the number of people you killed. There might have been more if they hadn't caught some of your goons installing gas tanks in Boston. You know, after all this, I really only have one question. How'd you do it? The serum"

Annabeth shivered in the orange jumpsuit. "My dad's professor. He developed it. In class he said things he shouldn't have. On accident. I could always get my dad to talk about it, he thought it was fascinating. But the most important part was the serum itself. I stole some of it. When I had some, I was able to run tests and figure out the composition. That, along with the clues from my dad, was enough. I tested it out in the woods on myself and it worked. That's when I passed the formula off to Phillips and I told him to come back and I'd bring him another vial just to keep my alibi in case I got caught."

Benny nodded. "And Mitson?"

"He was the fall guy. The face. If he got caught, we could still keep going. He was the one who turned the serum into gas. Everyone we hired was someone he knew, that way everyone would accept him as the leader. He was the one who found Philips. Philips got us into the ACC computer system which gave us access to tracker tags. That's how we planned our attacks."

"Where did all the money come from? You landed an attack helicopter on the roof for goodness sake."

Annabeth shook her head. "That's a secret I'm not ready to tell yet."

"Why not?"

"That's my bargaining chip out of here. Someone has to lead the awakening."

Benny shook his head. "You're never getting out of here. You know the penalty for terrorism."

"I'm done talking."

Benny turned and knocked on the door. "Oh, and Annabeth?"

"Yeah?"

He spat on the ground. "You're evil." He left the prison.

EPILOGUE

The judge looked out over the room before beginning his final speech. There were SWAT everywhere. Everyone in the room wore a gas mask. Just to be sure. "Annabeth Watson, the jury has returned a unanimous verdict of guilty for domestic terrorism, manslaughter, and conspiracy involved in the Stanton Bank Attack, Cottonwood Elementary Attack, Weber Fremont Joint Prom Attack, which occurred a year ago from this day, as well as the attempted John Hancock Tower Attack in Boston. You are hereby sentenced to death and by the demand of the justice system and the executive powers, your execution has been ordered to take place one week from today." The judge pounded the gavel.

Annabeth looked down at the orange jumpsuit she wore and wiped away a tear with her shackled hands. "I'm not finished yet," she whispered to herself.

After everything was settled and the jury was dismissed, Annabeth was led from the courtroom, head hung low. As she was led down the hall, she could see into the lobby of the courthouse, where two men laid on the ground at gunpoint. One of them looked up at her as she walked past and could only mouth 'sorry' before an officer pushed his head back to the ground with his boot. "Stay down."

Annabeth was led into a small room a week later. There was a bed in the center. If it could be called a bed. It was where Annabeth was to lay as she died. Several men in suits stood at the fringes of the room, only one made eye contact. The coroner. He wore a white coat over his clothes and a syringe sat on a paper towel next to him. "Annabeth, if you don't mind, my associates and I are going to help you get situated." The coroner gestured to the death table.

Annabeth nodded and climbed on top. The coroner and two other men began securing straps over her. Another man she didn't recognize stepped forward. "Annabeth, do you have any last words before we begin? Now is the time."

Annabeth closed her eyes. "Make the world a better place and finish what you start, because the night is darkest just before the dawn."

The coroner nodded to himself as he picked up the syringe. He tapped Annabeth on the shoulder to let her know it was coming. Then he gently poked the needle through her skin and depressed the plunger.

Annabeth's heart began slowing down. She closed her eyes, only to feel her eyelids grow heavier. She tried to move her fingers, but they were paralyzed. Within moments, all she could feel was a wetness in the corner of her eye.

WANT MORE?

The story continues in Vol. II The Foederati coming Fall 2025! Join what's left of the crew as they discover that Annabeth's legacy lives on!

"It's about Annabeth. She sold the formula. After three years, they've finally started capitalizing on it. People are disappearing everywhere. There's a new program, the Anthrope Crimes Agency. Anything involving anthropes, our jurisdiction, including internationally. And like last time, we've got permission to color outside the lines."

Check our website thedeadmenco.com for updates! Or follow us on Instagram @ thedeadmenco or Facebook @ The Dead Men Co. for all new release information.

Please leave us a review! Your review helps this story be told!